1986

THE 13th MAN

THE 13th MAN

Murray Teigh Bloom

MACMILLAN PUBLISHING CO., INC.

NEW YORK

For Dellie, the subway spy

Copyright © 1977 by Murray Teigh Bloom

Macmillan Publishing Co., Inc.
866 Third Avenue, New York, N.Y. 10022
Collier Macmillan Canada, Ltd.

Library of Congress Cataloging in Publication Data

Bloom, Murray Teigh, 1916–
    The 13th man.

    I. Title.
PZ4.B6543Th   [PS3552.L6394]   813'.5'4   77-8400
ISBN 0-02-511770-X

First Printing 1977

Printed in the United States of America

Then the elders of his city shall send and fetch him thence,
and deliver him into the hands of the avenger of the blood,
that he may die.

—DEUTERONOMY 19:12

FEISEN CONRAD WYCHOWSKY & D'ALEMBERT

470 Park Avenue New York 10022

Telephone 608–6100

December 3, 1973

Dear Jack,

Here is the manuscript I discussed ░░ by phone today. I'm sending it down by shuttle with one of our associates for hand delivery to you. That's how nervous it makes me. As you can see I'm even typing this letter myself. So far only Frank and I have read the manuscript and I bet he wishes he never saw the damn thing.

We're asking you because 1) You were once on the DA's staff and 2) your three years in Foggy Bottom puts you in a better position than any of us on assessing the international and domestic effects if this thing ever got out.

A little background on the author of the enclosed. Harry Hanan was--is?--a client who came to see us through his older brother, Warren, whom we represented the many years he was president of a VW regional distributorship. We also represented Warren in his divorce action and we were counsel for the estate when he died. Harry was executor and in that period we got to know him fairly well. Pretty level-headed for the handsome charmer he seemed to be. From bits and pieces in casual conversation--and from outside confirmation--we know that his curious official background is no bullshit. Incidentally, we also prepared his will and have a good picture of his net worth. From the sale of his 7 1/2 percent share of the distributorship, the sale of his Georgetown house, and various other assets, I'd say he's up there in the $400,000 neighborhood.

The manuscript was left with us--me--in late March with an attached note that if we hadn't heard from him--by personal visit--in more than eight months we were to turn the manuscript ░░░░ over to the District Attorney of New York County.

Down to basics: 1) Should we turn the manuscript over to the DA? Yes we have a client's instructions and all, but as you'll see, the explicit details place him in various kinds of jeopardy legally. Misprision. I haven't heard the word since law school so I checked Black's. It's "failure in the duty of a citizen to prevent the commission of a crime, or, having knowledge of its commission, to reveal it to the proper authorities." A bright, eager Assistant DA could easily come up with a lot of other crimes our client seems to have committed according to his own account. Sure, he was under a severe and credible ░░░░░░ threat to his own life, but is that enough to get him off the hook?

2) Once the DA gets it, I can't see him sitting on it as just another crank manuscript. This isn't dynamite--it's fissionable. The
repercussions could be lasting and international. Frankly, there are
some clients in the house--you know which ones--who would be pissed
off at us for a) being involved at all and b) letting such a manuscript
get out.

About the manuscript itself: I've verified that the handwritten
portions were written by Hanan. We have several samples of his hand-
writing. The typewritten portions were done on an Olivetti portable
which is still in his apartment on Central Park South. (Actually it
was his brother's apartment but he's been using it until the estate
sells it.)

Okay, counselor: counsel. And don't worry about it being too wild.
Frank and I have already run through a dozen scenarios that would
nourish our Bar Ethics Committee for years.

                                        Russ Conrad

January 6, 1973. Dr. Stichman's Office.

There was still some disagreement on the X rays. One of the radiologists said the lump in my lung was the size of an orange; the other insisted it was only lemon-size. Stichman, who's known me since I was twelve, said:

"Harry, this means you go in right away. I called a friend at Memorial and they can take you Sunday." I started to say, what's the hurry. He grimaced. "Don't futz around. If they can take you Sunday for a Monday operation, you go. No good hospital around here, particularly Union Memorial, wants patients with a prognosis like yours. Every surgeon around puts the pressure on them to take the tough cancer patients to satisfy families. You get them into Union Memorial, shows you tried everything."

He looked away. "Two packs a day twenty years you got no surprises."
He said a fine thoracic surgeon, Arthur Andresen, would do it.

January 7, 1973. Union Memorial Hospital.

Room 910. The ninth and tenth floors of the hospital are probably
the world's most expensive places to die. The rooms here average $370
a day and there are forty of them. They're nearly always full because
moneyed people dying of cancer mostly want to do it alone. The surgical
resident who came up tells me that the medical staff prefers to have
single-room occupancy to cut down on possible cross-infection. Still, a
lot of cancer patients don't want to be alone, no matter what. They take
them on the lower floors.

The room is thirteen by seventeen and has a large private bathroom,
a color TV, and a radio. From the bed I can look out on a private bricked
terrace with once-white garden furniture and some flower tubs. The
surgeon, Andresen, came in about 6 PM. He's short, talks a lot, and has
a crooked nose. Deep-set gray eyes and the butter-soft hands of a man
who has to scrub two, three times a day, five minutes each time.

"I hate to shake hands," he said after we did. "They always give me
that funny double-take when they find my hand's so soft. Sometimes I
want to explain: just a touch of leprosy, nothing serious.

"I get a lot of patients with lung cancer who want to die, some even
feel secretly, they deserve to die. A lot of the rest are scared shitless. And
there are some who just don't believe it. Nothing pains them too much.
In spite of what they've read, pain isn't a frequent consequence with
cancer. You can have a hell of a big chest tumor and not feel it for a
long time. Most doctors don't tell their patients they have cancer. And
patients help out. They talk of their infection, their cough, their weak-
ness—never their cancer.

"What you have is a shadow in the upper lobe of the left lung, almost
the size of an orange and partially hidden by the heart shadow. When
I listen to a healthy lung on the stethoscope it sounds like leaves rustling

in a tree. When I listen to you it sounds like a squeaking door—or a broken reed on a sax."

He observed me observing him and laughed silently. "I'm giving you the A-spiel—the straight-from-the-shoulder one. The B-spiel is: you gotta trust me, have confidence, I've done hundreds of thoracotomies, chest openings. We have lots of new gimmicks and marvelous new postoperative radiation therapy and your chances are good.

"I go by looks, the years. You're thin, under forty, and your heart's in good shape. The risk *is* good. But I want to get you kind of mad. After I've opened you up and removed the cancer I don't want you to be a friendly, cooperative patient. They die real quick. You should be a complaining, resistant, cantankerous patient. *They* survive.

"Tomorrow morning I'll make an opening about five by eleven inches to get at the lung. In your case because you're thin, I bet I can get at the lung twelve to thirteen minutes from when I start."

I was lucky, he said, because it was my left lung. The right lung is more important: it performs 55 to 60 percent of the breathing function anyway. Also, I had an advantage: I was Jewish.

"Jews come in early, they got doctors in the family; Catholics, they're late. Nuns, they're worst of all. They just struggle when they find the pain and lumps. God must be punishing them. We had a Jesuit monsignor who had cancer of the penis and it was three years before he came in. Christian Science practitioners are just as bad, but hell, they have a business reputation to maintain. . . . Okay, any group I haven't insulted yet?"

Maybe the A-spiel was right for me. I felt better after he left.

January 8, 1973. Union Memorial Hospital.

When I came out of the anesthesia a nurse was standing near me. I blinked at her. "Do you know what time it is, Mr. Hanan?" I shook my head. "There's a clock on the wall right in front," she said, pointing. "Read it." It seemed very important to her. I read it in a croaking voice.

"Nine fifteen." That made it real: 9:15 meant I was a discard, a surgical failure. The operation began a little after 8 AM. If it was only 9:15 the three-hour operation had been aborted. Andresen would have stopped only because there was no point to it.

About 11 AM I was back in my room and Andresen came in. His face showed he knew I had put it all together. "Nothing's right today," he said. "You should now be in an intensive care unit wired up like an astronaut with your whole left side cleaned out like a chicken."

I had you open in twenty minutes, he went on. "The trouble was the cancer had spread too far. All over the covering of the lung, the pleura, and right down into the diaphragm. Now I turn you over to the radiation and chemotherapy boys."

What were the odds? "Whatever the latest medical paper says they are. Doctors fooling around with statistics are as fallible as anyone. . . ."

What happens now? "They'll keep you here a couple of days but really they'll want you out of here as fast as possible. In the books you're terminal now. They don't want another bad statistic. We have three to five people dying here every day."

How long? "More bad guesses. You could buy it in two weeks and if God loved you you might live to be seventy-five. It happens. Offhand, I'd say anything up to six months—sooner, if you really want to die. It helps if you have something to do; something that has to be done— something that keeps you from becoming detached from your surroundings, from spending long stretches dozing or in a state of total withdrawal. . . . You with State Department or something?"

I nodded. "Well, if they really cared they'd tell you there's an important diplomatic negotiation you've *got* to handle for the next two years, something to keep you going all the time so that you can't think about this thing inside trying to kill you. It might help if you were compulsive. You a migrainer?"

I guessed what he meant and shook my head. "Too bad. You'd feel compelled to finish the job, no matter what. Apart from that all I can say is: don't accept it. Fight it. I'm a stupid son-of-a-bitch and the medical profession doesn't know a fucken thing. Now, I wish you weren't Jewish: they have an exaggerated regard for doctors."

I wasn't a very good one, I said. "Well, just start fighting. You're not married?" I said I was a widower. Turned out that was a merciful thing to be under the circumstances. "Often the wives of men with lung cancer develop symptoms identical with the ones the husbands show— chest pains, headaches, shortness of breath." He shook hands and moved to the door. Before he went out he said, "Ahh, I'm sorry I couldn't help. . . . She didn't die of cancer, did she?" I said it was an accident. "That's a help. At least you won't feel the cancer caucus is out to exterminate the Hanans. Don't go quietly. Be mean about it."

Ever since Stichman's office on Saturday I'd been trying to recall the Dickens lines in exact order. They open a travel book he once did on Italy. When Andresen left, the words fell into place. "On Friday, as he was dining with other prisoners they came and told him he was to be beheaded the next morning, and took him away." I cried for several minutes.

Miss Velez, the orange-blonde Puerto Rican nurse with the port-wine spot on her neck, came in and handed me an envelope. "Someone left it at the desk when I am away." She managed to avert her eyes. Terminal cancer is a great off-putter. The envelope was block printed: Harry Hanan, Room 910. No return address. The flap was tucked in, not sealed. I took out a saffron sheet, folded over once. The letters were about a half-inch high and seemed to have been done in black ink with one of those block-printing sets kids used to play with. A letter for each block. The thing was as incomprehensible as a Chinese laundry ticket. Except I knew the letters were Jewish—Hebrew? What the sheet had on it was:

$$\text{(13)} \quad \text{הַדָּם} \quad \text{גָּאֵל}$$

They didn't look friendly. The Menace of the Heavy Verticals? Thirteen what? Who knew I was in Memorial? Stichman, of course. Andresen. Miss Velez and God-knows-who down in the admissions office. And McCready in Washington. I had phoned him Saturday afternoon and told him I was going in for surgery. I didn't have to tell *him* what for.

He must have smoked at least three cigarettes in our ten-minute talk.

Some kind of subtle appeal from UJA or Federation of Jewish Charities? But how did they know I was here and where was the return envelope? Try this: maybe there was a secret cure for cancer, an Israeli medical nut had come up with it. If you could read the note you'd know who to contact to get the magic cure. That way only Hebrew-reading Jews would get the word and the cure. Who else did I know who could translate? My house in Georgetown on N Street was near a synagogue.

I once dreamed about the place. Someone comes rushing out of the synagogue one morning and knocks on my door. I have to come: they need a tenth man, a *minyan* for services. I stand there and tell them I can't read Hebrew, I wasn't even bar-mitzvahed, and I was married to a Gentile. As I'm giving them reasons why I'm not a good prospect one of them pulls a gun. "No trouble, Hanan. Come." I look at him more closely and I realize I'm checking his face against all the family albums we had in Ankara: Soviet "chauffeurs"; Czech wire-tappers; Rumanian female seducers; East German gay workers. None of them. I finally sense dimly the man with the gun is really my father with a paisano mustache and dark glasses.

I didn't notice Manny come in because I was going off into a teary doze. In some ways he was the one person who would be just right if I was going to die that week. The dying should only be reminded of the good they did during their life. And for Manuel Menahem Zdravko I had been a temporal savior: his life; getting him into the safety of America, and a good job. And the Lord had made things even sweeter: he arranged matters so that I *liked* Manny.

A visit to a patient in a cancer hospital is a venture into needed hypocrisy. But we knew each other well enough to dispense with nearly all of it. "Al called me from Washington," he said.

He wanted to know about all the medical miracles he'd read about. Cobalt bombs, new drugs, fancy X-ray stuff. I said the surgeon wasn't very hopeful about any of it. "We never had much luck with the Technical Services people, did we?"

I first met Manny when I was running a cross-border operation out of Turkey. Someone sent him to me because he spoke Serbo-Croatian, Bulgarian, Rumanian, and a little English. His opening line was: "Menahem not good Englitch-talker. Mösyö talk Serbo-Croat?"

That first meeting with him was still vivid. He was distractingly desperate and in Istanbul on an outdated Spanish passport. He was being sought by some mercenary agents of the UDBA, the Yugoslav State Security Directorate. They had been involved in a gold coin operation. He used the UDBA characters to take the coins out into Italy and India. They ran out on him with the coins and were trying to shake him down for more. He was broke and hunted and all I could think as I looked at him was how the hell could he keep that suede jacket so clean after what he had been through. The suede jacket and the cleft chin and the straight Roman nose, dark skin, and thick black hair streaked with gray. His eyes were filled with a lurking humor.

We checked him out. He seemed clean. I told him what was involved —the risks and the reward. The risks were constant as a border-crosser and the main reward was that if he performed well—and remained uncaught—I'd recommend him for the green heaven of a U.S. passport. Lots of people used to volunteer. Some were just crooks looking for an angle or a pardon.

Manny became one of our best. The stuff we sought sometimes seemed trivial but someone important wanted it. Maybe the Air Force wanting traffic patterns and types of planes on a certain military field; or maybe another agency on the new kinds of border documentation you need in that country.

When your border-crossers are off on an operation you're anxious like the first time you let the teenager have the car. Sure, the crosser's expendable and all, but you want him to come back and end *your* anxiety.

Some of the crossers went over with those special, very light one-man balloons made by some outfit in Minnesota. We liked them because they were hard to pick up on radar, but they were at the mercy of the winds. Manny always went over on foot and the one time he asked for technical help we failed him. All he wanted was an effective dog repellant. Often farmers on the borders had big, vicious dogs. And all those million-dollar labs and technicians at the Agency's Technical Services couldn't come up with an effective dog repellant. It was a wryly useful finding for Manny: even America couldn't solve all his problems.

After each border crossing the agent was asked for a critique of the mission. Mostly we were looking for pitfalls others might avoid in the future; for mistakes made. Manny impressed me because while most of the others tended to criticize the arrangements made for them—their documents or clothing—Manny used to explore in great detail *his* mistakes: "I shouldn't have pissed when I did, when I rested behind the haystack"; or, "I shouldn't have smoked under the shelter." He had a refreshing level of honesty you almost never encountered in border-crossers.

Manny did it for eight months and I recommended him for the passport. Even better, I put the pressure on the Double-O section, the disposal section. Not James Bond's kind. Double-O got jobs for Agency people let go, and sometimes for border-crossers who won their U.S. passports. The first job they got Manny was with a life insurance company but he got one on his own a couple of years later—fund raising. Now he was working for the Hebrew Theological Seminary in New York. He was making $17,000 a year, lived in a red brick house in Bayside with his wife, a pretty Canadian, who brought in about $9,000 a year working part-time at a reading lab for kids. They had a daughter.

I showed him the note. "You must read Hebrew, Manny." Sure, I *read* it, he said, but I don't understand it so good. "In good orthodox Sephardic families like mine in Yugoslavia you have to learn to read for prayer. But there's no push on *understanding. . . .*" He made out one word. *"Hadam . . .* I think that means blood, the blood. *Goel . . .* Something I remember . . . something biblical but I'm not the one to tell you. . . . Harry, you're not going to be doing much when you come out of here. Come up to the Seminary and I'll buy you lunch and you'll meet one of the professors up there who'll give it you backward and forward and ten thousand words of its Talmudic significance."

January 10, 1973.

One of the things I wasn't warned about: when you're dying you retreat to childhood and adolescence. Items:

1. I found a pimple on my neck. I haven't had pimples since I was seventeen.

2. I had a wet dream. I haven't had any in years. She wasn't anyone I ever knew.

3. I've begun making lists as I used to when I was a teenager. This one is headed: Things I Must Do If I'm Only Going to Live Two Months. Another: One Month.

4. In dreams I've noticed lately that a lot of the images are pictures from old elementary and high school texts. Last night's was from my high school European history text: *Les dernières Cartouches à Bilan* by a minor French painter, de Neuville. The image of the French soldiers trapped in this farmhouse at Bilan near Sedan with their last cartridge came into the dream like a superimposed tableau.

January 11, 1973. Hebrew Theological Seminary.

At lunch Manny told me how to raise money. Mostly it involved getting a big man to be honored in his trade or profession. You traded *kuvid*, honor, for money. If he was the head of a hotel chain, say, you got his PR man to work with you getting all the hotel's suppliers to buy tables to honor the big man. All for the cause of the Seminary. Other tricks, too, but I wasn't really interested. Where was the Bible expert?

In the Seminary's catalog he was listed like this:

Yochanan Shorsh, Professor of Bible. BA, Temple University; MHL, Gratz College; PhD, Harvard University. Among other courses he gave one called Bible 714, two hours weekly. Two credits. "The Book of Deuteronomy." He also taught Bible 712, "Introduction to Jewish Medieval Biblical Scholarship."

"Yock knows everything," Manny told me. "Also, he's an amateur expert on arbitrage so he's in my investment club. He's made us some money on convertible stocks. He knows a little about my wild years in the Balkans and that you're a good old friend. You can't fool him so easily, so I didn't give him any nonsense about your being a writer checking on *goel hadam*. I explained you're a friend who's interested in the subject without mentioning the note. I don't think he'll be nosy and if you want to tell him, go ahead, but it isn't necessary."

He took me to Dr. Shorsh's office on the fifth floor, made the introductions, and left. Shorsh had a cast in his left eye, a neatly trimmed brown beard, and a tan shirt open at the collar. "Our mutual friend was a little mysterious. Said you were very interested in the *goel hadam* concept and what was behind it and things like that."

I was tempted to give him the note but I didn't. I said I was on sick leave from the State Department and doing a lot of reading. Somewhere I had come across this *goel hadam* reference and I was curious about it.

He smiled. "So you went right down to the library and pulled out the appropriate volume of the fine new *Encyclopaedia Judaica?*"

No, I hadn't done that. "I'll take it as a compliment. Manny piled it on so about my expertise you assumed I'd know even more than H.H.C. who did the encyclopedia article. That's Haim Herman Cohen, an associate justice of the Israeli Supreme Court, who really knows, but he's in Jerusalem and I'm here so let me tell you about it."

The *goel hadam,* he went on, was an avenger of blood in biblical times, the person who was authorized by the law or local custom to kill a murderer. Private revenge was legal in Israel as well as in a lot of ancient civilizations. It wasn't just murder. It could be for rape or mayhem or other grievous injuries. The patriarchs were in many ways fairly unidealistic. They *expected* vengeance to be taken and if it was taken boldly and without excess, it wasn't condemned. In fact, the action was honored. Vengeance had been exacted. Who could be the avenger, the *goel hadam?* Almost any next-of-kin entitled to inherit. Some commentators think it also included even maternal relatives who ordinarily weren't in line for inheritance. Even women qualified as avengers. Where there was no next-of-kin an avenger would be appointed by the court.

By the time of King David, though, the institution was on the way out. The existence of a strong monarch made it less necessary for a family to take the law into its own hands. Still, there are some Talmudic scholars today who regard the killing by the avenger of a murderer as no more than unintentional manslaughter. And every now and then there are cases in Israel, particularly in Yemenite family feuds, where blood vengeance is offered as a mitigating circumstance. The courts haven't accepted it but ancient customs like this one die slowly.

Vengeance is mine saith the Lord, but some of the biblical characters didn't listen too hard. Take Jeremiah, the one prophet about whose personal attitudes we know something. He's a hell of a vindictive character. He asks for the punishment of the Israel which would not respond to him. He prays for vengeance *on* his personal enemies in general and no longer prays *for* them. If you go to the psalms there are a lot of them that have prayers for vengeance on enemies and prayers in thanksgiving for the answer to such appeals. God was the universal *goel* who saw to it that every man got his just desserts, but meanwhile here on earth it wouldn't hurt to take matters in hand directly—in case He wasn't looking just then.

There was, Shorsh went on—assuming rightly I was a total illiterate about things Jewish—a great Jewish scholar, the Saadia Gaon, who lived in the ninth and tenth centuries. His full name was Saadia ben Joseph al-Fayumi, and he was wise and subtle, particularly in his major work, *The Book of Beliefs and Opinions*. Shorsh pulled down a book from a shelf, went through it looking for something. He found it, translating as he read:

Others maintain, again, that the best thing for man to strive for in this world is to take revenge on his enemies. They assert, namely, that the satisfaction of the thirst for revenge removes from the soul the worry with which it is laden and relieves it of the sorrow in which it is wrapped. It affords it the pleasure of seeing the discomfiture of its enemy, assuages the vehemence of its wrath, puts an end to excessive brooding, and prevents a second enemy from daring to do what the first was bold enough to attempt.

This was what *others* said; the Saadia Gaon was against the seeking of revenge. But in a more recent study, Merz, in his *Blutrache bei den Israeliten,* showed . . .

I was feeling as awkward as an adolescent caught in a pointless lie. Why prolong the show? "I'm sorry, Dr. Shorsh. I should have showed you the note right away. . . ."

He grinned. "Why should you, *really?* You don't know me and in your work I assume that discretion and concealment . . ." He broke off to take the note. He felt it, turned it over, nodded.

"All right, now we're all on the same side. The amenities have been observed and now we can talk like *menschen* instead of all this fencing around. I think it would be a good idea if you talked to somebody about this. Let me phone him and see when you can get together."

He hung up after a brief conversation. "I assumed you could make it today at four PM. He has an office on East Fifty-fifth Street and if by some bad luck you have another appointment, please break it and go see Vogelsang. You two need each other."

The first real pain came on then. Someone had placed an old tin can in my lung and was opening it quickly. Shorsh immediately was at the chair to keep me from keeling over. He got me some water and I took one of the Dilaudids they gave me at the hospital. They said the pills were five times more effective as a painkiller than codeine. I felt better in about ten minutes.

"Maybe I should cancel for today. You might need a doctor more than you need Vogelsang."

I said a doctor wouldn't help but maybe Vogelsang could satisfy my growing curiosity. Why me? Obviously, I wasn't the only one who had gotten the note or Shorsh and Vogelsang would not have been all prepared for me.

Shorsh said yes, I wasn't the only one. But it was important that I see Vogelsang right away because I was the only one who was still alive.

2

It had been a hotel off Madison converted into offices. Small PR firms, consulting offices, advertising services—a bunch of people in the communications field who were trying out an idea, a gimmick, a magazine, a new service as inexpensively as they could. If they hit they'd be out of here as quickly as possible. The papered corridors had the palpable feel of transitoriness, of waiting to be called—up or out. The directory indicated that the Peter Vogelsang was in Suite 511—no mere rooms here, only suites—and I ran over the other names and found that 511 was also the place where you could find the Technical Information Syndicate.

The office, a single room looking out on an enclosed court, still had the original hotel furniture, slightly worn armchairs, a matching couch, a modest desk, some files, and—surprise—a Telex machine off in the corner. Vogelsang was in shirtsleeves looking at a message clacking in on the machine when I entered. He waved me to one of the chairs then came over to shake hands. About six feet three inches, a completely bald head, an eroded face. Maybe sixty. He locked the door and sat down on the couch.

He said, "Okay, you want to know what the hell this is all about?"

The voice was a slow deep croak. The Southern frog prince with laryngitis.

"You guessed? I'm a laryngectomee. They took out my voice box. Cancer. Then I spent a year at the New Voice Club up at Mount Sinai learning to speak by controlled burps." He opened his shirt to show me the opening in his neck through which he breathed. The mouth of a metal tube was visible.

I said he was lucky.

"I get carried away. I still feel it necessary to explain, so I just forgot they don't have anything to replace lungs. When you first realize you'll never talk normally again you want to cut your throat. A lot of them do. It's a hell of a way to talk but it works."

We smiled at each other, the surgical amenities out of the way.

"I'll tell you everything we got but you've got a piece of information that might be more important than anything we've got. So, please . . ."

You're *supposed* to get nobler when you're dying.

"I promise I won't die on you before I tell. Just fill me in on what you and Technical Information are all about and why I'm here."

His croaky guttural fascinated me. I found myself trying to detect what sounds he deliberately avoided. There didn't seem to be any. He said:

"I work for the American Hebrew Leadership Council, which is a kind of central consultation organization representing the whole set of key Jewish organizations in the country. Most of them are always battling one another over policy, ideology, and occasionally rival fundraising but there are also certain vital issues on which it is necessary to have agreement even if they're already to cut each other's throats on the everyday issues. Could I see the *goel hadam* note you got?"

I took it out of my wallet and handed it over. "Thirteen! We've missed some. But it's the same paper and printing. It's the McCoy, all right. Welcome to the club—and congratulations on still being alive. Now please, start at the beginning, getting the note and all the rest."

Beginning of *what?* Where-I-was-born kind of detail?

"Just where were you when you got the note, like that. The *immediate* stuff. We'll worry about the rest later."

I worried about it now. "Why does the American Hebrew Leadership Council need a cover like Technical Information in a place like this? It's a legitimate operation, isn't it? Why the cloak-and-dagger stuff?"

"Yeah, kid stuff, but it might be necessary. I promise you'll get the *whole* story. Just for the record, fill me in on the note you got. Trust me for two minutes, Hanan."

I told him. I was on leave from the State Department because of two deaths. First, my wife died in an accident in Turkey. Then my brother, my only close relative, from a heart attack in New York. I had an interest in my brother's business—he was a regional distributor of Volkswagens —and I asked for leave to clear things up. I was the executor under my brother's will. I got chest pains and went to a doctor who sent me to specialists and I ended up in Room 910 at Union Memorial Hospital where on January 8 I was told my lung cancer was inoperable, and where I got the note delivered by hand.

He took the same routes I had gone through. Who knew I was in the hospital? What visitors? Did I ask the nurse if she had seen who left the note? A big nothing.

He rubbed his cheek as he thought. "Thirteen. We're sure missing some in-betweens."

I was getting tired. "Vogelsang."

"Sure, I promised. I bet you're . . ." He broke off and hit his forehead in mock self-anger. I absolved him. "It's all right, Vogelsang. I am *dying* to know. Just tell me: what the hell is this all about?"

He told me.

The first one they knew about was a fifty-four-year-old accountant living in Marin County above San Francisco. That was in 1967. His name was Howard Lucksig. He was married, had three children, and made about $40,000 a year out of the partnership in a medium-sized accounting firm. The death took place in Los Angeles where he had gone to give a talk to the Directors of Finance/Treasurers section of the League of California Cities meeting. He talked about the new audit standards for local government units. The morning after his talk he was found in his hotel bathtub, drowned. He had a few drinks in him, the autopsy showed, and there was an inclination to call it an accident: he fell asleep in the tub. When his stuff had been shipped back to his widow she went through the wallet and found a *goel hadam* note like mine, only his was numbered: (2).

Because it was in Hebrew his widow, a convert to Judaism—she had been Harriet Strong of Butte, Montana, once—took the note to the rabbi of the Reform temple Lucksig went to on Rosh Hashanah and Yom Kippur. The rabbi vaguely remembered the *goel hadam* concept and it occurred to him that maybe Lucksig had been murdered. He discussed it with a seminary classmate who was now working for the American Hebrew Committee's San Francisco office. Understandably, the widow didn't want the whole thing reopened as a headline. She knew that Howard had no real enemies. It had to be an accident.

The second one was in February 1968 in a Caracas, Venezuela, suburb, El Paraiso. This time the victim was a forty-seven-year-old Jew named Jaime Wolynski, a manufacturer of insulating materials. He had been killed by a hit-and-run driver in Caracas. Weeks later his widow found the *goel hadam* note in his safe deposit box. The police were only politely interested. They were sure there was no connection.

Victim Number 3—although his note had the number (5) on it— wasn't Jewish. His name was Maurice Faucon and he owned a nursing home in Aix-les-Bains in southeastern France. Although baptized at birth, it did turn out that his father had been Jewish, a Moritz Fassnacht. He had married a French Catholic and Maurice had been raised a Catholic. His body had been found in Lake Bourget and it was assumed he had committed suicide. He had been in poor health.

Vogelsang was going through his notes about Number 4 when there was a knock on the door. He was a little embarrassed. "We don't get casual visitors." He opened the door carefully a few inches and then, suddenly, much wider. I could see his face light up with great pleasure. "Come in, Elly, come in." When she did he leaned over as if to kiss her and then, almost imperceptibly, decided not to.

As I got up he brought her forward almost gaily. "Elly, this is Harry." I think the realization of Vogelsang's unexpected adoption of a tradi- tional intelligence technique—first names only—must have hit us both simultaneously. She was smiling when she came closer and extended her hand: "How do you do, Mr. Harry Harry?" There was a faint accent, a remote overlay. *"Enchanté,* Mademoiselle Elly Elly."

Vogelsang was only slightly abashed. "It's all your fault, Harry. You made me too security-conscious."

She gave him a manila envelope she had been carrying. "This is you-know-what," she smiled. "Oh great," Peter said. "Matter of fact, we were just talking about you-know-what."

He excused himself, took the envelope to his desk, and started going through some typed pages. Elly looked at me with a half-smile as I was doing the adding. About thirty with a youthful pixie face, a broad mouth, gray eyes, heavy black hair cut close to the head. She was wearing a double-breasted navy blazer and a navy-and-white herringbone skirt. No wedding band but a lapis lazuli free-form ring. She was very attractive.

Years ago the Agency had an advanced identification course. They'd flash photos on the screen for five seconds. Two people standing near one another: a man and a man; a man and a woman. What you'd have to do was not only describe each in detail but deduce their relationships.

What was Elly's relationship to Peter Vogelsang? Employee-employer, obviously, but there was much more here. He was at least twice her age but what came through on all antennae was some kind of romantic relationship. Tilted probably more on his side. She to him: friendly, liking, warm. Had they been to bed together? I didn't think so. I couldn't spot any of the muted tension, the knowingness of slightly smiling eyes.

Vogelsang looked up. "You know, Harry, I'm not really good at this kind of stuff. My first instinct was to tell you both about each other. See how cautious I've become. But since we're all on the same side I'm sure it won't hurt to tell you Elly's been working with me on some of the foreign stuff. She's a great translator." To balance the one-sided equation he added: "Harry's going to be working with us, Elly. I think he'll be very helpful. You might say, he's vitally interested."

The coy euphemisms were beginning to depress me. "What Peter is telling Elly about Harry," I said, heavily arch, "is that Harry is Number Thirteen on the hit parade."

Her mouth opened—no gold, no gaps—and a long-fingered hand flew up to cover it. "You?" I nodded.

"I'm sorry," she said. "I really took you for someone from the Committee office." The mood had changed abruptly. She stood. "Call me later at home, Peter. If you need more." She shook hands with me gravely, nodded to Peter, and walked out swiftly.

Vogelsang was still looking at the door seconds after it closed. "She's a simultaneous translator, free-lance. Does a lot of work for the UN and international conferences all over. I met her when I was still at the ad agency and she was working an international consumer research meeting in Brussels. I wined and dined her royally but I couldn't persuade her. She moved to New York and I looked her up and again kept trying. Then a peculiar thing happened. I fell in love. Wanted to marry her. I'd been married twenty-eight years, fairly successfully, everything considered, but I wanted her more than anything. I rehearsed a little speech for my wife. I talked to my lawyer. And Elly talked me out of it so effectively I wasn't hurt too much. She liked me and wanted my friendship but marriage wouldn't make any sense for a lot of reasons. Well, you get a Dear John talk like that and you figure the least you'll get out of it would be a consolation prize: like going to bed with her. I didn't even get that. So I tried to work it around to another consolation prize: a protective friend–little friend relationship. That didn't work too well because she's a very private person and if you don't know what the problems are how the hell can you protect? So right now we're in the stage where I'm trying to figure out a new relationship. Meanwhile she does some work for us. She was out with hepatitis a couple of months and her income fell off pretty bad. Yeah, I'm still married."

He would have gone on, not with the desire to extract matching confidences from me, but because he was still struck with the wonder of having fallen in love again at his age and what a close thing it had been to starting a new life and all. Since I was primarily interested in bringing an old life to a more orderly close I closed my eyes as punctuation. "I thought you'd be curious about her," he said half-apologetically. I said I had been—a little.

The fourth victim they knew about was a real-estate investor named Monte Morden. He lived in Hastings-on-Hudson in New York and at

one time had been a successful real-estate syndicator with projects running into the millions. He came a cropper in the late '60s and then lost
a lot of money in a high-interest swindle operating out of New Jersey.
The *goel hadam* note had been found by his wife and attorney when
they were going through his papers.

On October 5, 1972, they found the fifth one. His name was Artur
Zelkowicz and he managed an electronics factory in Berlin. He had
gotten his engineering training in Manchester, England, and had fought
with the young Israeli Air Force in 1948. He returned to Berlin—where
he had been born—in order to take over considerable property he
inherited from his grandparents. Property the Nazis confiscated. In
addition he got $2,500 for the sums spent on his education abroad and
he and his wife—also German-born—received $1,500 each as political
or racial victims of Nazism. Zelkowicz's body had been found in his car
parked on the Ringbahnstrasse about a mile from the factory. He had
been stabbed to death. The *goel hadam* note came in the mail to his
home two days later.

The sixth and most recent was right here in New York. On December
11, 1972, the police found the body of Mike Gangwach, a forty-seven-
year-old locksmith who lived in a run-down residential hotel on West
End Avenue. His body was found in the hotel pool. Death was by
drowning. The pool was supposed to be closed because the lifeguard was
having dinner, but a lot of the hotel guests used the pool anyway.
Gangwach had a tiny locksmith shop on West Seventy-first Street near
Broadway but subsequent investigation revealed that he made about
$1,000 a week from a peculiar specialty: auto odometer "adjusting" for
shady used-car dealers up on Jerome Avenue in the Bronx. There he was
known as "Mike, the Clocker." He'd get $10 for every "clock"—odome-
ter—he "hit over the head." Apparently, he designed his own tools to
turn back the odometer of any car built. In less than three minutes he
could have an 88,000-mileage-registered odometer back to a more modest 34,000. He had never married and had lived at the hotel for more
than twenty-two years, in a rent-controlled room. The *goel hadam* note
had been found in the top drawer of a beat-up desk in his locksmith
shop.

Vogelsang paused in his recital. "Yes, we first did what you're doing now—look for the common denominator. What do these men have in common? They certainly weren't killed the same way—if, indeed, all were killed. As far as we could find out, they weren't related. Now if the number on your note—thirteen—is an accurate one, it means that we haven't heard about most of the victims. Which means (a) that they might not have received notes, (b) they received them but we haven't heard about it, or (c) there haven't been thirteen victims, or even twelve, if we assume you're not among them."

He went to one of the gray filing cabinets. "We have gathered a lot of information about each of the six. Looking for the common denominator, of course. We've spent quite a lot of money on the investigation, and right now, I'm sorry to say, we don't have the vaguest idea of what they had in common except the obvious: they were males; they were Jewish—or of Jewish descent; they were not criminals; they were not—as far as we know—spies of any kind or working for intelligence apparatuses. And they led, as the expression goes, comparatively blameless lives. Why should anyone want to kill them? Or you?"

I was curious how Vogelsang knew the men were not in intelligence work but he waved away questions for the moment.

"Of course, when you're presented with this kind of thing you go to the traditional puzzle carriers of our time: the detective novels."

He looked at me and I realized that his eyes had a slightly unfocused quality to them. "Everybody reads them at one time or another. Well, it's a whole damn industry. You have these hundreds of writers thinking up new ways of killing, new reasons for killing, and new ways of deceiving the reader. The theme of a series of unrelated murders is not uncommon.

"I hired Elly. I said work on this for two weeks: interview the mystery-story editors at the top publishers, go to a dinner meeting of the Mystery Writers of America and ask."

He waved at the files. "This isn't a paid job. I made some money a couple of years ago when the advertising agency I was a partner in went public. I sold out right away and decided fifty-eight was too old for the advertising business, even my end, which was research. I used to take it very seriously once. Even got a PhD, but by the time I was fifty-five I was getting restless and bored. I couldn't get excited by finding out if the market share for Pampers was going to be fourteen or thirty-four percent; or even what kind of images women worked up when they were spraying themselves with vaginal deodorants. A friend of mine was a big giver and he thought that they might find a man of my background useful at the American Council. Actually, they really had nothing for me then. Then I had the laryngectomy and spent a year learning to talk again like a neighborly foghorn. By the time I came back to the Council they were all excited about this *goel hadam* thing, and they asked me to 'coordinate.' You wouldn't believe how much we've had to spend on this investigation so far."

I said I'd believe.

"More than forty thousand dollars all told. We've really done a job even if we have nothing to show for it. . . . Okay, I was telling you about the mystery writers. Well, the main solutions to why a group of un-related men and women get killed in a detective story turn out to be like this:

"One. They were once on a jury that convicted an innocent man.

"Two. They once took part in a fraternity hazing in which someone was injured or even killed.

"Three. They're all heirs to a fortune and a more remote heir is killing them off one by one. Remember Alec Guinness in it?

"Four. They're all killed the same way but the killer only wanted to get one of them really; the rest are just to muddy the situation.

"Five. Turns out the killer is the first one on the list to be murdered. Only he isn't dead at all. But since no one can even think of him as a suspect he's able to kill off the others one by one. The mystery writers love this one even if they have trouble figuring out good reasons why he has to kill off a bunch of people.

"Maybe a few more, but believe me, Hanan, none of them make any sense for us here. None of these dead men went to the same school, and since they're several different nationalities they didn't serve on the same jury. And they're not heirs to some mysterious fortune. They weren't killed—if in fact they were all killed—the same way, either."

Vogelsang hesitated. "As one cancer victim to another, we can talk frankly, can't we?" Hadn't we?

"Take your case," he went on. "The killer thinks you're a terminal cancer case. You get the note and on your death he's credited with another score—even if he had nothing to do with it. Don't forget some of the notes were delivered only after the men died. A nut, sure, but a shrewd one willing to take all the breaks coming his way."

I asked who did the actual investigations.

"My role was coordinator, mostly. The fella really in charge of the investigations here and abroad was an old-timer who used to work for the American Hebrew Committee. Back in the old days he was in charge of getting undercover people into the Bund, into various militant anti-Semitic groups and things like that. He retired a few years ago, and he was called back to get this investigation started. He was able to use some men overseas, including some people who are regional representatives of the AHC. I think they did a pretty good job but we've had some problems with old Sammy."

For the first time he was looking at me directly, the gaze exactly focused. "You know, Hanan, you have us at a little disadvantage. We know almost nothing about you. Yes, I did look you up in the State Department Biographical Register before you got here, but that only tells me that you were until recently a FSR-4 and Political Officer at Istanbul and that you were appointed on April fifth, nineteen-seventy. That you were born in Paris on May fourth, nineteen thirty-three, and you went to Columbia for three years and didn't get a degree. You a naturalized American?"

I explained that my parents were American-born, that my father was the number-two man in the Paris office of Associated Buyers, which bought for a lot of department stores. That I came back to New York when I was six, in 1939, and I didn't finish college because I wasn't interested; I was spending more time playing bridge in Hartley Hall than in the library. I had inherited $4,000 from my grandmother and I flew to Paris in the summer of 1952.

"So now we know all about you," he said, meaning the opposite, of course. "A fella in a job like yours makes a lot of real enemies?"

Not real ones, I said, which wasn't true.

We descended into the treacherous, foggy valley where everyone has to work out his own careful orientation. Who's who and why and how far can you go along the same path in safety? He sensed the impasse almost as quickly as I did and since he had fewer cautions to hold him back he emerged first.

"We're on the same side, Hanan," he burped. "It just takes a while before you're ready to show all your cards. My problem is I've got to let you in on some embarrassment of ours *first* . . ."

". . . And you wish you had a little embarrassment of mine so we offset each other," I finished. "Why don't you have your people do as good a job on me as you did on the others. Look for connections, for possible enemies, who-knows-what. Inevitably, you'll come up with things I'd rather forget and, at the same time . . ."

He was quick. "At the same time it'll give you a chance to see just how good our cockamamie investigators really are, how carefully they really went through the lives of the six dead men."

We smiled and shook hands. We were now talking like *intelligent* allies.

"Okay, now *our* problem begins. Number-one problem is old Sam I told you about who's been supervising most of the work. His name is Sam Urdell and right now he's pissed off at the American Hebrew Leadership Council and the American Hebrew Committee, for which he used to work. It's an awkward family mess and I'm in the middle. It's a dispute about his pension. His *pension.* A bunch of Jews are being knocked off one by one all over the world by some mysterious crazy killer and they're arguing about whether he was supposed to be in the original pension plan for Council employees or a supplemental one. Believe me, it's enough to make you an anti-Semite. Well, I put up a few bucks and some friends of mine anted up some and the Council bled a little and we've arranged an extra two thousand dollars a year for Sam. He's gonna accept, but meanwhile he's still kind of mad and without him and his contacts we're up the creek. But I think that if he met you and saw your note he'd want to get back in harness. He really wants to solve this *goel hadam* thing before he dies."

I couldn't resist. "Me, too."

January 12, 1973.

I keep running into people besides Vogelsang who are getting second chances. My last two cabbies had gone bankrupt in small businesses and were now building up a stake to try again. It sounded more than just a big tip come-on.

I drew up my will at Feisen Conrad et cetera. It's always a lot more complicated when there's really no one to leave it to. My wife's family? I never met them. My brother's two daughters, Helen and Audrey? Fine. I left them half. I gave a fourth to the American Cancer Society and separate $10,000 gifts to McCready and Manny and $5,000 to a couple of my other border-crossers who were still alive. Another $5,000 to the American Hospital in Paris and some money to Columbia. Were there any illegitimate children around, Russ Conrad asked me. None I knew of. If there are, he warned, they'll turn up. I almost hoped there were.

I stipulated there were to be no funeral services and that my body should be given to medical researchers who might want to utilize different parts such as the eye corneas or liver or heart or whatever. I had to sign several authorization papers. I would vanish.

I have two more pimples. I picked at one of them like a teenager. I looked in the mirror intently. I imagined a coroner saying: "What a way to go: he died picking a pimple." I'm tiring more easily. There's a generalized pain in my chest. Not sharp but very *there.* I took two Dilaudids today. Still not coughing blood but sometimes I spit out some dark blue phlegm with a metallic taste. When I left the hospital they told me in cases like mine the trouble comes when the cancer spreads to the liver or the brain. If it hits the liver first I'll get jaundiced and turn yellow. When it gets to the brain I can expect terrible headaches or strokes.

There was a letter from Andresen, the surgeon:

"You asked me what else there was to do and I vaguely talked about chemotherapy and radiology. Not with much hope. But sooner or later in cases like yours the thinking starts running in the direction of the unorthodox. It's only fair that you have some background on them even if I don't think much of them. But then I don't have cancer."

Included were a set of tear sheets from a medical magazine. Each was headed: Unproven Methods of Cancer Management. One sheet was about Krebiozen, which you could get in Chicago; another about Laetrile, available in a Mexican border town; the Issels Combination Therapy, which you could get only in a Swiss clinic or London. And the Gerson Diet for cancer, which was still available at a health resort in Escondido, California. How come no travel agency had put together a Last Chance Tour? Finished off with a final visit to Lourdes.

Andresen said it was bad to sit alone and brood but I would have gone out anyway. Saturday mornings in Manhattan had a special significance since I was much younger. It was a time for taking shirts to the Chinese laundry, for walking, for looking at New York faces, to marvel at being in the city. But this Saturday I was tempted to visit the Agency walking wounded who lived within ten blocks.

McCready had phoned from Washington with the bad news. A new Agency boss, Schlesinger, had instituted a major purge. Some 2,000 of 15,000 employees were being dropped. A lot of them got the word with a one-line note on Friday morning. As Al told it, all of Friday was given over to phone calls in the Agency: "I'm still here, how about you?" I was irked to find myself pleased Schlesinger wasn't Jewish. There were a lot of premature retirees, and one of them I knew was building up a business as a house painter. Another was going to run a plant nursery in Maryland. What made the forced departures grimmer was that the Agency had only recently instituted Family Day. It was a day to bring your wife and kids and they got a modified tour through the Langley Building. Mostly it was confined to the big library and computer operation and a talk by a deputy director. Usually he'd talk about some Agency feat that took place long ago, like the Berlin underground phone-tapping. It would all be topped off by lunch in the cafeteria. By then most of the kids would still be wondering what the hell daddy did for a living in this building with the gray corridors and brightly colored doors, the strange building made of interconnected steel vaults.

The ones I was tempted to visit this Saturday had departed the Agency long before the current purge. There was Kevin Dunn who had a co-op apartment on Fifth Avenue in the Seventies and had gotten very rich after leaving the Agency. He had been Chief of Operations in Turkey with a curious cover: steel imports. The trouble is he made so much out of his overt operations that when he had a tangle with a new, fussy Chief of Station he just quit. The messy details never emerged and Dunn wouldn't talk about it. Dunn had long ago become one of the Agency's legends, like Virginia Hall, our indomitable one-legged operative who was now retired and breeding dogs somewhere. Dunn had come up from the FBI into the OSS and then the new Agency. In the late '30s he had been successfully planted, as a supposed American Bundist, into Kaltenbrunner's RHSA apparatus in Berlin. He lasted there until 1941. He became a legend in part because he was such unlikely spy material. He had grown up in Evanston, went to a veterinary school, grew orchids commercially. He had once been a prize 4-H lad. Now he was wealthy enough to have a large co-op and part-ownership of a private bank in the Bahamas.

On East Sixty-fourth Street near Park lived Ferd Kentle who had been Chief of Station in Kabul, Afghanistan, a GS-15. Suddenly he's out of the Agency and living in New York. Why? I'm sure he's not a homo. Misuse of funds? Possibly. More likely he just drank too much.

And somewhere in New York was Louise Bertolotti who always blamed me because she was no longer in the Agency. And about 11:30 AM on this Saturday, as I'm turning the corner in the Plaza, heading for the Fifth Avenue entrance, she spotted me. She was about to enter the Palm Court. She wore a flecked gray pantsuit and about a dozen junk jewelry chains. And no bra. Her nipples were almost the size of quarters. The mink coat was worn over the shoulder; the Sortilège engulfed you.

She tapped me on the right shoulder. As I spun around she said, "Harry, the Prince Charming. Don't tell me they let you out in the current pogrom?"

I said, how was she, I was on leave, and yes it was too bad about the new firings. I was trying to remember if I'd have to file a contact report on her.

"You look lousy," she said cheerfully. "Maybe you ought to get out, too." I said I might at that. She smiled thinly. "Don't give me that. You found a home in the Agency. You'll outlast the next three directors. They don't have too many living legends left, you know."

Louise once worked for me. She had to leave because she never reported an affair she had had with someone from the Other Side. The affair had taken place in the early '50s and she hadn't known who he really was. In fact, it took a defector ten years later to turn up who he was. It was a sad mess, and she told everyone that it took the miserable ex-FBI types working for the Agency—all good Catholics out of Boston College—to get rid of an Italian Catholic.

Her olive Modigliani face was a little more lined, but her carriage had a grand sweeping grace. She was, she said, an account executive at an ad agency, making more than any GS-18 would at the Agency. "And now I can fuck anyone I want to—even you, Harry." I said it would be too complicated after all these years and we weren't really right for each other. She moued: "You're running out on me again." Her face almost rounded with sudden compassion. "I'm a bitch, Harry. I almost came to visit you at Memorial. Yeah, I heard about the operation. I don't owe you anything, but it hurts to hear things like that—even when it's a bastard like you." She went into the Palm Court. A plump gray-haired man was standing at a nearby table, waiting for her impatiently. Someone else had known I was at Union Memorial.

January 13, 1973.

Vogelsang called. Croakily apologetic. Sam was coming around. There were some people at the Council he'd *never* talk to again but Vogelsang was okay and if he wanted Sam to talk to this Mr. Hanan, all right, but Sam wouldn't come into the city.

"He's living temporarily with a married daughter in Great Neck. I said you weren't feeling well—somehow I didn't want to tell him the truth—and he's still grumpy. You gotta go out to see him," Vogelsang explained. "I can arrange a car to take you out. It's only forty minutes on the Expressway, but you're doing us a favor, so please, when can you make it?"

Well, he could have suggested an ambulance with an oxygen tank. I said I'd make it on my own. I still had Warren's Mercedes in the garage. It—and the apartment—were among the last items I hadn't disposed of as executor of my brother's estate. Vogelsang gave me elaborate directions but his heart wasn't in it. Wouldn't I rather have a car and driver? I told him I wouldn't die en route. He was a kind man and didn't ask me how I knew.

3

Sam phoned. It was all right to come today, a Sunday. It looked like a nice cold but sunny day and maybe I'd like a little country air. He repeated Vogelsang's directions. I took the Fifty-ninth Street bridge and the wrong turnoff, but finally got to Great Neck by way of the Cross Island Parkway and Northern Boulevard.

The house was an enormous surprise. I expected a rambling ranch, perhaps an older mock Tudor, an adaptable Southern colonial set on an inadequate plot; or even a Spanish fake from the '20s, roofed with the requisite red tiles. Set on two acres near the confluence of Long Island Sound and Manhasset Bay, the house was a showplace, adapted from what I suspected was a French model. It was a three-storied affair built of huge, golden-white blocks of stone studded with great windows. The drawing room was a forty-foot affair, two stories high, surrounded by a gallery-library. There were coca mats on the dark-stained parquet floors, several groups of Mies chairs, a fake Ming table topped by an arresting metal sculpture. The adjoining dining room had an enormous Aubusson tapestry, a glass-topped table with modern wicker-and-steel chairs. A decorator's dream.

"Some place," Urdell said admiringly. "My daughter Marcia. She's a big decorator. They got women who pay to come through on these fund-raising tours. You get it free."

We sat in a sitting room on the balcony level, overlooking the Sound. The only discordant note was a series of framed *New York Times* ads featuring photos of some life insurance company's salesmen who had again made their mark by selling more than $2 million worth of insurance during the past year. I assumed Sam's son-in-law was one of them.

Sam said I could stay for lunch, no? His daughter and son-in-law, Bruce Hazeman, were visiting friends, a condolence call. Sam's grandson was at Yale Law School.

We had coffee and he apologized for the trembling of his arthritic hands.

"I'm a pretty old party," he began, "who's discovered at the age of seventy that he's devoted most of his life to miserable work for miserable people. Nice, huh? But you didn't come here to hear how they screwed me out of a full pension, people with millions, they roll in the dirt for a few thousand. Listen, I don't need their lousy money, but all my life I wouldn't let bastards get away with stuff so I'm not going to begin when it affects my own pocketbook. Not Vogelsang. He's all right. He's gonna make them ashamed, and they'll come through because they need me. With you around more than ever, I figure."

He sipped his coffee slowly and appraised me. "You're a young man: I got advice for you. The time will come when they'll not ask you where you got it or how you got it; only, *have* you got it? You hear the story about this professor at the Harvard Business School? At his last lecture for the term he tells his students: 'Listen, *boychicks,* you been hearing for months about line and staff and management decision making and price-earnings ratios and all that book stuff, but the most important advice I can give you comes in two words.' He picks up his books and notes and walks to the door. They're on the edge of their chairs. What's the great message? Just before he's out the door he turns around and smiles: 'Gentlemen: the first thing you must do is—*get capital.*'

"So what did I do all my life? I got anti-Semitics and Nazis and Bundists and *nishgites* like that instead of getting capital. Sure it was dangerous work. I wasn't fearless; I was *brainless.*"

His words poured out, guided by the fierce stare of his slightly exophthalmic eyes. Years ago he probably bore a slight resemblance to Mussolini.

I said capital wasn't my problem. Only time and health. He relaxed. "Now that's a gentleman hinting. I talk too much. Vogelsang said you weren't feeling too well."

I was tempted to test him. Was he going to be an Oh-my-Godder; or a "Y'know the doctors could be wrong. Now I know this fella"; or, "There's this doctor the AMA is out to get. Well, he has this medicine and they won't let him. . . ." I told Sam and he surprised me. "You *believe* you're going to die soon?" That question was so unexpected it took me a while to respond.

"When you're this side of forty it's hard to *believe*. But unless the medical profession is completely hopeless I have three months, probably less."

He drank his coffee a little noisily.

"I'm gonna *need* you long as you got. Vogelsang is no pro. I read your biography in the State Department Register and it tells me right away you're CIA. I've read enough of those cover biographies so I recognize one. You got some talents we need in this investigation, Hanan."

"Right now my strongest talent is only curiosity. . . . Why *me* and what do *I* have in common with those six dead men? As the pain gets rougher I'm pretty sure that curiosity is going to drain away fast. I don't think you should count on me for too much help."

He unbuttoned his black alpaca cardigan while he sought to frame his answer. "What we need, Hanan, is fresh thinking and a lot of luck. So far what we got is worth yesterday's *pishachs.*"

It was Yiddish-testing time. I smiled. "That much I know." The word must have triggered him. He excused himself to pee. When he came back he was still tinkering with his zipper. "You know what's one of the terrible troubles of age in a man? Terminal dribbles. You never really finish peeing. Drip, drip, drip. It gets on your drawers, it gets on your pants. Every man my age must smell like a urology clinic." I said I'd settle for that. He sighed. "May you live to have terminal dribble."

Another cup of coffee got us down to the investigation.

Did I ever think about that ridiculous expression: "He led a *blameless* life"? Who's doing the blaming? Who's measuring? And by what standards?

"These six we know about. No indictments, no major scandals, no real hidden pasts. Fairly ordinary middle-class men, perhaps a little more prosperous than average. Maybe a little sharp-shooting now and then. Not one of them even divorced. Why should anybody want to kill them? If you see nothing straight ahead you start looking sidewise. Then you start seeing things. Take Number One, Howard Lucksig, the accountant. Okay, we know that he played around a little on trips. Girls, not boys. And he was once on the verge of trouble with the SEC on a cockeyed over-the-counter issue in which his firm did the accounting. He got a fair amount of the stock at ten cents a share. The stock collapsed and there was a civil suit that was settled out of court. Nothing really. But Howard has a younger brother, Harris, who is a research chemist with his own testing lab. Howard and Harris were behind a little company that financed research into a long shot that could have made them very rich and very hated. Harris spent ten years with General Foods working on synthetic coffee. He left, went on his own, but continued with his interest in the synthetic coffee problem. Turns out a lot of big outfits were in this. Made some South American and African countries very nervous. If real, flavorful synthetic coffee can replace coffee beans, a lot of national economies are in big trouble. It's one of the big research projects of our time. Very difficult. More than five hundred different components. They not only got to find them, but then be able to put them together right. Stabilize them, they say. Well, Harris Lucksig thought he had a shortcut and he and his brother were out raising more money. Word was starting to get out. Did they *really* have something? Who knows? But if some Brazilians or Colombians *thought* they had something, maybe they might be inclined to make sure that the discovery wasn't made. Now, you ask intelligently, if they were out to kill a Lucksig why the accountant and not the chemist?"

You had to follow the script:

"I ask."

"So I tell you there is no *good* answer. Obviously they killed the wrong Lucksig, and since they weren't twins or look-alikes maybe it wasn't over synthetic coffee. Mostly I dragged that part in to show you how thorough we went into this. We checked out all the detours and footpaths —looking for the footpads." His face enjoyed the wordplay. "Believe me, we went through a lot of idiot projects in this investigation. Wait, here's another one."

Lucksig, it turned out, was the surname of a particularly black family in Russian-Jewish history. Between 1825 and 1856 Nicholas I introduced forcible conscription into his army. Jewish boys, the "cantonists," were forcibly inducted for twenty-five years' service. In that time a lot of them were converted to the Russian Orthodox Church. The few middle-class families, the merchant class, were able to buy exemption for their sons but the poor couldn't. After a while the Czar introduced mandatory quotas for each town and community and the village elders had to supply the conscripts. This meant that choices had to be made in each village: who went, who stayed. The choice was generally on the side of the ones who showed an aptitude for study of the Torah. The stupid ones, the idlers, the misfits, were sent to the army. But after a few years, when the quotas were increased, some communities decided on another alternative: perhaps their quotas could be met by using Jewish boys from other communities. Jewish gangs, the grabbers, *choppers*, arose. On contract, they kidnapped Jewish boys from smaller communities and delivered them to the larger communities to fill their quotas. It became a big, shameful business and one family, run by a Chaim Lucksig, thrived on it for twenty years.

"Tracing Jewish family genealogies, particularly those from Russia," Sam went on, "is a very tough business. What we had to go on is that in eighteen ninety-one in London a member of the Lucksig family was killed by some irate Jews on the ground that he was bloodstained. The murderers were never caught. The chance that our Lucksig was related is pretty bad, but I mention it again only to show how we looked into everything, no matter how iffy."

Maybe, he went on, they looked too hard. "We got distracted by glittering footnotes that had nothing to do with what we were looking for. So sometimes, in the stories I tell you about these six men and some of the connections we worked out for them, it was important not to ask what the hell all this got to do with *goel hadam* notes. We had to work on the understanding that *anything* might lead to a connection that would tie them all together. So we had to check out everything. That's what made it so expensive."

He shook his head and smiled vaguely. "I'm like a seventy-year-old Pavlovian dog. Listen, Hanan, could you stand me smoking? I mean . . ."

Not one cigarette in a month and it hadn't bothered me as much as I was told it would. Anyway, I was never a cigar smoker. He went out to another room and came back with a Monte Cruz 210. "The best you can get legally here. My only real vice, and if those *momzerim* on the Committee hadn't fixed up my pension I would have—God forbid—had to smoke some U.S.-made *dreck.*"

He lit up ritually, inhaled, blew a smoke ring—I was beginning to feel like a wide-eyed nephew being entertained by a great storytelling uncle —and commenced the story of the peculiar Zelkowicz connection.

Zelkowicz, he reminded me, was the fifth *goel hadam* victim. The one who managed an electronics factory in Berlin. Married, one child, fairly well-to-do, no significant political connections or ideologies. True, he had fought with the Israeli Air Force in 1948 but that would hardly make him a target of any murderous Arab groups. Yes, they had explored that possibility, too. It didn't lead anywhere. Most of the Arab guerrilla groups love to boast of the killings they were responsible for. They'd hardly hide these under a couple of Hebrew words.

No, the peculiar trail this case investigation led them to was *treasure hunting*. Urdell waited for me to come up with an appropriate response. General Rommel's supposed treasure somewhere in North Africa was appropriate; Captain Kidd's, of course, wasn't. I threw out the missing gold bars of the Reichsbank of Hitler's Third Reich; the still-missing artworks taken by Goering's detachments from France to Italy. Urdell was obviously pleased. I was playing the game right.

"Books have been written about those treasure hunts," he went on, "but the one Zelkowicz was on hasn't been written about. One good reason might be that no one is even sure there is a treasure. And if anyone was sure, he'd also know it could be a very dangerous one."

No, what Zelkowicz was after was the missing fortune and documents of a strange man named Alexander Helphand who died in Berlin on December 12, 1924. Died in a magnificent estate, Schwanenwerder, on Lake Wannsee. At the time he died some estimated he was one of the ten richest men in Germany. Which was a peculiar state for him to be in because he was a fierce advocate of the idea of permanent revolution, an idea that Trotsky admitted he had borrowed. He was also the means by which Imperial Germany financed the Soviet Revolution in Russia to the extent of at least $10 million—$150 million in today's values. And finally, he negotiated the arrangement by which Lenin was permitted to cross Germany in a sealed train to reach the Finland Station in Petrograd and the start of the Russian Revolution on April 16, 1917.

As a multimillionaire revolutionary, Helphand was naturally suspect to everybody. The Socialists distrusted him in spite of his enormous assistance to the revolution because of his life-style. His estate on an island in Lake Wannsee had liveried footmen and butlers in white cotton gloves. There were lavish parties and open houses for Socialist leaders, young and old. A lot of the older Socialists distrusted Helphand because he was a great lover of fine old wine and beautiful young women. They were suspicious of him because they suspected his financial dealings—he had made millions dealing in coal during the war and more millions before the war as a grain dealer operating out of Constantinople. And finally, some of them were certain that a lot of the money the German Imperial government had paid out to finance the Bolshevik Revolution had ended up in some of Helphand's bank accounts in Switzerland. He was the dangerous black sheep of German Socialists. Trotsky, who had been a good friend, broke with him on ideological grounds. Lenin, who owed his safe return to Russia to Helphand's covert operations, used to warn comrades not to have anything to do with the millionaire revolutionary. Some said that Helphand had a dangerous dossier on Lenin, providing proof of untold shameful incidents.

When Helphand died in 1924, his son and friends searched his Schwanenwerder estate for his political papers. They found nothing. His widow—a much younger woman—had, and presumably still has, a collection of bank vault keys. But she didn't know what Swiss banks they were for.

Since 1924 several efforts have been made—some by Soviet agents, it was believed—to solve the mystery and get at the supposed dossier. Others have tried just to get at the money and securities Helphand is supposed to have secreted in the vaults. Artur Zelkowicz got involved because a classmate of his at Manchester University had become a European historian. He interested Zelkowicz in the treasure hunt. Zelkowicz had unearthed the Helphand widow—she still lived in Berlin—and had been allowed to make impressions of the keys she still possessed. A week before he was killed he wrote his historian friend that he had come across a new and vital clue but didn't say what it was.

When he finished the story Urdell put his hands on his lap. "All right, now what do you do with details like *that.* I don't think there's any kind of damn connection between this and why Zelkowicz was killed, but you have to try to check it out. You know, Hanan, when I put the pieces of the story together I always see Sydney Greenstreet and Peter Lorre in the movie. Helphand was a big, fat party and very, very intelligent. The trouble is Zelkowicz wasn't a Lorre type."

Urdell's daughter returned to the house about noon. She was in her late forties, a short, fairly slender blonde with deep-set green eyes—and the offsetting burden of rather heavy legs. Was she not wearing a pantsuit because she was courageous? Masochistic? Or just stopped caring? In the past ten years she had built up a great business as an interior decorator. She wanted to know about the types who were in charge of decorating U.S. embassies abroad. I knew very little about it but filled her in on a few decorating disasters I remembered hearing about in the embassies at Athens and Ankara. I nibbled at the luncheon —clear soup, a quiche, cherry torte, and coffee—and about one o'clock Urdell suggested we take a little walk around the area "to settle his stomach." When he saw that I tired after walking only a hundred yards we returned to the house and the den.

There are some heavily laden historical names that die out because no one dares carry them. You can't pick up the Manhattan phone book, he said, and find, say, a Thomas Torquemada; or maybe spot a George Jeffreys in the London phone book. Terrible names. A lot of terrible *Jewish* names came out of the Nazi terror in Eastern Europe. The names of Jews who had willingly cooperated with *them* either because they hoped to endure, enrich themselves, or, occasionally, because they thought the Nazis had to win and maybe there was a sliver of room for a proven Jewish collaborator. There was Chaim Rumkowski, who ran the Lodz ghetto for the Nazis, and Leib Kudish, who ran a smaller one in the Ukraine and celebrated his silver wedding anniversary with a week-long feast which the fearful ghetto residents had to pay for.

But in Warsaw, where the ghetto fighters put up their great, fierce resistance to the end, there were also a dozen miserable Jews like Abraham Gancwajch. He was the leader of a group who served as agents of the German Secret Police. He expected the Nazis to win and the only hope, as he saw it, was that he and his group would be on record as working 100 percent with the Nazis all along. Crazy, Urdell said, but don't forget there was even a tiny band of Jewish Nazis in Germany in 1933 until the real Nazis told them to get lost.

Victim Number 6, Mike Gangwach, the odometer-fixer and locksmith, bore a name that remarkably resembled that of Nazi collaborator Abraham Gancwajch, but Urdell's group couldn't establish any connection. In running down Gangwach's background they did find out that he was a heavy and unlucky speculator in commodities. "There was one firm that practically lived on his trades," Sam recalled. "You could have gotten rich doing exactly the opposite of what Gangwach did in the market. Also, he slept with the same whore, a Norwegian girl, every Saturday night for more than three years. He gave her fifty dollars every time and on Christmas he'd bring a big box of Barton's chocolates. Yeah, we checked out the Norwegian girl. She had no reason to kill him: he was her steadiest customer and she really liked him. He replaced the locks in her apartment so that no one could get in without a special key."

The last crazy story we got, he began, as he lit another Monte Cruz —he waved it like a question mark before he lit up and I nodded—is about the Frenchman, Faucon. The one who died a Catholic in Aix-les-Bains. "This is the wildest one. At least with the synthetic-coffee character and Zelkowicz and his treasure hunting in Berlin we have pretty good documentation. This time we got documentation but how good it is, is another matter." He and the cigar made love for a minute.

"Once when I was a boy on the Lower East Side I did what a lot of boys did then: I sold papers. But I was a little different. I used to read the papers, too. Well, once there was a front-page interview with Andrew Carnegie somewhere in Scotland, and he was talking about some big amalgamations taking place and he came up with a marvelous line that still sticks with me like the smell of a bakery early in the morning. He said, 'They throw cats and dogs together and we call them elephants.' I kept repeating the line and I'd laugh to myself. Went on for days. That one line and the rhythm I worked out for it could get me to laugh for years after. So, for that one line and his public libraries I always liked the *momzer.* "

He went on. "Sometimes in our investigations it must look as if we're working too hard to put cats and dogs together and then get tempted to call them terrible elephants. But we never did. When they didn't add up to elephants we were the first to say, listen *boychicks,* we only got pups and pussycats, so let's forget it. And it wasn't easy because every one of those 'let's-forget-its's cost us several thousand bucks, believe me."

"The Faucon case," he said, "made us think maybe we had something new. For the first time a *goy* was involved. But we learned pretty quick that his father had been a Jew who had changed his name when marrying a French Catholic. But it wasn't Maurice Faucon who interested us. He was a nothing; but his pop, Moritz Fassnacht, there was a man destiny played with. If we can believe him."

Fassnacht was born in Constantinople in 1880 in a middle-class Jewish family. He was always ashamed of the way his family made money: they ran a couple of whorehouses. So he managed to get them to stake him to about $5,000, which was a hell of a lot of dough then, and he lit out for Vienna because he could talk German. He futzed around awhile and then settled on manufacturing stuffed toys. He was a bachelor, and it was a pretty good business. He employed about thirty people and his toys were shipped all over Europe. Mostly he was knocking off Steiff stuffed toys, which a lot of sharp operators were doing then. One day on a whim he bought an automobile, a forty-horsepower Métallurgique, a two-seater built in 1912. It was a crazy thing for him. In those days only the rich or the nobility had sporting cars in Vienna. Because he was a Jew he wasn't even eligible for membership in the Royal Austrian Auto Club. He bought the car because it was a slightly used bargain. One of his suppliers of velvets and plushes was on the verge of going bust so he sold the $2,800 car to Fassnacht for $1,200. The bargain also included driving lessons.

The details of the way destiny toyed with Fassnacht came from an account that he had written in German in 1936, two years before he died. He left the account for his son, but actually the adventure with the Métallurgique had become part of the family folklore because he used to like telling the story. Except that after 1940 it became a very dangerous story to fool around with. Somehow Urdell's French agent had managed to get a copy from Madame Faucon—presumably for a modest payment—and Urdell had had it translated.

Urdell had a few pages of the translation with him—the important pages. They went this way:

So now we come to 3 February 1913, a Monday. About 3:30 that afternoon I had a sudden and terrible compulsion to get out of my factory. To go for a drive. Anywhere. It was not a nice day. During the long winter months in Vienna the sky hangs dark and sad with heavy banks of clouds. The winds are cold. But something, God knows what, was forcing me to go driving that afternoon.

I drove aimlessly on the Ringstrasse, to the Karlsplatz. Then, still without thinking, I headed for the Maximilianplatz and the Votive Church. . . . Suddenly I was almost on the two men.

They had stepped off the curb about the same time and were almost in front of me on the Maximilianplatz. It was beginning to get dark and I could make out not much about them except that I sensed they were not together. As I approached they both turned their faces to me and the car and they looked panic-stricken, stuck in place. Without thinking I turned the wheel so that the car would turn out and away from them. But in my confusion and sudden fear I turned the wheel in toward the curb and them. In that second they had come to life and taken a couple of steps. I was going about 60 km an hour. Instead, by turning in, my left wheel and fender knocked them to the ground with a glancing blow.

I braked immediately, stopped, got out and ran back to where they were still lying on the street. The shorter one caught my eye immediately. His yellow eyes were pouring hate into me. I did not expect him to be happy to make my acquaintance under such circumstances, but I had the feeling all drivers of autos such as mine were his bitter enemies. His skin was sallow and pock-marked. He had a thick nose, a heavy mustache, and a low forehead. He wore a black hat and a heavy dark coat.

The other man had a thin, hungry face covered with black beard. His hair was long and unkempt. He wore an oil-stained long brown coat that looked a little like a ghetto caftan. His greasy black derby had been thrown to the ground when he was hit. For a moment I thought maybe he was Jewish.

They picked themselves up, moved their arms and legs, and seemed surprised that no bones were broken. The short one with the yellow eyes spat at me and said something in a Slavic language—Bulgarian, Russian, Serbo-Croatian—it could have been any one of them. The other picked up his derby and took a step toward me. I was sure he was going to ask me to give him something for his troubles and I started reaching for my wallet. Then he suddenly walked away.

When they left, going in different directions, I was about to go back to the car when I saw a sheet of gray paper on the ground near me. I remembered the one with the yellow eyes was carrying a cheap portfolio that had burst open when he was hit. This was a sheet from it. I picked it up. The script was tight and harsh and Slavic. I pocketed the sheet. Driving very slowly back to my apartment I remembered when I had seen the taller man before.

There was a Hungarian Jew I knew, a fellow named Neumann, who bought old clothes and remnants. Twice a year he'd come to my factory to buy the remnants of plush and velvets left over from cutting. The Lord knows what he did with those odd pieces. He was a bachelor and lived frugally in a run-down hotel for men at 27 Meldemannstrasse near the Danube. Well, the year before when Neumann came to pick up his remnants he brought this fellow with the long black hair and beard. He was an artist and Neumann thought he could draw some signs or posters for me. He was a good artist, Neumann assured me, even if he had some wild ideas. It happened I had nothing for the artist but I told him I'd keep him in mind. The day after the accident I sent word to Neumann I had work for his artist friend who also lived in this men's hotel on Meldemann-strasse. Three days later the artist came to my factory.

I am sure he didn't recognize me as the man who had nearly run him over —those goggles and thick muffler and cap would hide anyone's identity—and he showed me samples of his work. There was a poster of Teddy's Perspiration Powder; a postcard of *Le Bonhomme Noël* selling colored candles and things like that. I told him what I wanted: a drawing of *Le Bonhomme Noël*—a Santa Claus—with a pack full of my stuffed animals. I didn't really need it but I could use it in my catalogue. He asked for some of the toys and I put a few in front of him on a counter and he sketched rapidly. After a while he said he'd be back with the finished product tomorrow.

When he left I remembered the sheet of gray paper of the shorter man. I called in my foreman, a very intelligent Russian. He slowly deciphered the scrawl and translated the writing this way:

"Not the national but the agrarian problem decides the fate of progress in Russia. The national problem is subsidiary to it. . . ."

The artist came back a week later and showed me the watercolor. It wasn't bad for its kind but stiff and ungraceful. I paid him a little extra—to ease my conscience—and he left without thanking me. I was beginning to feel better.

Sam stopped reading. "You're a smart feller. You figure out who . . . ?"

I could but it didn't make much sense. Hitler and Stalin in Vienna in February 1913? Almost too perfect: like a needed construct for one of those time-machine fantasies in which the past is tinkered with to create a less catastrophic present.

Sam went on: "That part was easy. They *were* in Vienna in February nineteen thirteen. Stalin was there working in the State Library on a book to be called *The Problem of Nationalities and Social Democracy.* Hitler had lived in Vienna from nineteen ten to nineteen thirteen and made a miserable living doing commercial art."

Checking on Fassnacht's story was a little trickier, though. The manuscript had been written in 1936, long before much was known of Hitler's down-and-out days in Vienna. Only after World War II did details start emerging, such as that he had lived in the crummy men's hotel on Meldemannstrasse and that a Hungarian Jew named Neumann *had* befriended him. On the Stalin end there was a yellow photostat that Fassnacht had made of the sheet Stalin had lost in the accident.

"The original?" I asked.

Sam began reading from Fassnacht's story again:

As I write this in November 1936, Hitler and Stalin are absolute dictators in their countries. The more I read about them the more I am certain that in my stupidity, in my inability to distinguish right from left—and spare me your smiles of irony—I had been responsible for one of the truly great tragedies of history. I was supposed to kill two men by accident that day in Vienna and I had failed. An instrument of fate who had fumbled his one assignment. . . .

After he wrote his account, Fassnacht sent Stalin a letter telling him what had happened on that February day in Vienna.

I begged him as one who had once held his life in my steering wheel to reconsider his course, one sure to lead the world to destruction. And I sent him the sheet I had picked up in the street. I also sent the watercolor and a similar letter to Hitler. I got no answers. I really didn't expect any. Both were megalomaniacs and atheists. Neither could believe God played any kind of role in their lives or that He, once in His great Prescience, toyed with the idea of removing them from this earth before they attained the power of universal death and destruction.

I was very tired and put my head carefully to the back of the Mies chair to keep from fainting. I passed out for a minute but remained upright. When I came to, Sam was putting a wet towel to my forehead. He helped me over to a couch with luxurious fur-covered pillows and I slept awhile. Later he drove me home. I was able to take the elevator up to the apartment and I went to bed.

4

January 17, 1973.

The pain, Andresen warned me, would come because the growing cancer compresses root nerves or invades blood vessels. The painkillers would help awhile but they had side reactions: my mood would turn down miserably, I'd wheeze like an asthmatic, and I'd get dopey. I could expect lots of nausea and vomiting. "It's not what you might call living," he admitted. Also fever. As the cancer destroyed the invaded body tissue there would be high fever.

It started Sunday night and ran up quickly. I managed to take my temperature about eleven, 104. It went up but I didn't have the energy or will to find out. I remember the phone ringing a few times but I couldn't answer. Before the fever went up I put out a pitcher of water, a bottle of aspirin, and some rubbing alcohol with a towel on the bedside table. The end of the line would be 112.

Sleeping inside a roaring furnace isn't sleep. Incendiary Inertia? A fact: a twenty-four-hour period of fever results in the destruction of one percent of the body's protein. The process was irreversible. I would shrink steadily and then when I could no longer stand the heat I'd have a cool bath. I'd let the water run out, go down the drain, and thus bring my life to an end with my first remembered fear.

By Wednesday morning the fever fell to 101 and I managed to get to the bathroom to see how much weight I had lost. Four pounds. Suddenly I felt ravenous and I chomped oatmeal cookies and apples. About noon I found a note near the phone: I should call Vogelsang when I could. If I had had hallucinations about another person being in the apartment I was right. He had phoned Stichman who managed to get a nurse to come over Monday and Tuesday. She was committed elsewhere the rest of the week. But a nurses' registry had promised to have someone in on Thursday and Friday, if necessary.

I phone Vogelsang to thank him and let him know the fever was down now.

"When you feel up to it," he went on, "come by. For the first time we have something that ties in most of the victims. We ought to have it nailed down in a day or two." I asked, me, too? "Well, not directly, but it does include the Hanan family. Come by Friday."

I phoned a delicatessen on Sixth Avenue and ordered a roast beef sandwich, onion rings, and some cherry strudel. Just ordering it made me feel healthier even though I wondered if I could eat it all. I opened the door and checked the dropleaf table near the elevator where the doorman usually left the mail. The only interesting item was from Yochanan Shorsh, the Hebrew Theological Seminary professor. Apparently I was now officially on the *goel hadam* team, for the letter was a carbon. Mine was probably the least legible one as befitted the newest team member. It was headed, "Items of Interest from the Talmud and Rambam and Clues to the *Thinking* of the Killer." On my copy he had thoughtfully put an asterisk in ink next to Rambam, and at the bottom of the page he wrote: "Maimonides: a twelfth-century rabbi-savant who organized the vast mass of Jewish oral law. You knew?"

Shorsh had made some nice points about the *goel hadam*, ancient law, and modern murder.

The Sanhedrin, the highest criminal court in Palestine in biblical times, was empowered to inflict four methods of death for major male-factors: stoning, burning, slaying by the sword, and strangulation. The order was important. The severer the crime the likelier that retribution would come by stoning or burning. Beheading and strangulation were considered more merciful. But these rules didn't apply to the *goel hadam*. He could kill in any way that came to hand. Just like our *goel* is doing apparently.

Seder Nezikim of the Talmud provides the sanction for the catch-as-catch-can murder by the *goel:* "But where it is not possible to execute him in the manner prescribed . . . one may execute him by any means possible. . . . The avenger of the blood shall himself put the murderer to death." If the murdered man has no avenger of blood, the *Beth Din*, the high court, must appoint one. Thought: where does our *goel* get *his* sanction to kill? . . .

Can we consider killing a man by running him down with a speeding car akin to stoning? A remote connection, but still we have the death of Jaime Wolynski struck by a hit-and-run driver in Caracas.

Two of the known victims died by drowning. Can we assume this to be a modified version of the Talmudic death by strangulation? N.B.: Medical examiners have long known and worried about the fact that if a person is rapidly disabled and thrown into the water, the findings will often resemble an accidental drowning. George Joseph Smith, the English bride-in-the-bath multiple murderer, drowned his successive wives by simply holding their knees out of the water while they were in the bathtub. This, of course, made it impossible for them to lift their heads above water. Many medical examiners think the cases experts miss most often are homicides in which the victim is smothered or strangled. In strangulation the signs can be extremely subtle; and in smothering there are almost no signs. If the killer knows how to place the victim's head right after death, it's just about impossible to detect the fact that murder has taken place.

In the Talmud, six specific crimes called for death by strangulation: having intercourse with a married woman—by other than her husband, of course; striking one's father or mother; kidnapping a Jew; an elder rebelling against the decision of the court; prophesying falsely; and prophesying in the name of an idol.

How come no female victims? Is Verkko's law involved? This Finnish criminologist says: "In countries of high frequency of crime against life, the female proportion of those killed is small; in countries of low frequency of crimes against life, the percentage of female victims is large."

I suspect our *goel* doesn't worry about Verkko's law—or any others.

Maimonides, like all later interpreters, is against the taking of private vengeance. But we mustn't assume that to understand all is to forgive all. Psychoanalysts agree the need for revenge is present in most of us. Here's Reik: "Only fools, hypocrites, or sick people deny the deep and voluptuous staisfaction adequate revenge can give, deny the extraordinary feeling of liberation, indeed, redemption from stifling psychic pressure, which follows successful revenge."

Let's not assume vengeance is old-fashioned, unintelligent, unsophisticated. Take Heine, who spent a lot of time and energy banging out at the romantic notions of his century. "My frame of mind is most peaceful. My wishes are: a modest hut, a thatched roof, but a good bed, good food, milk and butter—very fresh, flowers in front of my window, beautiful trees outside my door, and, if the good Lord wishes to make me *completely happy,* he lets me have the job of seeing hanged on those trees about six or seven of my enemies. Deeply moved, I shall forgive them before they die all the wrong they inflicted upon me in their lifetime. Yes, one must forgive one's enemies, but not until they are hanged."

While waiting for the deli order, I decided to get dressed. I went to one of the bedroom closets and found the overhead light wasn't working. I couldn't quite reach the bulb so I looked around the deep closet for something to stand on. Off in a far corner I spotted a compact, gray metal toolbox about eight inches high. I pulled it over, stood on it, reached the bulb, unscrewed it, and got another from the pantry closet to replace it. When I went to push the metal box back into the corner I heard a rattle inside. I took the box over to the window and found it had a flimsy lock, which I opened with a screwdriver.

It was Warren's memorabilia box. My brother was ten years older. The box had some track medals won while he was at Fieldston; a couple of gold Kings Crown awards for work on the Varsity Show at Columbia; some columns he had written for the Columbia *Spectator;* several tradepaper clips about his setting up a Volkswagen distributorship in 1953; letters he received overseas in World War II—he had been a Transportation Corps Captain in France—and my grandfather's pocket watch. It was a gold Elgin. On the inside of the cover was engraved in ornate italic script:

> For M. Hanan. From His Many Loyal
> Friends in the New York United
> Benevolent Association
> October 1, 1905

I had heard about the watch. Warren got it from Grandpa Hanan when he was four, which was about five years before Grandpa died. That was before I was born, of course.

I remembered little about Grandpa. He had made some money in real estate; he had once been a minor Tammany pol; and when he died in 1923 he left a number of heavily mortgaged buildings which were eventually foreclosed. Fortunately, there were some trust funds left for my grandmother. She died in 1934 and left the money for my parents and bequests for Warren and myself. Mine I was to get when I was twenty-one or graduated from college. With interest it came to $4,000 and I left college without finishing when I was twenty-one.

There was never much talk about Grandpa Hanan. In the few pictures of him I remember seeing, he was florid-faced, heavyset, with a turned-up mustache. They never smiled in those old portraits, but even so there wasn't the remotest touch of benign grandfatherliness in any of them.

At the bottom of the metal box was Warren's old stamp album. Like many youngsters, he started collecting and forgot it after a year. Most of them were low-value U.S. and Great Britain, perhaps two to three hundred in all—typical philatelic junk. And at the back, near the fading cover, was a postcard. An ordinary U.S. penny postcard. It was addressed: "M. Hanan, 204 West 38th Street, City." The postmark was New York and dated April 12, 1908:

NEW YORK UNITED BENEVOLENT ASSOCIATION

Brother: You are requested to attend the funeral of our beloved Sister, Katie Polta, which will take place on Wednesday, April 15, 1908, at 1 o'clock sharp from Sigmund Schwerin, 141 Second Avenue. For not attending: $2 fine.

By order of the President: J. Schlifka,
Secretary

The deli order came and I took it into the living room overlooking Central Park and the skaters, and I found I wasn't as hungry as I thought. Also, I wasn't feeling quite as exultant as I had earlier. The fever was pretty much gone but some of the old pain was coming back. It wasn't going-out weather, after all.

Perhaps the Urdell-Vogelsang team had already solved the mystery of the New York United. If they were anywhere near as efficient on my forebears as they had been on the other *goel hadam* victims, they could save me a lot of curiosity. I phoned Urdell in Great Neck. His daughter answered. Her father had gone back to the city. She gave me his number. He lived on West Eighty-first Street. I phoned. We exchanged health reports. How were they coming on my background check?

"Suspended, everything's suspended. Vogelsang is sure he's got the answer and your background doesn't matter anymore."

I said he sounded as if he didn't think Vogelsang was on the right track.

"He's not even on the right continent. I bet him a box of cigars he's wasting time."

What was the tie-up?

"It's his little Edsel. Let him sell it to you. Reminds me. After my wife dies my daughter and son-in-law send me on a Far East tour. In Kyoto I'm sitting in a hotel room while it's raining pigeons and I see this book under the telephone. Like a Gideon Bible. Only turns out to be *The Teachings of Buddha*. I open it up at random and what do I find on page sixty-two? 'Where, then, is the source of human grief, lamentation, pain, and agony? Is it not to be found in the fact that people are generally ignorant and willful?' So you see even Buddha had his own Vogelsangs. . . . Listen, I don't know what it is in Sanskrit but in Hebrew it's *malech hamovis*. Stay inside. On a day like this the angel of death is real busy in New York with old cockers like me, so maybe he'll overlook you if he doesn't pass you on the street."

I phoned Manny and brought him current on my miseries.

"How would I check on an old Jewish benevolent association?" I told him the name and the date when it was around.

"One of the old *landsmanschaften*. There were thousands of them and they're dying off fast. There's someone at the New York State Insurance Office who helps liquidate them. Mostly, they had cemetery plots which are filled and maybe they had a few thousand bucks in the treasury. The old ones die off. None of them could get their sons to go into the organization, so what you have is two or three members with a few thousand dollars, and they don't even bother holding meetings anymore. In the old days every Jewish fund raiser went after them, but it doesn't pay anymore. The best way to find out who's around still is to call the funeral home handling their burials."

Sigmund Schwerin, untkrs, was still in the Manhattan book. And still at 141 Second Avenue. I got Newman Schwerin, who must be at least the grandson of the original Sigmund. What could he tell me about New York United? I said that it was a family matter and we were interested in the plots.

Well, New York United had a big set of plots at Washington Cemetery in Brooklyn. The man to talk to was the current president, Morris Clapman, who lived in Forest Hills.

I told Clapman I was inquiring because my grandfather had been a member. He asked the name. "Oh yeah, I seen that name on a stone. Way before my time."

He was one of sixteen surviving members. "One time we got two hundred and we hold regular meetings at the Central Plaza on Second Avenue, maybe fifteen, sixteen years ago. Me, I joined only in nineteen thirty-two. Most of the men left are in their sixties now and they joined in the late Twenties and Thirties also. It was a good outfit to join. Had lots of money. Widows got two hundred fifty dollars and a free burial."

Any women members? "You kiddin?"

Could there have been women members back in 1905? "Impossible. You got us mixed up with another outfit." He went on about how sad it was that an organization like New York United was allowed to die out. None of the sons of the members wanted to join even though care on all the plots in the two cemeteries was paid up until 1990. The treasury still had $15,000 in war bonds purchased in 1943.

I tried another tack. What businesses were most of the surviving members in? "Businesses? They just try to stay alive. Most of us are near or past retirement. We got all kinds. Cab drivers, storekeepers, one guy was buyer for a restaurant chain, another one was a furrier. We did whatever Jews in New York did."

I asked, feeling very foolish, if they had any kind of history of the organization.

"They stopped taking minutes twenty years ago. All a history would have is: Brother so-and-so died, and then Brother so-and-so. A long, sad list, that's all. . . . Six months ago, maybe more, I get a call from someone who asked me the same thing."

A history?

"Yeah, we got some kind history of the New York United? You know what I figure? Some writer down on his luck hears we got this fifteen thousand dollars in the treasury, maybe he can latch onna piece. Turns out it's a missing-heir investigator. Finds missing heirs, and he's looking for someone who might have belonged. It sounded some kind of con job, a little dipsy-doodle, so I didn't listen too close but I remembered because he also started out asking if we had a history, like you."

I thanked him for his help and he said, anytime.

January 18, 1973.

Vogelsang was filled with anticipatory pleasure: I'd see how professional a job he had done. "How well did you know your brother's private life?"

I said I was ready to be knocked over.

"We've linked your brother with three of the victims: Howard Lucksig, Maurice Faucon, and Monte Morden."

The connection was established when they were checking the late Monte Morden. He was, Vogelsang reminded me, victim Number 4, who had once been a successful real estate syndicator and died broke. He lived in Hastings-on-Hudson.

"Soon after he died his widow and a state inheritance tax examiner and her lawyer went to the bank and opened his safe deposit box. In it they find stock certificates worth about four million. Now get the picture. The widow knows her husband is practically broke. He's in hock to everyone, the house is mortgaged to the hilt, he's borrowed on his life insurance, and suddenly there's four million in beautiful stock certificates. Her lawyer is open-mouthed. The state tax fellow is impressed. And the widow is just glazed. She fingers the certificates again and again. They're all made out to Monte Morden. You can imagine the moods she runs through in a few minutes: first, how could this be? If he had this kind of money, why were they so in hock? Why didn't he tell her, and so on. Then she has to discard all the negative moods. Okay, maybe he had his reasons. But no matter what, here's a lot of dough for her and their three kids. For that she'll take the knowledge that Monte hadn't leveled with her, had put her through hell for a couple years.

"They make a list of the stuff, the stock certificates are taken to a broker in New York, and he's told to sell them. A week later the lawyer is called in to the broker who says, Hey, what you trying to pull here? The certificates are phonies, counterfeit. The broker talks of running down to the DA, to the Bar Association Disciplinary Committee on West Forty-fourth Street; the lawyer, who's sweating bullets, explains how the certificates turned up; that he's just the lawyer for the executrix of the estate, nothing more."

They didn't find out where and how Morden got the certificates but they figured out how he used them. He'd pledge them as collateral on various real estate loans from banks he negotiated in connection with his syndication operations. In a rising real estate market he could pay off the loans on time and the banks never had any occasion to examine the certificates closely—or even try to sell them—so he was able to get away with it for years.

"But that's not the connection," Vogelsang went on. "It merely showed what a very sharp, conniving cookie Morden was. And that makes it all the funnier that he was taken on an obvious swindle. Along with Lucksig and Faucon and your brother."

It started with a gnomish stub of a fellow named Teddy Richmond who ran a group of bus lines in New Jersey. Back in 1954, he let a few friends know that he could pay 12 to 14 percent interest on loans—at

a time when the going rate was 4 to 5 percent. How? Well, he had to
buy a lot of new buses for his lines and the state of New Jersey allowed
him a return of 7 percent on his total investment. No reason why his
friends couldn't benefit if he had to borrow money at high rates to
finance the bus purchases. He showed everybody balance sheets of his
bus companies and they were obviously making money. Gradually
friends began telling friends, and pretty soon he also had a group of
finders, mostly lawyers and accountants, who helped bring in new money
—for a 3 percent finder's fee; a fee that would be renewed every year
the money stayed in. And the money stayed in because the interest
checks would go out every month like clockwork. In 1964, Monte
Morden became one of the finders. Like most of them, he let his 3
percent fee stay in. Very few of the finders wanted their payout in cash.

When the scheme collapsed in 1967 it turned out that there were
more than 4,400 victims and they had about $60 million on loan. It had
to collapse because Richmond needed at least $8 million every year just
to meet his soaring interest costs. He wasn't even borrowing from Peter
to pay Paul anymore. He was borrowing just to pay Paul's interest.

Most of the 4,400 lenders were Jewish families in the New York and
Los Angeles areas. One family had more than $4.5 million; another New
York family, $655,000. But there were also some foreign lenders. One
of them was Maurice Faucon, who had lent $5,000. Howard Lucksig,
the San Francisco accountant, had been a finder. He had persuaded
clients to put in about $400,000 and had gotten his 3 percent finder's
fee in cash. A very shrewd fellow, obviously.

"Your brother Warren had lent Richmond thirty thousand dollars in
nineteen sixty-four and instructed the monthly interest payments to be
sent to a Doris Janeway someplace in Westchester."

Vogelsang looked at me, expectantly.

I nodded. "So that's what the item was." I explained that in going
through my brother's accounts we had found a mysterious withdrawal
of $30,000. The check was marked payable to the Tejay Commercial
Corp., and no one had been able to figure out what it was for.

Vogelsang smiled. "A lot of girl friends and mistresses were getting
these monthly checks from Richmond. Great gimmick. Richmond
didn't file ten-forty tax reports, so it was unreported, untaxable income
for the recipients of the interest payments."

I told Vogelsang about Doris Janeway. "She wasn't his girl friend. She was his slave. She was efficient, quick, and a total blah in looks and personality. She worked six days a week for my brother and if he asked her to, she'd lie to a grand jury or anything. Her whole life centered around her job, office manager, and my brother. She never married and I sometimes wondered if she ever went to bed with anyone. What happened was, she developed myasthenia gravis. She was covered for a couple of years on the firm's health and medical insurance but when that ran out Warren must have set up this thirty-thousand-dollar fund for her. At fourteen percent interest she was probably getting forty-two hundred a year from it. That and social security payments and a little money she had on her own, paid the bills at the hospital. She died two years ago."

You could almost feel Vogelsang wince. "Would it make any difference if she had been his mistress, Vogelsang? The whole linkage is a big nothing. You have four men—and one of them, my brother, is linked indirectly. Okay, two of the men were getting a percentage of the money they persuaded people to lend this Teddy Richmond. One of them was also victimized because he let his commissions ride on loans. So, in effect, three of the four were victims. Three out of forty-four hundred who were mostly Jewish. But why on earth should anyone want to kill them because they were *victims?* If someone had tried to kill Richmond, that would be understandable. But *these* three? Just because they were foolish enough to get involved in a Ponzi-style swindle? Come on, Vogelsang."

It suddenly struck me that I hadn't had as much asperity in my voice for a long time. Maybe I was feeling better.

5

January 19, 1973.

I wasn't. Feeling better two days was only a prelude to feeling much worse longer. Fever again. I had canceled the nurse, so it was a lonely business featured by remote reveries of a book I had read when I was twelve because there were supposed to be lots of dirty parts in it. The hero, in Restoration England, is knocked out by the Great Plague of 1665 in London and he's nursed by the heroine using her own folk medicine. He's saved and they climb into the sack forever. That was the book. *Forever Amber*—and it must have been 1945 when I read it.

The inner heat abated by 11 AM. I got out of bed to confront a primitive reminder I must have set up while I was in fever. I had placed two books on the floor to form an L. For library. I was to call the New York Public Library, Reference Division.

Wasn't there a *New York Times* book index to all the obituaries they'd run? There was, she said. Could she check on an obit for a Max Hanan who died around 1923. She looked and said there was no obit for a Max Hanan. My disappointment was greater as a grandson than as a researcher. Had he been so minor a politician his death didn't rate even a few inches in the *Times?*

Urdell phoned. Was I in shape to talk? It was time for *us* to have a good long talk—now that Vogelsang had blown himself out of the ballpark with his big fart of a theory. I said come over and if he would, buy me a good-sized Cranshaw melon. I had to have it. Urdell said maybe I was suddenly pregnant with useful information. I said I was only gestating some useless questions about a relative of mine. And I'd pay for the melon, of course. He said he knew *that;* I didn't have the crummy bookkeeping tricks of the Committee.

He brought the melon. Some $8 at Charles & Co.

I ate the whole thing; gobbled it, slurped it like a famished child. I didn't care if Urdell watched me or not. He didn't. He looked out over the skaters in Central Park.

He finally sat down facing me, lit a cigar, and looked at me with a faint smile trickling forth from the proscenium arches of his massive eyebrows. "Such a big man in the Agency!" he said. "Chief of Station, no less. Ankara. Scheduled to be Deputy Director of Plans. A legend, a GS-Eighteen at thirty-six thousand a year. Some *boychick!"*

Obviously, the Hanan dossier had been going forward diligently. A lot of it wouldn't be that hard to come by. There were now hundreds of ex-Agency employees floating around.

He was reading from a pocket notebook. Hired Paris 1955 as a one-year contract agent. Permanent full-time 1956. Fucks his way through Europe.

I said he was off by a few years. *That* came later. He wasn't listening.

Does a great job as a charmer. What does an Agency charmer do? Used in special situations to develop a particular warm relationship with some key parties to give him total entrée so that he is in a position to influence that person. Hanan's particular target: King and Queen of Greece. Doesn't lay her and doesn't pimp for him, but makes himself so useful, so needed, so helpful, they depend on him; turn to him for advice and counsel. Develops reputation. Even British agents say Hanan could charm a fly off the butter dish. Given reward after a year: made a full-time staff agent with permanent status.

Charmers ordinarily resented by other agents because charmers spoke better, dressed better, and lived better. Charmers who stayed bachelors too long are suspected, so they put him on the box—the polygraph—about every eighteen months. Solid heterosexual. Involved somehow in Operation Barkside in late '50s. Forged Swiss bank letters sent to key Soviet officials working in satellite countries, telling them of large deposits made to their account. Big stink from Swiss and complaints at the UN. Operation stopped and Hanan given cross-border operations out of Turkey. . . . Does well on annual efficiency reports. Promotion boards love him, he moves up. . . .

We were wasting time. I said, "Okay, Sam, I'm impressed. But give me something you or your people couldn't have picked up in two days of questioning in Washington and Paris and God knows where."

I was saving that, he said. The unfriendly stuff. He continued reading —or reconstructing as he went along—from his notes.

"Hanan has big rep as Agency cocksman. Buys house in Georgetown during stateside assignment in nineteen sixty-one. Agency people always buy homes in Washington instead of stocks. Lease out furnished houses when abroad. Agent's wealth generally rated on basis of houses: Is he a two- or three-house man? Hanan has only one, but it's a great one. Also invests money earlier with his older brother in Volkswagen distributorship. Does everything right and smart until marriage fiasco in nineteen sixty-nine in Ankara, Turkey. He's Chief of Station with State Department cover and now he falls in love and decides to get married. Terrible complications because woman he marries is an Agency report officer in Ankara. Her name is Dorothea Fowler and she's thirty-one and very plain. From Mansfield, Ohio."

I hadn't said anything, but Urdell looked up. "I'm giving it to you like it was coming from the raw files. It's faster that way. But if it's going to get your back up . . ."

Curiously, it wasn't. I was listening to the gossip about someone I once knew but hadn't talked to in a while.

Anything about a peculiar item on the bulletin board, I asked. He had nothing on *that.* I often wondered who had put it up. What it was, was a Xeroxed page from a book by Konrad Lorenz, *King Solomon's Ring.* He had a section on social order among jackdaws. There was one, Double Aluminum—named after the rings on his feet—who had returned to the colony, conquered the ruling tyrant, and became number 1. Double Aluminum fell in love with a young female jackdaw. As a result, she automatically took Double Aluminum's top ranking among females in the colony.

The extraordinary part was part was the amazing speed with which the news spread that such a little jackdaw lady, who hitherto had been maltreated by eighty percent of the colony is, from today, the wife of the president and may no longer receive so much as a black look from any other jackdaw. But more curious still, that little jackdaw lady knew exactly what she could allow herself and she made the fullest use of it. She used every opportunity to snub former superiors and she did not stop at gestures of self-importance . . . she always had an active and malicious plan of attack ready at hand. In short, she conducted herself with the utmost vulgarity.

Urdell continued. "Everybody talking at embassy. How come handsome Harry marries dowdy Dorothea? How come smart Harry throws a monkey wrench into the social order? As wife of Chief of Station, Dorothea acquires immense social status but at same time, as minor employee, she rates so far below the salt she's practically in the kitchen. Terrible protocol problems. But Harry, superb handler of people, manages to minimize the problem. Then comes tragedy. . . . I don't have to go into this, Harry."

He wanted me to stop it. The point had been made. A thorough investigation had turned up quite a lot about Harry Hanan, whose background was tougher to investigate than the other six on the *goel hadam* list because he was an Agency employee. Ergo, Urdell and colleagues had done a thorough job all along on the dead men.

I suppose I could have relived the past through his notes if it would serve any useful purpose. But I'd get started on trying to explain why I married Dorothea and a fuller explanation of the "tragedy." Useful catharsis, perhaps, but I didn't need that now, not with Urdell.

"You got the picture. What turned up on my father, grandfather, and so on?"

He coughed a laugh. "Listen, we could spend the next three months just checking the enemies you made in your Agency career. Who has time to waste on your pop and grandpa?"

There used to be a course at The Farm, something called Teacher Training. You had to learn how to explain things from scratch. For example, *tell* someone how to tie a shoelace. Not show. *Tell.* You had to assume total ignorance. Not only did it call for great patience but you also had to break the problem into its sequential parts exactly. Now I had to explain to Sam why he shouldn't waste time on trying to run down my obvious enemies.

"Sam, we used to figure it cost us about thirty-five hundred dollars to check someone out to handle top-secret stuff. There just wouldn't be enough money around to check out, say, a hundred people who might have wanted to kill me, or even thought of it, at one time or another. And of all of them, I think there's only one man—and an American at that—who still thinks of killing me. He wants to kill me because I know about his shitty secret. He was once a U.S. military attaché in Rome. One day the locals pick him up drunk on a doorstep. They search his apartment and I get to know about it because I had done a favor for an Italian opposite number. What our American had in his bedroom was a collection of lumps of shit from each of the women he'd slept with in the past few years. He kept each in a large glassine envelope and had the woman's name attached. What happened is that I used to have to run into this guy at embassy functions and he'd always insist on shaking hands. And it took a real effort to shake hands with so kinky a collector. Well, that moment's hesitation on my part finally convinced him that I knew about his collection, and that major hated me for knowing. *He* could have killed me. But he wouldn't send me a *goel hadam* note."

I took another tack. "Sam, there are nine million people born on the same day I was. That's a link but nobody is going to follow that one up. There are lots of links, Sam, but none of them matter a damn. All the present links are beside the point. We've got to go deeper into the past. I know you've tried that, but something's eluded you. All my hunches, instincts, and training tell me that's where the answer is. And hunches are what got me a GS-Eighteen."

Intelligence, I went on, was important in the Agency—in spite of all he had heard from its critics. But intuition was even more important. Take the "charmer" job I had for two years. On the surface it sounds like all it calls for is an agreeable gopher: someone who is always around as a fourth in bridge, who can get tickets, who can plan pleasant outings, say the right things, be an obliging intermediary and all that. But the trick of the charmer is much more: first he has to intuit a minute or two before it occurs to the ones he's working on—the charmees—what it is they're going to be wanting, or even thinking of next. And he has to suggest it just as it's percolating through their minds. It's a little like the ability good magazine writers are supposed to have: they have to think of the reader's questions in advance—and have the answer in print just a second before it occurs to the reader.

When they took me on in the mid-'50s, the Agency was mostly Ivy League college types. Most of them had lived in Europe awhile with their parents when they were kids. Well, I had that, too, and my French was fluent, but don't forget I was a Jewish kid from New York and maybe Columbia is Ivy, maybe not, but I wasn't even a college graduate. I didn't have any special skills and no how-to-rise tricks. We had one character who went around with a pocketful of Ivy League rings and he'd put on the appropriate one when going in to see a superior officer. No, what I got by on was basically intuition. I could spot a Bulgarian official we could reach; I could tell, most times, who would make a good border-crosser. Even on the Barkside operation I knew who would be particularly vulnerable to those phony letters. You might say I rose on intuition. Why I didn't apply it to my life is something else. Maybe you're not allowed to—like the mediums who yap they'd lose "the gift" if they went out to the track to make their fortune. All right. Now what I'm telling you is that my intuition says we have to go back, maybe way back, for the answer on this *goel hadam* thing. The six were killed and I was warned not because of anything we did or were, but because we come from certain families. Fathers, grandfathers, maybe.

The Italians have a marvelous metaphor, the tail of straw. Most of us, it turns out, have one. What is it? All the dirty facts of your past, the stuff you want forgotten, the things you're afraid someone will turn up and shame or discredit you. Why tails of straw? Well, it's what keeps you from coming too close to the fire of controversy, the blaze of politics, the heat of corporate in-fighting. I think you've been chasing the wrong straw tails.

Urdell assessed me. "I hear grandfather a few times. You don't mean me even though I'm a one-time member of the fraternity, so it must be in the Hanan *mishpocha*. What makes you think we have to go that far back? I'm sure we can come up with a good dozen who would wish you dead or are even capable of killing you for reasons that have to do just with you, yourself."

I was tired and depressed. "Sam, we're wasting time. You know there's not a real thing that ties me in with any of the other six. I've had two bouts of high fever and they're very realistic introductions to death. Both times, I almost didn't want to come out of them. One or two more, you can cross me off the list of your little helpers."

Sam nodded. "Okay, my partner says cut velvet, we cut velvet. Tell me about your grandpa."

I started giving him what little I knew when he put up his right hand in a traffic cop gesture. "Ahh, I'm playing stupid games, again. I *know* all about your miserable grandpa.

"Hanan isn't that common a name and the only one I knew was this old Tammany crook and fixer, Max. So what I did one day while you were burning up is go down to the Health Department's Vital Records section and get your father's death record and right there it turns out *his* father is listed as Max Hanan. I get Max's death certificate and he dies on September twentieth, nineteen twenty-three, and leaves a wife and one son, Robert, your pop. Max's occupation is listed as 'real estate' and he was born in Austria. He dies of diabetes.

"In the old days I knew a clerk in the *Times* morgue who'd look up clips for me but he's dead and they're converting to a computer retrieval system so I went through about twenty years of *New York Times* annual indexes in the library and there were a few references to your grandpa, but actually I remembered more than they had, anyway."

Max Hanan, he went on, isn't listed in the indexes of the two or three standard histories of Tammany Hall but that doesn't mean he wasn't important. He started out as a lieutenant of Martin Engel, the Tammany leader of the Eighth Assembly District, which was 1880 to 1910 probably one of the most graft-ridden districts in the U.S. "You start talking graft, corruption, everybody says well it couldn't have been like Chicago in the Twenties. It was worse. In De Old Ate, they used to call it, *anything* went. You could get a guy killed for fifty dollars; a fourteen-year-old virgin kidnapped, raped, and placed in a whorehouse for less. You could gamble any way you wanted; drink anything you wanted anytime; and get all the opium, cocaine, or anything you liked. What your grandfather was, was in charge of payoffs to the cops. That's the way he *started.* . . ."

The phone. Vogelsang, anxious to talk to Urdell. The seventh dead man had turned up. A Singapore Jew named Miguel Karir. He lived and worked in Mexico for many years before he moved to Singapore. He had more but he wondered if Sam would come over to the office; I was welcome, too, if I felt up to it. It sounded as if I had been forgiven for my asperity when I last saw Vogelsang.

"It's very small of me," Sam said, "but whenever I hear him on the phone it makes me think that one of those talking computers has gone a little on the blink. Still, a couple of crocks like us, I bet we change places with him foghorn and all. For me it would be a good switch. He's eight years younger and a million bucks richer."

What would he do if he suddenly came into a million?

Sam laughed hoarsely. "You're thinking: what the hell can this old cocker *do* at seventy? No, it can't be women. And you've correctly lined me up as not being the kind fella gotta leave his daughter and grandson a pile. And I don't want to subsidize some name writer to do a nice big puff book of my adventures in the Thirties and Forties with the Nazis and the other louses. So what can it be? I'll tell you. I want to rearrange my obit. You get my age, obits are favorite reading. What did Balzac say? 'Fame is the sunshine of the dead.' No, it's not just the self-congratulation of how many other characters your age you've out-lived. . . ."

He read the impatience in my eyes and shoulders. "Okay, I'll omit a few thousand well-chosen words on the art of rearranging obits and jump to the fact that your grandfather didn't rate an obit in the *Times* or even the old *New York World.* I checked. He didn't because there wasn't much good they could say. He was a kingpin in what was, really, the Jewish Mafia. From eighteen ninety to nineteen fifteen there was a hell of a big Jewish underworld. Among them you could find the city's leading killers, arsonists, holdup men, pickpockets, pimps, horse poison-ers, whorehouse operators, con men. They were protected by Irish Tammany—in return for turning out the vote on election day and making sizable political contributions—and they properly paid off the Irish police force. They preceded the Italians just as the Italians came before the blacks and the Puerto Ricans in those roles. What Max Hanan did was make sure the payoffs went through right. Then he graduated and became a big owner of saloons, hot-bed hotels, and gambling joints. Most of the arrangement faded by nineteen fifteen. Jews were moving out of the East Side to Brooklyn and the Bronx. There were a few investigations and a lot of characters moved out of the country, and by the end of the war the Italians were in a position to take over. Prohibition really pushed them way up, and by then Jews weren't in the dominant position they once had. Sure you had remnants like Murder Incorporated and incredible survivors like Lansky, but the days when the city was their crime turf was over."

He was a little winded. "Now I know I'm running down. I used to be able to talk forever. Anyway, that's it. Does it make any sense anyone's trying to kill you because of what Max Hanan was sixty, seventy years ago?"

I said he must have left out a lot of juicy detail. "Sure, sure. You wanna research I can tell you where to look, but believe me, it's a big waste."

Sparing each other's feelings, we walked slowly to Vogelsang's office. Neither suggested a cab. Presumably he wasn't too old and winded and I wasn't too weak.

A little past the St. Moritz I sensed we were being followed. I said: "Sam, walk slower and after a couple of steps just put your arms around me as if you're passing out." He did and I held him after making a half-turn. Butoma. Pyotr Butoma last seen in Ankara. When? Maybe '68, '69. An opposite number. Memorable only because of his cute tricks. We had a new kid over from the States. He brought a wife and four-year-old daughter, and he didn't have embassy cover. He was a buyer and seller of antique guns. He really knew them and there were a lot of these items floating around Turkey so the cover wasn't bad. But after two months the four-year-old comes home with a note and gives it to her daddy: "A nice man gave me this and said I should give it to you." The note was in Russian. Translated into: "You have a very pretty daughter." Their way of telling him they had made him and no more crap about antique guns. Butoma sent the note.

He approached me, smiling broadly. "I was going to come sooner but I am not sure. You have changed so much. We hear about your illness and I try to tell some of our old friends we ought to send some flowers to the hospital but they fear you might misinterpret."

I said that was very nice and I would have understood. He said if I ever got over to the UN *soon* I should look him up in UNITAR, the UN Institute for Training and Research. I said if any of my old Washington friends needed some research I'd send them to him. The smile faded as he turned to Sam: "I hope you are feeling better. Your friend has made a lot of people sick." He walked back to Sixth Avenue.

Sam was delighted. "A real Russian spy, hoo hah. That little spy talk at the end was that you got a lot of his people or something?"

What happens, I said, is that spies also go to movies and watch TV and they gradually acquire the proper way for spies to talk and act. I explained how I had helped make Pyotr Butoma an internationally recognized character in the spy world. When he first came to Ankara, with diplomatic cover, we had a bug in his room at the hotel. Another diplomat-agent came over and we heard Pyotr ask him in English— maybe it was his week to practice language—just three questions: "Vare do ve get a voomin? Can ve take the voomin back to dis huttel? You tink de locals are vatching us?" Well, the accent, the inflection, and Pyotr's distinctive bass were so funny that we played the part over and over for laughs. Later I sent the tape to the Agency when they were preparing a course for new people on phone-tapping, hot-miking, and stuff. I included the Pyotr tape for laughs and they used to play it for a light moment in the new-agent courses. And then one of the Agency instructors sent a copy to an opposite number in London. I think they played it for their people, too, and gradually everybody in the spy world had heard Pyotr. Well, the laughs ruined his dignity and somehow demeaned him; the Russians are very sensitive, and they put him in the UN boondocks. Sam said spies lived in a tight funny little world and to show me he hadn't missed the main point added: "That means that Butoma also knew you were in Union Memorial Hospital. You sure there wasn't an announcement in the *Times?*"

Vogelsang was conciliatory. "Maybe I went a little overboard on the Richmond connection, Harry. But you must admit it was worth following. We never had so many names tied in before." The walk from the apartment hadn't tired me as much as I had feared, we had laughed a lot en route—my first real laugh in several weeks—and I felt myself getting consciously cute. "Right number, wrong nexus." Vogelsang laughed. "You *must* be feeling better. Anyway we got this new one and this time we got ourself a real international crook, not like that speedometer tinkerer, Gangwach."

The latest victim was a sixty-six-year-old Singapore Jew named Miguel Karir. He had an office on Orchard Road where he was in "investments" and a house on Orange Grove Road in a fashionable suburban area. His body was found in the bathtub by one of three servants, a man named Karrupiah bin Katamuthu. The CID Special Investigations Section decided that drowning was accidental. A week later Karrupiah, the valet-houseman, brought an envelope to a friend of the dead man at the synagogue. The envelope had a crudely drawn skull-and-bones on it—Karrupiah was certain it had been drawn by his dead employer—and inside the envelope was a *goel hadam* note. Karir's friend didn't turn the note over to the Singapore police because of the continuing synagogue battle and he felt the note might be related, in which case it was better that the local police not get involved.

The quiet little Jewish civil war, Vogelsang went on, started in July 1971, when a little notice was posted on the bulletin board of the synagogue on Waterloo Street. The notice, on the stationery of the Jewish Welfare Board of Singapore, said that the Board "views with extreme seriousness the conduct by certain sections of the community in their approaches to tourist visits to the synagogue. This nuisance must stop and the Board will take full measures against any individual who receives any money from any tourists. All monies should be deposited in the box in the synagogue and no individual regardless of his capacity should receive any gratuity."

Inevitably factions formed: for the sexton and against him; for the Board and against them. Most of the synagogue members had been around a long time, so inevitably attention began being paid to one of the combatants, Karir, who had been in Singapore only three years. They knew he came from Mexico City and that he once had a fine house in the posh Mexican suburb of Tecamachalco until his wife died. Well, one of the members on a business visit to Mexico decided to check up on Karir and soon he had quite a dossier.

Karir came to Mexico in the summer of 1930—from Buenos Aires. He had some money, a lot of curiosity, and apparently some underworld connections. He quickly saw the possibilities in rationalizing an old racket, *el timo del baúl*, the swindle of the trunk as the Mexicans call it.

Vogelsang broke off with a footnote. "With a PhD in psychology and as a fellow who's made a million bucks in advertising, I should be the last to say my Committee research has appalled me with the levels of human gullibility. Between the Teddy Richmond racket and this one . . ."

This one turned out to be the old Spanish prisoner swindle, one of the most lucrative con games ever conceived. It had started in Spain about 1890 and then spread to Havana in 1910 and finally came to Mexico in the mid-'20s. There were minor variations but essentially it came to this:

The would-be victim gets a typewritten letter from Mexico,

A person who knows you and who has spoken very highly about you has made me trust you a very delicate matter of which depends the entire future of my dear daughter, as well as my very existence. I am in prison, sentenced for bankruptcy, and I wish to know if you are willing to help me save the sum of $450,000 U.S. Cy, which I have in bank bills hidden in a secret compartment of a trunk that is now deposited in a customhouse in the U.S.

Turns out the money was stolen by the writer, a Vera Cruz banker, who planned to skip to the U.S. The trunk was sent but he was arrested at the border. In order to release a suitcase which contained the receipt for the very valuable trunk, his fine and certain trial fees had to be paid. This came to $3,650 in U.S. currency—in the '30s. If the trusted person came to Mexico City with this money the imprisoned banker would be happy to turn over a third, or $150,000, to the good Samaritan. Naturally, he'd also meet the banker's beautiful daughter.

After coming to Mexico in 1930 Miguel Karir saw the immense possibilities of the racket—if it were properly run. When he looked in on the gang running it he found they were trying to use crude mimeographed letters in their first come-ons. He found an inventive Mexican mechanic who rigged up a bunch of typewriters that could be made to type letters from a master keyboard. He also added the important touch of enclosing simulated newspaper clippings telling of the banker's arrest and one containing a tear-filled interview with his beautiful daughter whose picture was run. These clips Karir had run off by the tens of thousands, as he did with official-looking court documents and "judicial receipts." All with suitable translations, of course. The new methods produced fine results and all through the '30s Karir's little gang averaged two U.S. victims a week, running down to Mexico City with their $3,650 each. The $7,300 a week wasn't all profit, of course. About 15 percent went for overhead and mailings. A fourth went for the necessary police protection. The real profit—about $4,400 a week—went mostly to Karir, the boss. He invested in apartment houses, gold, and Argentine real estate. For the time it was an enormous income. When Mexico entered World War II in 1942 the president's emergency powers enabled him to jail all foreign-born criminals for the duration. Karir and his aides were jailed. He was inside only two weeks when he worked out a deal—for $25,000—under which he was permitted to leave for Argentina. He returned in 1945 and thus equipped himself with an insurance policy—a certificate from the mayor of a remote Mexican village attesting to the fact that Miguel Karir had been born in that village. Now he could no longer be deported as an undesirable alien. After the war he found that the *timo* racket had been taken over by a bunch of Spanish con men who had come over in 1936, following the fall of Republican Spain.

Karir, who now had a net worth of about $600,000, set himself up as an industrial banker, lending money at the traditional high Latin American interest rates to struggling businessmen. He continued to prosper, married a much younger woman, a Spanish refugee, and blended into the business community. He had two sons, who were educated at military academies in the U.S. and then went on to Stanford. One of them was killed in an auto accident near Bakersfield, and the other now was the head of a small, prosperous electronics firm near Boston. It had been started with money from his father. Señora Karir died in Mexico after a too-long-delayed operation for uterine cancer. Soon after, Karir sold his large house and moved to Singapore. Now he was dead at sixty-six.

Presumably Miguel Karir had a lot of enemies: hundreds of victims who had been taken. Most were so ashamed they didn't even complain to the U.S. Embassy in Mexico. But even those who did complain didn't discover the head of the racket was Miguel Karir. And he had never gotten intimately involved in the Mexico City Jewish community. His sons had been raised in his wife's faith: Christian Science.

When he finished, Vogelsang looked at me: "I know, I know. What do we have on this character *before* he came to Mexico, and the answer is not much. Police records down there that far back aren't in good shape right now, but we do know he wasn't born in Argentina. The name is Sephardic, of course, so he probably didn't come from Poland or Russia the way most Argentinian Jews did. We're working on that part."

Sam said: "He must have been involved down there with crooks. No one suddenly becomes a smart crook just by moving to a new country. And why Mexico? Most Argentinian crooks just move on to Uruguay across the River Plate when things got too hot temporarily."

Elly came in, took off her suede coat, and kissed Sam lightly on the cheek. "I love it when Sam goes into his thinking-like-a-crook bit." Vogelsang held up a hand. "Only Sam rates a kiss around here?" Elly was bubbling. "He's the only safe one around here and I'm not too sure of him sometimes." I was distantly amused that she was right. There were stirrings in me I hadn't felt in weeks. Sam interpreted it quickly: "She's right, Harry. For the first time since I've known you you look like you still might have a dirty thought in your head. You must be getting better." I said it was probably just reflex. "Listen, Harry," Sam went on, "Elly helped prepare that dossier on you. She knows what a dirty young man you were in those early *Wanderjahre* in Europe."

I think the discussion was making Vogelsang a little uncomfortable. He brought us back to business. "Turns out we don't have such a blameless little crew of victims here. Gangwach and Karir were out-and-out crooks even if the locksmith never did time. Monte Morden was using counterfeit securities to con bankers, and I suppose if we dug more on our California accountant, Howard Lucksig, we could find a passel of white-collar criminal finaglings of one kind or another. . . ."

I said at one time or another every adult was a lawbreaker of some kind. Minor, perhaps, but still. . . . If the *goel hadams* were going to bump off every lawbreaker, there would have to be a million of them working eighty-hour weeks. We were back in a dead end. Some pain came on suddenly and I had to sit down. I managed to get out a Dilaudid and by the time I had it in my mouth Elly was there with a cup of water. They stood around looking at me—which I hated—and Elly took the initiative again. "If you like I can take you back to your place. I'm taking a cab to the Essex House anyway." I left with her.

In the cab she explained there was a chapter meeting of the International Association of Conference Interpreters, their trade union. It was going to discuss raises in the daily minimum of $114.50 and the traveling day's rate of $35.75. But since she had long graduated from the minimum scale, what she actually was going for was to see two other New York-based simultaneous translators who were going to work with her at an international conference in London. They had a useful glossary of French, German, and English management terms she wanted to bone up on. Ordinarily I would have been curious about the whole business but there was something nagging me.

"I had the feeling that you stepped out of character back there kissing Sam and the 'he's-the-only-safe-one' business. As if you were trying on a new role."

She was amused. "People confuse translators and interpreters. The first are desk-bound, introverted. Most interpreters are very lively, outgoing, and, in a way, actors. We even call the top ones *les grands ténors*. I guess we're performers. So we try on different roles, too. It's not just an ego trip. To be good at it you have to have, besides the obvious language knowledge and memory and ingenuity, the ability to *think* and even feel like the person you're interpreting."

She had the cabbie make a U-turn on Central Park South to let me off at 117. "I'll walk to the Essex House," she said at the door, "if you think you're all right now." I thanked her and said the pain was about gone.

January 20, 1973.

I was refilling my pillbox with the Dilaudids I carried around—from a larger plastic container the pharmacy had sent up—when I noticed the pharmacy sticker inside the plastic container was no longer level but tilted at a sharp angle. Being terminal and paranoid sounds like a pointless combination but you react as trained. I got a sheet of wax paper from the kitchen and carefully laid out all the Dilaudids on it. There were about twenty-five. The pills are the size of saccharin tablets. Flattened cylinders with well-defined edges. That is, all except one. The edges weren't as sharp and it was a trifle higher than the rest. It could, of course, be just a slip-up in the quality control department, but there was another possibility. I rubbed a finger lightly across the top and put it on my tongue. No taste.

Surely this was a time for testing in the Agency's Technical Services department. But asking for favors of that kind would be awkward; if it turned out to be something deadlier than Dilaudid, there would have to be lots of explanations which suddenly I didn't want to have to make to *them*. I realized how much distancing had taken place. I was thinking like Sam and Vogelsang: this was a Jewish affair. Let's keep it to ourselves. There was another way.

The pet shop was on Fifty-eighth Street off Eighth. It was a good walk, offset by a pimply lout dealing cards for a new massage parlor. He didn't think I was eligible. The shop owner was busy netting some tropical fish for a customer and I waited and sniffed. Every pet shop hoarded smells that must carry all adults back to childhood. It wasn't just the puppy-in-the-window sentiment; the collective smells annihilate time. I was back in 1937 at the Paris Exposition. I was four and a half and my brother a lordly fourteen. We were taken to the Exposition on a Sunday in September. On the island in the Seine were a lot of native bazaar keepers and strange smells. The Algerian and Tunisian quarters had tinkling fountains, atmospheric patios, and camels. But it wasn't the camel smell I remembered. I cried because they wouldn't let me sit in a two-cylinder, thirty-two-horsepower Taupin monoseater sports plane. I had fallen in love with the tiny plane on exhibit and wouldn't leave it. I was dragged away, crying bitterly. To assuage the loss I was later given a gerbil as a pet. It was the gerbil smell that was coming back.

The pet shop owner came over to where I was looking at two caged rabbits. How much? Ten bucks each, but if I wanted to go to a better class of bunny they had fancies, tricolored rabbits. I said these would be fine and offered him $25 to conduct my little experiment. On the way over I had tried out several different cover stories: some pal was secretly trying to get me to go on an LSD trip; I was afraid my wife was putting something in my coffee to make me less randy. But both sounded pretty silly and didn't fit me. I said in this experiment I wanted to try out a couple of white powders. The worst that could happen was one rabbit would die and the other would be drowsy for a few hours. In any case the rabbits stayed with him, dead or alive. I put the $25 on the counter and let him size me up. He did—very intelligently. "You don't look like a nut; what I got to lose?" I took out two separate paper spills in which I had placed some of the powder scratched from the suspect pill and some from one of the others. I had put an X on the suspect powder spill. He took the latter, worked it into a cleft in a piece of carrot and fed it to one of the rabbits. He did the same with the other powder to the other rabbit, which had a fist-size black marking near his tail. We both stood and stared at the animals for a while and all he said was, "They don't buy bunnies for kids the way they used to. Smart people should buy them and raise them for meat but how you gonna do that in a two-and-a-half-room apartment?" In two minutes the rabbit given the suspect powder keeled over. He reached in the cage—the other was very drowsy and inactive—and said the bunny was dead all right. I said in that case the other one would probably be okay in an hour or so. He said didn't I want to know what killed the rabbit? I said it didn't matter; enough of it would also kill a person. I think by now he was vaguely making mental notes on my appearance for what he was sure would be an eventual visit by the police in some poisoning case.

When I got back to the apartment Sam called. "If you're still hot to find out more about your *zayde,*" he said, "I can give you a couple of references that will save you a lot of time. First look up the *New York Times* for December sixteenth, nineteen eight, and March second, nineteen thirteen. It's only partly about your relation but you might find it interesting."

I thought of filling Sam in on the poison attempt but decided there was nothing he could do to help find out who had placed the pill in with my Dilaudids. If we got hold of the *goel hadam* or the gang—it was becoming less and less likely that just one avenger of the blood was involved—we'd know. At the rate Sam and Vogelsang were going I'd be dead long before.

You had to put your head fairly deep into the microfilm projector in the special reading room on the third floor of the New York Public Library. The film was scratchy and it was hard to focus clearly. The December 16 item was of all things about a criminal libel action instituted by Martin Engel, a city councilman and Tammany wheelhorse in the Eighth Assembly District, against a crusading East Side butcher named Norberth Pfeffer who had circulated a little pamphlet alleging all kinds of misdeeds and criminal activities. He said Engel was a perjurer, blackmailer, stool pigeon, conspirator, and professional bondsman.

As it turned out Pfeffer had been counting heavily on making a case, also, against one of Engel's lieutenants, Max Hanan. For this he had been depending on the testimony of someone from London named Felix Solomon who was the managing director of an organization called the Hebrew Association for the Defense of Women and Girls. Pfeffer said Solomon was willing to come over to testify but unfortunately Pfeffer couldn't afford the round-trip fare from London.

The other item Sam referred me to was also in the *Times*—March 2, 1913. The front-page headline was GRAFT TRAIL LEADS INTO TAMMANY HALL. It was so perennial it was probably kept in stock. A reform DA, Charles S. Whitman—later to become governor—was after the men who made the payoffs to keep "gambling houses and bagnios in business." It was only far in the story's jump that Max Hanan emerged:

From information that came to Mr. Whitman in the last few days he is convinced that the alliance between the crooked politicians and the crooked policemen is so close that to expose one will mean the exposing of the other. Perhaps the one man in the city who stands closest to the politicians, the saloon keepers, and the disorderly resorts is Max Hanan.

There were no further references to Max Hanan and it was, Sam thought, the last time his name appeared in the *Times* except for the paid death notice in September 1923.

A reference librarian on the third floor thought the best place for more information on the London-based Hebrew Association for the Defense of Women and Girls might be the British Information Service on Third Avenue.

Turned out the Hebrew Association was long out of business, having been absorbed by the Jewish Board of Guardians in London. They also turned up a tiny obit on Felix Solomon, who had been killed in an air raid in 1942 as he was leaving the Hendon Synagogue where he was the senior warden. He left a son, William.

January 22, 1973.

About 9 AM I called the Jewish Board of Guardians in London. It was 2 PM there and after a while they put me through to a Peter Hutman, their press officer. No, they didn't have any records of the Hebrew Association—most of it had been destroyed during bombing raids in 1941—but Hutman knew that Solomon's son, William, had a lot of his father's personal stuff. He knew that because the family was negotiating with the Mocatta Library of London University to give the material to them for cataloguing. William Solomon was now on the faculty of the Graduate Business Centre of the City University, Gresham College, which was located in the City of London, not far from the Bank of England.

Lucky day. I got through, first time, to William Solomon at his college office. I said I was doing some historical research for the American Hebrew Leadership Council and I was going to be in London in the next week or two. I wondered if it would be possible to go through his father's records of the time he was head of the Hebrew Association for the Defense of Women and Girls. When he got over his natural surprise that a historical researcher was using the transatlantic phone to check on material seventy-five years old he said he'd be glad to help. The material was unassorted and a bit scrambled but I was welcome to look at it. Perhaps I could let him know, in advance, of my actual arrival and he'd try to have it in better shape.

The idea of going to England hadn't really been that sudden. William Solomon simply provided a practical reason. There was a far more important psychical one. In London was a man who could partly relieve, assuage, lingering guilt.

A half-hour later I was wondering what kind of stupid idea the whole thing was. I could see it all, even smell the aromas from the galley as I died in great pain aboard the 747. One of the stewardesses on arriving in London testifies she's sure the dead passenger committed suicide: she saw him take pills before he died. Then the brouhaha at Langley. Why is a dying Hanan flying to London? Another Mason flap? A few years ago Mason, one of the Agency brass, eloped to Mexico with his secretary, who was about twelve years younger. They went over on his blue diplomatic passport and one of the Mexican border officials was sure that it was a major defection. He got a call in to one of the Agency people in Mexico City and it was a hell of a fuss all weekend until they determined that the couple wasn't defecting, just eloping. Anyway the sleeping passport rule came into effect. Those who had the blue diplomatic passports would turn them in when they returned Stateside. Only the very top brass were exempt. Since mine had been turned in it meant if I was serious about the trip I'd have to (a) find my old passport and (b) renew it and hope that the name on the passport application wouldn't trigger any computer readouts in Washington.

I ran through the stuff Andresen mailed me about the unorthodox cancer "cures." I phoned McCready in Washington to bring him up to date. I had heard about a fellow who had a so-called cancer cure in London. Probably a quack, I said, but someone was supposed to have been helped by it and what the hell, what did I have to lose. I asked about Dave Quittle in London. Turned out he took early retirement— at fifty-one—and he joined up with a cousin, a retired army colonel who had some kind of missing person agency he ran from England. He'd try to get me an address or phone number.

The word would percolate in certain Langley levels and when my name would appear on the passport-control lists they'd know why I was flying to London. I'm sure McCready didn't believe the cancer-cure stuff. He knew me well enough to know that some kind of absolution from Quittle was far more important to a dying man.

Old passports generate memories faster than light. Who is this blond, stiff, wavy-haired youngster of twenty-one staring blankly at me? The kid who battled his parents about leaving Columbia before graduating, about taking grandma's bequest for a trip to Europe in 1952? We compromised: I'd seriously think about coming back in the fall to finish my senior year. They hoped but no one believed it. I remember two years later when it was obvious I wasn't coming back I wrote my mother and grandly quoted somebody: "Young people suffer less from their own mistakes than older people's wisdom." I won't make another list: words I regret having spoken, lines I wish I never wrote. I don't have *that* much time left.

At the Rockefeller Center passport office they said I could have a new passport in a week if necessary. I made a flight reservation for February 3, a Saturday. It was for a morning flight, which I figured would give me a better chance to avoid jet lag since it would land me at Heathrow in the evening for a night's sleep. And with luck maybe I could catch Solomon on Sunday at his apartment in Albert Court. It was one of the very few times in twenty years I was paying for my own transportation and the quick debate between first class and tourist was resolved in favor of the favorable seating: in February the plane would be mostly empty and if necessary I could stretch out on four seats in tourist. In first you'd have to remain upright on one, more comfortable, perhaps, but upright.

I phoned an agency that specialized in cooperatives and told them I was ready to sell and they could show it after February 3. They knew the apartment since my brother had bought it through them. The market was sticky for co-ops, she said, but she still hoped we could get $100,000 or so for it.

The ten days passed fairly quickly. There were lots of neglected odds and ends in the estate. I averaged a Dilaudid a day and the blue phlegm with the metallic taste came up twice in that time. Still, I was able to walk as far as Saks for a birthday gift to be sent to my niece Audrey, who lived outside San Diego.

There were bits and pieces from Vogelsang:

1. Harris Lucksig, brother of the dead California accountant, was still working hard trying to come up with an acceptable synthetic coffee. A syndicate had put up another $300,000 for expanding his lab. At a recent dinner party in Palo Alto he was heard to say, "We're getting so close on this coffee thing, I'm getting scared."

2. Artur Zelkowicz's classmate—the Manchester University historian —reported to the university security officer that over a weekend someone had gone through his office files. But nothing was missing as far as he could tell.

And there was another carbon from Yochanan Shorsh at Hebrew Theological Seminary. This time headed simply: "Items of Interest."

It was a curious academic grab bag, footnote trivia, and illuminating insights. If only we knew which were applicable.

• In Islamic theology, God had ninety-nine cover names. Number 81 was *al-Muntaqim*, "The Avenger."

• From an article by a Moses Buttenweisser in the *Journal of the American Oriental Society* for 1919: " . . . In Israel as well as in Greece the prosecution and punishment for murder and manslaughter was at bottom a religious act."

• A quote from Hermann Hesse's currently sacred book for the under-thirties, *Steppenwolf:* " . . . we do not kill from duty, but pleasure, or much more, rather, from displeasure and despair of the world. For this reason we find a certain amusement in killing people. Has it never amused you?"

• From the *Code* of Maimonides, Book of Torts, something that seemed to apply to my case: "If one kills another who suffers from a fatal organic disease, he is legally exempt even though the victim ate and drank and walked about the streets."

• Inevitably we'll have to consider the possibility we're dealing with a psychotic. If so, paranoid schizophrenia seems the likeliest classification. They're the ones who might murder strangers en masse. Some reported cases involve nine, ten unconnected murders committed because the paranoid schizo was trying to keep earthquakes from coming to California, Martian mind-controllers from taking over the earth, and so on. But—and a big but—most of them operated within a small orbit, seldom more than a few miles from where they lived. And all of them were long-winded in their explanations. None so far reported as spare as our *goel hadam*. A possible solution but the present fit is a poor one, I think.

• Rollo May: "Deeds of violence in our society are performed largely by those trying to establish their self-esteem, to defend their self-image, and to demonstrate that they, too, are significant. . . ."

• George Bernard Shaw: "All the people I ever hated died. A deadly but horrible emanation comes from the hater to his victim."

• Up until the '30s, Budapest Jews fought duels against anti-Semites who had impugned their honor as Jews. In Herzl's vision of the future Jewish State the duel was to be an honored institution.

An item I could also take as intended for me—someday:

• "The Torah has said: 'If a man comes to kill you, rise and kill him first.' " (Ex. 22:1).

Finally, an exasperated coda:

• "The Germans have a unique science: *Die Wissenschaft des nicht Wissenswerten*—the science of what is not worth knowing. I'm tired of practicing it. Give me a *motive*. Then I might be helpful."

January 26, 1973.

Manny phoned from the Plaza. He was concluding details for a fund-raising dinner the Seminary was going to hold and he'd be finished earlier. Would I like company?

We were friends but I was also his original sponsor and great American guide. Now he wanted vocational advice. He was tired of fund raising, of being a *schnorrer*. He was forty-four, happily married; he and his wife had saved about $18,000 and they had a $25,000 equity in their Bayside home. From being a hunted Yugoslav he had become a moderately prosperous naturalized American. He was grateful for the opportunity, that his daughter was American born, that life had been really very good to him ever since I had helped him get an American passport. But he was getting restless. He had been tempted to invest with his brother-in-law in an auto-transmission franchise but he knew that wasn't for him. What was? Well, he had this wild idea he had been thinking about for several months and with the recent heavy cuts at the Agency he thought it was time for action.

"Harry, you know I'm not a foolish person." If he needed such an apologetic prologue the idea must *really* be wild. "You know what makes it so hard to talk about? It's like telling someone about a childish daydream."

As a comparative stranger in our midst he was struck by the American fascination with espionage. Look at the wild success of the James Bond films, how anything to do with the CIA will draw out dozens of reporters and investigative writers, how well spy books sell.

He'd been reading lots of them lately. One of the commonest templates in them was: Some young fellow, usually a loser in life's sweepstakes, gets accidentally involved with an espionage caper. Through luck, daring, and ingenuity he comes through unscathed. Not only does he outdo the professionals but he gets the girl—at least he lays her—and, best of all, the admiring pros offer him a full-time job with them. What a tribute to an amateur!

Surely out there in America there were several thousand men who would love to feel they were part of the intelligence organization. And pay for it, too. Obviously he didn't mean a fan club or lobbying organization such as army and navy suppliers had. What he had in mind was a real training and *ersatz* participation.

It would mean taking over a small resort hotel, perhaps in the Bahamas. The trainees would be recruited by word-of-mouth—you obviously couldn't openly advertise this peculiar school—and would be charged a $5,000 fee. What would they get for it? Well, first there would be two weeks of basic training in lock-picking, wiretapping, flaps and seals— undetected opening of letters and packages—small-arms fire, hidden-camera work.

He anticipated my comment: "I know Harry, you can't do much with that stuff in two weeks but it will give them the *feel* of it, the feel of belonging. Nobody there will know anyone else's real name. And they'll be competing but nobody will wash out."

After two weeks the fun would begin. Each "graduate" would be given a mysterious assignment overseas. He'd get a plane ticket and instructions to meet his contact in London two days hence in front of, say, Fortnum & Mason. There'd be code words and stuff and the graduate would get a small package that he was to take to Paris. To keep up the excitement he'd get mysterious phone calls changing the Paris assignment slightly. In Paris he'd deliver the package and get instructions to take some seemingly innocuous photographs of any young woman coming out of the Solferino metro between 3 and 3:15 in the afternoon—provided she was carrying a gray umbrella and wearing an orange scarf. He would then deliver the roll of film to a contact in Geneva. . . . It went on and on—Manny had worked it out like a detailed scenario—and it would culminate with a happy coupling in Geneva or Zurich with an attractive fellow agent who would, of course, be a discreet call girl. After that the graduate would be instructed to return to New York, dial a certain number, and report in detail. Then he'd be told to return home and await further instructions. He was now in the "Reserve." If he had any friends or acquaintances he thought might be interested in "joining the Reserve," why there would be a number for them to call.

It was one of those fantastic floating ideas—between Hitchcock and parody—for a spy-stung age. The pitfalls had been measured by Manny long ago. The graduate might—just might—by his spylike antics get picked up by police or, less likely, some counterintelligence people. So what? He'd have nothing incriminating on him. And if under pressure he told about his training? Well, that might be a problem. But for the rest, really: he was meeting people, running errands, making phone calls, and finally having a one-night stand. So what?

He had worked out the economics of the operation fairly well. The total costs per "trainee" would come to no more than $2,500, so that $2,500 would be pure profit . . . if they could average only eight students a month, or $25,000 monthly profit . . . and worked out to, say, a ten-month average . . . why. . . . Yes, the potential was there if the idea could be worked. There were crazier ideas that eventually worked. . . . But the longer I had to suppress the laugh the worse it would emerge.

"It's not the *idea*, Manny, or even your natural assumption that no woman would spend $5,000 for this. No, it's just wild enough so that it *might* work. Count me in. What made me laugh so impolitely was that in your own way you reinvented the 'bouncing game.' We stopped doing it a little before you became a border-crosser for us."

It went this way. Adjoining countries X and Y are engaged in a cold war. The intelligence head of X gets an idea: let's empty our insane asylums and let the inmates wander across the border. At the very least they'll be able to tie up many interrogation teams. At the same time the

X intelligence boss gets access to a couple dozen con men and black marketeers held in the local prisons. He tells them they can get out if they do one thing for him: he gives them a series of rendezvous on the other side and other suspicious actions that are bound to get them picked up. More interrogation teams and puzzlement for the opposition, which means, of course, they have less time, are less alert to your real agents among them.

Manny became defensive. It wasn't a con job because for those attracted to the idea it would be worth the money. He admitted one of the problems would be they wouldn't be able to talk about it—not that it would make sense to anyone else. And, of course, if they told it all from beginning to end why there might well be some hard-nosed characters who would simply say they'd been taken. He even had worked out veiled classified ads that might attract prospects. And the scheme would provide employment for some of the Agency people let go. He thought he'd need about $100,000 to start. I said he could put me down for $20,000—but only after he had raised the first $50,000. He said he didn't think things could move that quickly. "Manny, now I can tell the doctors I've got to live longer because there's a wild idea around and I got to see how it works out."

He thanked me for listening and for liking it. I was the first one he had described his daydream to.

January 31, 1973.

The passport came. I called a Georgetown real estate agent to tell him my house on N Street was for sale as soon as the lease ran out in May. The present tenant, an official of the Canadian Wheat Board, agreed to let prospective purchasers go through weekends, if there weren't too many.

I'd have to tell Sam about my London trip. I said it was personal business and also I thought I'd look in on a local clinic that was getting some results in cases such as mine. In any case I didn't plan to be away more than a week. He said he was having trouble with Vogelsang, who was getting very discouraged and felt maybe the *goel hadam* thing needed international publicity. Sam and key officials of the American Hebrew Leadership Council had overruled Vogelsang. They couldn't see how publicity would help.

"You'll be happy to know," Sam concluded, "that Vogelsang gave up his latest theory about the killers in just two days. I must be a small, miserable old party to be telling you this."

I said it was a virtue to solace the dying. Sam continued: "His latest theory was maybe, just maybe, we were dealing with some kind of hidden-Nazi plot. Why would they use the *goel hadam* motif? Well, some of the most murderous Nazi Jew-killers proudly admitted their knowledge of Hebrew—to know the enemy better. And everybody knows Adolf Eichmann spoke Yiddish and Hebrew. But Vogelsang reluctantly gave this up because it just didn't add up to anything. Then he wondered maybe some of them had been helping the Israeli Secret Service in running down hidden Nazis. He dropped that one pretty fast, too. It has not been a good week for Vogelsang."

I said if we're at that desperate stage maybe I shouldn't hold back. I could also throw a pretty wild theory into the pot.

"So why have you been saving your little gem?"

"Well, for one thing there's no easy way we can check it out. For another I don't think this rates any odds better than one-in-a-thousand. And to really check this out means bringing my old firm into the act and I don't think anyone wants that right now."

So I threw out my very wild card solely, as I said, for Sam's amusement and for his general store of useless but portentous knowledge—in case he had ever had to slug it out with Shorsh.

Right after World War II the Russians had several key espionage networks blown as a result of the Gouzenko case in Canada. So they had to recruit new people abroad, mostly through local Communist parties. But the Military Intelligence Center, the Razvedka in Moscow, decided that they had to be sure the new man, no matter how certain they were of his political attitudes, was ready to risk his life in direct action. So before a new man was really ready to take on a post he'd be told that he first had to commit a major event that would make the papers: a train derailing, the blowing up of a small bridge or an ammo dump. Of course, it would have to be done at a certain date and at a certain place so that the new man couldn't take credit for a chance disaster.

Then a new Razvedka chief—this was still in Stalin's time—decided the method was fine but the target could be simplified: a human target. Not a wino or a bum but some local figure whose death would make the papers. It would be a whole lot more economical in terms of innocent lives lost and just as effective. All right. Let's say the policy is continued until the '60s and some new director says why not let the death policy do double duty. Let's have our new people prove their loyalty and commitment and at the same time let's make trouble for those miserable Jews. So the called-for killings take place and this time a sly little *goel hadam* note is left so it can be discovered.

Sam was taking it too seriously. "Maybe it's not such a lousy possibility."

It's still way out, I said. "Don't forget most of these deaths got little or no press coverage. Most of them weren't even considered murders at the time. How would Razvedka know it was the work of the testee instead of just a routine death? No, it's just not the way they'd work."

Sam shook his head: "I wish you hadn't told me. I'll keep rolling that possibility around for a few days and I'll get to think hey, this could be it. Then I'll try it on Vogelsang and he'll start believing it. . . . Harry, you sure this couldn't be it?"

I laughed. "Sam, I threw it at you because I knew I could depend on your basic skepticism. Take my word, and I've been in the business a long time, this is still pretty damn remote. Forget it and don't tell Vogelsang. He'll kill a few weeks on it."

Sam nodded. "I'll try to get rid of the idea but it's a little like the old game: I dare you not to think of a yellow giraffe with blue eyes and six feet. You know what you are? A dangerous *kochleffel,* a big cooking spoon, stirring up the pot. What you gotta do now is come back from London with something *useful* for us."

I said I liked him better as suspicious old party.

6

February 4, 1973. London.

At JFK I stopped at the insurance counter. Years ago there was a psychological ploy I fell into and used sometimes. When I'd fly on Agency business I'd deliberately take out a flight policy for the maximum available. I think it was $250,000 and the policy would cost me about seven or eight dollars. The beneficiary would be the current favorite. I'd fill out the form and mail it off. When I got back the embrace would be warmer and intimations perhaps we weren't just going through a passing thing and how thoughtful, how sweet, and so on. Mostly I'd be curious to see how she'd handle the subsurface guilt: after all, there must have been long moments when, without actively wishing me in a crash, she thought how nice it would be to come into $250,000. Obviously I wanted her to have the money if something happened to me en route and if something did happen she would grieve awhile. Still, there would be memories of the moments when she'd visualize the crash, the shock, and the numbing delicious moment when the insurance company would turn over $250,000. There was only one who responded properly: she decoded the trick message properly and took out a $250,000 insurance policy with me as beneficiary when *she* took a flight back to the States. It wasn't done in an innocent if-you-love-me-that-much, why-I-love-you-that-much, too. She did it because she knew exactly what was going on in my mind and heart. After we had played to a 1–1 standoff she said: "Okay, my love, enough of that *merde.*" She was unusual in other ways, too. I think she was the only Agency staffer we had in the field who used the cover of a call girl when she worked on the Riviera. Later she married a German ferrous-metals tycoon and I was invited to the wedding but couldn't go.

This time the beneficiary was Sam Urdell. It was a slight expression of my guilt: I was going to London without telling him what I was chasing. I should have, probably. But mainly, if by some utterly remote chance the plane didn't make it, why $250,000 would give him enough cushion to pursue the *goel hadam* even if the Committee lost interest.

I thought a bit about which hotel and finally narrowed it down to the Hilton and the Europa. Both were near the embassy, which would indicate I wasn't trying to hide from anyone. I finally reserved at the Europa, which was even nearer. I *had* been able to stretch out on four center seats. That and the fact that I didn't need a Dilaudid made it a nice flight.

William Solomon lived on Prince Consort Road in Kensington and we arranged I'd come over for a drink about three Sunday afternoon. His wife and two children would be down in Seaford, Sussex, where she had an interest in some carnation greenhouses.

The apartment was enormous—probably twelve rooms and I saw about five of them. The building, Albert Court, is a huge cooperative of the turn of the century with eleven-foot ceilings and a fair amount of central heating added on later. Still, an electric fireplace helped make the linen-walled sitting room habitable. Solomon is tall, red-haired ("considered terribly unlucky in Jewish families, y'know") with a carefully tended Van Dyke. He was also marvelously disarming. Instead of proceeding to knock out the palpable absurdities of my "historical research" mission he went on to relate the absurdities of his own situation. Only a total cad would refuse to be equally and engagingly frank.

He was, he said, the beneficiary of several shaming contradictions. "Really, on my academic salary, which comes to about ten thousand a year in your terms, I have no business living so grandly. A cottage in Wanstead should be my level. Since I teach security analysis at Gresham College it would be so nice to remark offhandedly, 'Well, I've had a bit of luck in the City, y'know.' But that would not be true, either. In fact, the few flyers I've taken haven't turned out too well. No, when you come right down to it the Solomon prosperity, such as it is, is due solely to the fact that a totally uninformed amateur—my wife—did something rather foolish, quite spur-of-the-moment, didn't consult me at all. As a result she made thirty-two thousand pounds or roughly seventy-six thousand dollars. It was a staggering blow to my pride and friends here for dinner or tea will still refer to the flat as Freda's Fruitful Folly. Envious scorn, you might say."

What happened, he went on, was that his wife's mother died in White Plains, New York, where she was living with another daughter who was married to an American. Freda, his wife, flew over when her mother was dying and stayed on for the funeral and the settling of the small estate. Turned out the old lady's sole assets were two savings accounts she left for her two daughters in trust—each for $5,000.

While there Freda became friendly with her sister's neighbor, a woman who worked as part-time secretary for a promoter bringing out a new stock that was going to sell at $2 a share. It was a medical device supposed to help rheumatics and arthritics. Freda was so impressed she invested $4,000—2,000 shares—in the silly machine. When she returned to London she told her husband what she had done; he was furious. "Dammit, that was half a year's salary. What business did she have *gambling* it away in a country where they're always looking for gullible foreigners. Oh, I went on for hours. Then when I lost some of my vapors I made some inquiries through a branch office of Merrill, Lynch here. Mind you, it was then about three weeks since my wife acquired the stock in New York and I hoped I'd have time enough to unload without too much loss. I resented having to inquire about some dreadful penny stock—for all I know it might be one of my former students who'd be fielding my inquiry—but I bucked myself up and I did. And I fainted. Fortunately I was seated so I didn't do myself an injury. Of course I didn't believe them at first so I checked at another brokerage office and there it was: this silly swindle of a stock, this ultimate cat and dog, this ha'penny holdup, yes, it was now worth thirty-eight dollars a share! I recovered my blood pressure, my voice, my composure and self-esteem, and ordered a friendly broker to sell the two thousand shares. We got out in three days, I recall, and incurred a mess of cable charges and suddenly we were worth seventy-six thousand of your dollars. Of course we had our capital gains tax here but when it was all over we had more capital in hand than my father had earned in his entire lifetime, I think. And more, for that matter, than I was ever likely to make even in a five-year period. To make matters sweeter, two weeks after we sold, the damn stock started falling precipitously and I think it ended being worth fifty cents a share or something like that."

What the Solomons did was acquire their present apartment and Mrs. Solomon, who loved carnations, bought a half-interest in a small but profitable greenhouse operation in Seaford which included a habitable cottage they used on weekends.

It was clearly my turn. It would have been simpler—but much longer —to have told him the whole story but since I hadn't cleared this with Sam and Vogelsang that was out. Instead I told him about a belated interest in my family background, particularly my grandfather. I showed him a copy of the *New York Times* item which led me to the London-based Hebrew Association for the Defense of Women and Girls. I added that another important reason was to see some friends in London and clear up one or two business matters. I described myself as a prematurely retired businessman.

He read the *Times* item twice.

"I'm afraid it sounds as if your grandfather was in my father's black books—along with several hundred other of our coreligionists."

I made it clear I had no illusions about my relative. He had obviously been several kinds of rogue.

"The difficulty is," he went on, "it's a little harder for some Jews to think that there are Jewish crooks and Jewish swindlers, Jewish pimps and Jewish murderers, and even Jewish fascists. But even when we grudgingly accept the obvious, Jews are not better—or worse—than any others, there's still a lingering feeling it's best to keep quiet about the miscreants among us. Don't we have enough enemies out there without making more by telling them about these miserable creatures who also happen to be Jews? I'm being a bit tiresome about the obvious, perhaps, but I have to explain about the peculiar nature of my father's files before you look at them."

He was arranging his thoughts as he delicately adjusted two japanned tin vases on an enormous marble-topped table in the room. "You have to understand first something about Jews in England. Their development here has been quite different from the U.S. Before eighteen eighty there was in England an Anglo-Jewish élite—Rothschilds, Montefiores, and Goldsmids. They were an élite with a number of humbling restrictions. Until the middle of the nineteenth century they couldn't enter a profession, hold municipal office, own land, or enter Parliament. As late as eighteen seventy they couldn't even graduate from Cambridge or Oxford. Still, they did well in the City and they built a network of Orthodox synagogues and Jewish schools and they ran their own welfare system. No Jew was allowed to be a public charge. They even founded the Jewish Board of Guardians for the relief of the 'necessitous Foreign Poor' and that's when their troubles started. The eighteen eighty-one Russian pogroms brought in thousands—a hundred thousand by nineteen ten—and the influx aroused intense opposition. One magazine, *Country Life*, commented that these 'aliens bring with them not only filth and poverty but crime.' Another publication had them as 'loathesome wretches who come itching and grunting to our shores.' "

The élite Jews at first welcomed the newcomers, but after a couple of years there were just too many of them and they tried to divert them —to the U.S., to provincial cities, and they even had a scheme whereby they paid a small bonus to any immigrants who would return to their homes on the Continent.

Things were so difficult in London, work was so scarce, some 50,000 accepted the bonuses to return. Behind this scheme was the Jewish

Board of Guardians, which also was getting increasingly concerned that a number of Jews were becoming thieves, pickpockets, burglars, fences, pimps, and prostitutes.

A lot of girls sent off to London from Russia, Poland, or Galicia by their parents—too poor to make the move themselves—never got to the relative whose name they had scribbled on a piece of paper. They were easy prey for Jewish white-slave agents who congregated at the main railway stations and the ship landing berths. To protect them the Association for the Defense of Women and Girls came into existence around 1885. They set up refuges for young girls and homes to rehabilitate prostitutes. They had agents at the docks who worked closely with the police; they kept check on suspected white slavers. And the Association issued annual reports which the newspapers quoted. A lot of English Jews had very mixed reactions: some felt the Committee was exaggerating; others felt the activities of these unsavory Jewish types shouldn't be broadcast so that the many enemies of the Jews would have additional ammunition. And there were some who simply refused to believe that Jews could be doing such terrible things to fellow Jews. But they had to believe when Dr. Hermann Adler, the Chief Rabbi of England, said it *was* so. Solomon read sonorously from a speech the Chief Rabbi gave in 1910:

We know that agents of these vile traffickers induce girls to leave home under the pretense that they will obtain remunerative situations in other countries. In many instances these villains offer them marriage. Their ignorant and credulous parents imagine that their daughters' future has been secured, and lend a too-willing ear to the representations of these miscreants. . . . They are in total ignorance of the existence of this trade. . . . It is therefore our bounden duty to spread full information as widely as possible. . . .

Solomon looked up from the sheet. "I love the Victorian perorations. Miscreant. Vile traffickers. Bounden duty. The only difficulty is that it manages to conceal certain truths. In Eastern Europe girls *were* an economic drag on a family. They needed dowries to get husbands, so every father looked the other way when there was a chance to get rid of one or two. Tevye, the hero of *Fiddler on the Roof*, was not that typical, I fear. What's that great line of Marx's? 'Money annuls all human relations.' Many of the girls knew damn well what they were getting into. A lot of them figured it couldn't be much worse than what they would have to endure in Galicia."

He found another sheet containing a talk given at the same 1910 conference by another prominent London rabbi, Dr. Moses Gaster, who described the incredible misery of Jewish families in parts of Galicia:

You cannot imagine the terrible poverty which exists where people fight not for a crust, but for a crumb. . . . If then, a man comes with gold which means untold riches not to one, but to all members of a family, can you wonder that a girl is entrapped, that she accepts a dowry even though she may be told that it is a prelude to shame? They will not believe that to her it is salvation, escape to a life of hope, of the enjoyment of these things denied to her, but the birthright of more fortunate girls; she will have enough food, fine clothes, amusement, a life of ease and pleasure. . . .

Solomon broke off with a smile: "At that point the old boy probably realized he was beginning to sound a bit like a recruiting madam so he went into his final plea: 'We must go there and alleviate the misery. . . . It is for us to prevent the fall, not to try to rescue only those who have fallen.' "

He poured himself another Scotch and sipped slowly. "For the Jews of London it seemed a uniquely shameful situation when, of course, it wasn't anything of the kind. Chinese families had been selling daughters into prostitution for eons. African tribal leaders had sold kinsmen into lifelong slavery for centuries. Thousands of French peasant families had nudged daughters into prostitution to get them out of the miserable house. But no outcries: how could Frenchmen and women do this to other Frenchwomen? You did it because it was one way of surviving. *Mrs. Warren's Profession* in eighteen ninety-eight could just as easily have been *Mrs. Warschavsky's Business*. But in fact the Jewish end of the business was quite small. There was a much larger trade getting British, Welsh, Scotch, and Irish virgins into houses in Belgium and France. It was an enormous British and non-Jewish trade and there were outcries in some of the press and Parliament but curiously no cries, how could Britons do this to other Britons? No, only the Jews had to personalize it, racialize it: how could Jews do this to Jews?"

The *London Jewish Chronicle*, he went on, had an item not long ago that Israel now had 5,000 whores in the nation. It didn't cause much fuss, really. Instead there was even an old quotation of the late Zionist poet, Bialik, "A normal Jewish nation will have arrived the day the first Jewish horse thief is arrested in Tel Aviv." By extension, then, the presence of 5,000 whores makes it clear the Jewish nation has certainly arrived.

Solomon apologized for going on at such length, at his own peroration before a captive American audience. Anyway, that was what his father had been involved in all his adult life. By 1939 he was probably one of the world's great authorities on the international white-slave traffic.

But what interested me, he went on, was anything in the material on my grandfather and that would probably be in the 1908 file, if the clipping was an accurate guide. The difficulty was that the material was still being indexed, and if I could wait a day or two he could see to it that it was in shape for me to go through it. He'd phone me tomorrow afternoon to let me know.

February 5, 1973. London.

Dave Quittle suggested lunch at Scott's. "They've charged it up since the move from Piccadilly but it's still great seafood." We agreed to meet there at one.

The Agency used to have an Inspector General staff of sixty and it was cut back in the recent wave to about forty. And Quittle was one of the men who chose early retirement at fifty-one. The Inspector's staff makes regular visits to all Agency outposts to see if directives are being followed; if budgets are adhered to reasonably; to make sure discretionary funds aren't being handled too indiscreetly or wastefully; to listen to gripes by the field hands against the Chief of Station or other superiors. And from time to time their job would be to lecture us on excessive use of black-market currency operations which were often necessary if you weren't going to be clobbered by the artificially maintained government bank rate. Or excessive use of cable charges; or overclassifying material in order to get it priority transmission. They were our auditors, chaplains, policemen, and efficiency experts.

What happened was I killed my wife.

We had gone to Izmir, which is still Smyrna to the Greeks. It was to be a four-day holiday and we had a fine room in the Büyük Efes with a balcony overlooking the sea. We drove back by way of Manisa where we were going to picnic and visit—at Dorothea's insistence—weeping Niobe, a huge reddish rock that looked remotely like a weeping woman. She's crying her eyes out because she talked too much: about how beautiful her fourteen children were. This got to the gods and Apollo and Artemis were ordered to kill the children. As the story goes nothing was left to Niobe except tears and a moved Zeus turned her into stone and when water oozes out it's obviously Niobe's tears. Dorothea was very strong on what she called the classical antiquities and in high school she won a prize for knowing the name of every Greek and Roman god and goddess and what they were supposed to do. So I also heard about Lamia, the Libyan queen who was loved by Jupiter. Jealous Juno had Lamia's children stolen. Instead of trying to get back at Juno, Lamia vowed vengeance against all children. She'd entice and devour them. Dorothea's hidden messages didn't lend themselves to simple decoding.

The Niobe rock had become a tourist attraction with flower gardens, a restaurant and bandstand but we were going to picnic on a grass ledge higher up. We got up with the picnic stuff and were opening a wine bottle when a soldier came up and said, *"bir patlak,"* illustrating the flat tire with one palm coming down slowly on the other. I went down to where we parked the car and the right front tire was flat and I remembered, too, I had done something stupid. I opened the trunk and took out the expensive Fendi attaché case Dorothea had given me on my birthday. There was some office material in there I shouldn't have taken with me and there was the .38. Ordinarily there would have been any number of locals who would have offered to fix the flat for a few lira but on this noon the place was deserted. I took out the spare and was about to begin with the jack when I realized that Dorothea would be annoyed with my leaving her alone on the picnic ledge. I shut the trunk, took the case with me, and trudged up again. When I got there an *onbasi,* an army corporal, was trying to force a huge brown prick into her ass. She was flat on the ground and immobile. What registered in that frozen moment was the corporal had a long scar on his right thigh, that his dark olive-brown uniform gave him a strict U.S. Army look and his mouth was open and he was nodding as he tried to force his penis into the tight, viselike anus. The other soldier, a private, was masturbating. He had just come and he was still holding his cock to milk it for more. As I opened the attaché case to get the gun the private dropped his cock to reach for his rifle. I fired before he had the piece in position. The bullet went through his heart and the corporal on Dorothea got up terror-stricken. At first I assumed he was reacting to me and the gun but he kept looking at Dorothea's inert body. Only later did that make any sense. In any case there was only instinct, not thought, and I shot him too. I aimed for the groin but got him a little higher.

Buggering by Turkish soldiers was an old story. There had been another incident in the late '50s involving the French chargé d'affairs and his wife picnicking near the Çubuk Dam, eight miles north of Istanbul. The soldiers buggered both and slit their throats. The French raised a terrible stink and so did the British, paying a little homage to the memory of Lawrence of Arabia. The soldiers were caught and executed.

As it happened, when the barman from the restaurant below came up he saw me standing there and says he heard me mumble, *"Karakol, lutfen"* (police, please) and in time the police were there and then someone from the office of Commander of the Allied Forces, Southeastern Europe, which is headquartered in Izmir. He was an *albay,* a colonel, and he had met me once or twice in Ankara. By then I dimly realized that Dorothea was dead, too. The bullet which killed the masturbating private went through his heart, ricocheted off a rock between two dwarf oaks and some wild hollyhocks, and came back to sever the femoral artery in Dorothea's right leg. This, of course, came out much later. For a while the police and the colonel were very nervous about the situation. Perhaps the two soldiers were killed to hide a simple wife-killing and so on.

What helped greatly, Dave Quittle said, was one, I had used round-

ńosed bullets. A round-nosed bullet will tend to ricochet easily whereas
a flat-nosed or square-pointed one will be more likely to dig in. And it
was a low-velocity bullet. With high enough velocity or a weak jacket
a bullet will generally break up on hitting a surface.

But mostly, he said, the traditional Hanan luck was still working. As
it happened, that very week there was a meeting in Istanbul of the
International Academy of the Forensic Sciences. Among them were the
world's two greatest experts on the curious business of death by ricochet,
a Calcutta medical examiner named Jauhari and an American ballistics
authority named Berg from Minnesota. They were called in early—I
never found out who at the embassy was that knowing—and established
beyond doubt that Dorothea had been killed by the ricocheting bullet.
There was no publicity on the case but later on one of the experts did
a report—no names, of course—for the *Deutsche Zeitschrift der gericht-
lichen Medizin*. It was becoming a classic case.

Over brandy Dave said that he had taken charge at the request of the
ambassador who had gotten together with Çaglayangil, then handling
the ministry of foreign affairs. Also it was Dave who decided that it was
best to keep me sedated for a few days until they got things established.
"So if you still have a blank for the aftermath blame me." I thanked him
again, as I had several times before leaving Ankara. A reporter from the
popular daily *Hurriyet* had been tipped off, probably by the barman, but
nothing was allowed to appear.

"Oh, there were one or two people in the embassy," Dave went on,
"who were convinced you were out to kill Dorothea anyway, to get out
from under the marriage. I wish I knew who they were so I could ask
them why a Protestant and a Jew couldn't get a simple divorce. Anyway
the technical evidence was so flukey, so special, no one really believed
it was deliberate. The odds against that particular ricocheting bullet
killing Dorothea was, the experts said, one in ten million. Everybody
knew you'd never rely on that kind of odds if you really wanted to kill
her. It didn't hurt you at Langley. As it happened your promotion and
transfer to headquarters went through a week later. I don't think it was
simply to get you out of the country, although, I suppose, that could
have been a small part."

Dave is stocky, white-haired with a glazed face and mustache to match. A New York face, I told him. But he was a Jack-Mormon from Moab, Utah, who had been in World War II and Korea and had two Silver Stars.

" 'Why did he marry her?' I kept hearing at the embassy," Dave went on, "and I remember once I said maybe he needed her and the answers would always be, hell, he could have had anyone he wanted."

I owed him a lot, but I couldn't sort it all out that evening. "You're in the neighborhood," I said. "I did need her then. It was a bad time for me. I was depressed as hell. The anxiety was not only floating free but it was down at my soles, too. She had a kind of mock cheerfulness that was just right for me then. And she was a great ego-sustainer."

I asked him what he was doing in retirement. "I didn't quit. I was kicked out like a few thousand others. What the hell can I do? I'm too old to go back to school for a law degree. I can't see myself getting in with a lie-detector firm or doing security work for a plant in Oshkosh. I've got a daughter in college. My ex-wife and I both help out and I suppose I could get along on the pension quietly but I'm not ready to lie down and die."

What he was doing was working with a cousin in London. His relation, Sam Garrett, had lived there more than twenty years and was in a peculiar business: finding missing heirs. Mostly it involved U.S. estates where there were no known heirs—and no will. Some were pretty sizable. If no heirs turned up the estate would be taken over by the state. The heir-hunters would try to find legitimate heirs—usually first or second cousins who never knew the dead person—and establish the relationship with birth and death certificates and genealogical charts. For his successful efforts the heir-hunter would get anywhere from 25 to 50 percent of the estate on contract with the found heir. It was a business that had been around for more than ninety years and while it had a lot of sharpshooters and con men it also had its legitimate operators who did well. Most of them were men who got started in the '30s when regular jobs were scarce. He and his cousin were often brought into cases by U.S. heir-hunters who suspected that likely heirs were to be found in Britain or Ireland. The job was to find them, get them to sign contracts, and then prove they were the rightful heirs. It was a small field with about a dozen operators in the U.S., two or three in England, and a few more on the Continent. Most of them knew each other and often worked in tandem on international jobs.

"My trouble is I can't see it as a job for a grownup," Dave said. "But I'll hang around awhile. Puts off having to think what the hell I'll do when I finally go stateside."

I remembered a missing-heir hunter had been poking around in the old New York Benevolent Association. I asked Dave if he could get me a list of the stateside missing-heir hunters.

Naturally he wanted to know why. The truth was too involved. I was feeling quite tired and a little queasy so I said one of them had been poking around about my brother's estate of which I was the executor. He politely accepted my version and promised to get me a list. When we got up to leave—I picked up the tab after a bit of fencing—I saw Elly at a table near the entrance. She was with a tall brown man who looked Indian. I walked over and asked where she was staying. She introduced me to Triguna Hathi, a director at the International Industrial Research Management Association, for whom she was interpreting a meeting. She was staying at the Hilton, where the meeting was taking place. I said I'd phone and perhaps we could get together before I returned to New York.

Dave watched us from the entrance and said as we left, "I know her from somewhere." I told him who she was. As he walked me back to my hotel he said, "What gets me is that someone who was involved in a one-in-ten-million long shot should be nabbed by something as common as lung cancer. It doesn't fit." I said, sounding like a voiceover on a thirty-second public health commercial, if you smoke common cigarettes a lot you can earn a common death. He asked how long I was supposed to have. I shrugged: three days; two months; or seven hours. We shouldn't have walked. I needed my first Dilaudid in three days.

Waiting for it to take hold, two ancient urges surfaced. I must run through the London phone book to see if there was another Harry Hanan; and I should phone MAI 45–59, our old Paris number, to see who now lived in our house on Rue Perronet in Neuilly. I didn't do either and for the first time I felt I was really going to die soon.

February 6, 1973. London.

William Solomon's office at Gresham College is on Basinghall Street. Modified Dickens with a touch of the grasping modern: on the first and fourth floors of the college building the Commissioner of Income Tax for the City of London holds forth.

Solomon had been able to bring me his father's correspondence files for the years 1907 to 1912 which he thought would cover most of his involvement with my relative. The indexers had finished with those years. If I wanted to Xerox any stuff I should ask the secretary he shared with two other faculty members. He was off to a class.

The files were random pincushions. In an age before paper clips, staples, and Scotch tape the collective noun was the pin. There were copies of letters, some typewritten, clippings, and cryptic memos. Some of it was in Yiddish but nearly all of it had accompanying translations. The first one that caught my finger was a rusty-pinned Yiddish pamphlet whose only English words on the cover indicated it was published by the Hebrew Publishing Company of New York in 1911. And written across the top was "Trans. U.S. Immig Comm rept., 1911." Providentially, the Immig. Comm. rept. was only a half-inch away.

The report was headed, "Importation and Harboring of Women for Immoral Purposes." There were lengthy analyses of the differences in the ways Japanese, Chinese, French, Italian, and Jewish gangs worked in bringing women over, breaking them in to the life, and exploiting them.

The report went on to mention the headquarters where French importers, procurers, and pimps congregated, received their mail, and transacted business; that the Japanese groups, headquartered in California, imported only Japanese girls but that the Chinese, while importing their own, also used American women. And the Italian pimps were more feared than the others.

The Jewish gangs also imported but mainly they "prey upon young girls whom they find on the street, in the dance halls, and similar places and whom, by methods already indicated—love making and pretenses of marriage—they deceive and ruin. Many of them are petty thieves, pickpockets and gamblers."

Like the Japanese, Chinese, French, and Italian pimps and procurers, the Jewish groups also got together. But more businesslike:

Perhaps the best known organization of this kind throughout the country was one legally incorporated in New York in 1904 under the name of the New York United Benevolent Association. As stated in the articles of incorporation, the objects were benevolent, providing for a weekly payment to sick members and for burial. They had a cemetery plot in Flatbush where members were buried . . . but the main object of the association was to assist its members, many of whom were keepers of disorderly houses, pimps, or procurers, in carrying on their business, and especially in defeating the law. When one was arrested for committing a crime, money was raised to assist him. Money was also raised for protection fees.

When a prostitute was murdered because she had discarded her pimp, every member had to attend the funeral or pay a $2 fine. Now the strange postcard I had found made sense.

Solomon had his own notes on the New York United.

Their headquarters was the International Cafe at 60 Second Avenue. Run by a man named Joe Siegel, it was also the mail drop for the New York United's scattered members. There was a long, rambling letter from a New York reformer named Frank Moss. Solomon had underlined some passages:

There has grown up as an adjunct of this herd of female wretchedness a fraternity of fetid male vermin who are unmatched for impudence and bestiality and who reek with all unmanly and viscious humors. They are called "pimps." A number of them are in the roll of the Max Hanan Association. They have a regular federation and manage several clubs, which are influential in local politics and which afford them the power to watch their poor women victims, to secure their hard and ill-earned money, and to punish them when they are refractory.

Moss, apparently, had been counsel for the Society for the Prevention of Crime and had had a court run-in with Max Hanan. Once in a vice trial Moss found that a man present in the court had warned a defendant so that she evaded arrest. Then, Moss went on:

A good judge, Voorhis, was on the bench. I apprised him of the circumstances and pointed out the man. He directed the officers of the court squad to bring him to the bench. They looked at him, their faces paled, and their feet refused to move. I turned to the officer in command and said, "Why don't you bring that man here?" His teeth chattered. I said, "If you don't, I will."

Boldly, Moss walked up to the man and pushed him toward the bench and the witness chair. The judge asked him his name:

The answer came, "Max Hanan." I had never met that important personage before, and at once understood the terror that had seized the court officers. Apparently Judge Voorhis did not know him. He gave Hanan a scathing lecture and ordered him to keep out of the court. Hanan went immediately to the counsel for the defendants and asked him if he thought it would cost over $100 to demolish my face. He then went out on the sidewalk and harangued several hundred of his followers. Our devoted little band of detectives were hustled, threatened and repeatedly struck by the leading members of a crowd of at least 500, who chased them all the way to the Bowery. . . .

So I had a whoremaster for a grandfather, but it didn't get me any further on a theory on the *goel hadam* murders and threats. Then in the 1911 file an orderly Solomon had placed a clipping from a Yiddish paper, *The Jewish Tageblatt* of New York.

Incredible as it may seem it is nevertheless a fact that almost the entire traffic in women in the city of Constantinople is in Jewish hands. It is not done secretly, quietly and in a hidden way so that it is known only to a few, but openly and boldly so that one cannot help but notice it.

When you come to Constantinople and begin to get acquainted with Jewish life and take note of Jewish institutions, you are forced to notice a Jewish congregation of white slavers. This is a community of full autonomy. It has its leaders, officers, sextons, almsgivers, and even a synagogue. It is a community of two hundred families, comprised of Jews from Russia, Galicia, and Roumania. They form a separate town for themselves.

In Galata, the poor quarter of the city, ten or twelve streets belong entirely to these white slavers. There is their government, their stores, their houses, their merchandise, and their clubs and when you pass through those streets you shudder. In the open doors and windows there lie around semi-nude girls. The newly established B'nai B'rith Lodge in Constantinople, among other good things, is fighting the transport of Jewish girls for immoral purposes.

I almost missed the great clue because Solomon when making his translation had penned in the bottom margin, a note to himself: "Write

Tageblatt. Inform our work here, elsewhere." He wrote a tiny, crabbed script that didn't invite casual reading and I readily assumed the translation ended there. When I put the sheet back in order, the light from the window hit it and the translucency revealed that there was more on the back. It was a continuation of the translation:

> The head of this shameful community is an Austrian, one Franz Fassnacht. . . . The Turkish government is satisfied that this trade shall remain in the hands of foreigners. . . .
>
> If the B'nai B'rith succeeds in breaking up this traffic, it will have done something beautiful, something great from the Jewish standpoint as well as from the standpoint of humanity.

Solomon appended another note to himself: "See Fr. Pappenheim ltr." He was neat and systematic and it appeared further in the accordion-pleated file. Fräulein Bertha Pappenheim of Frankfurt was a German-Jewish coworker in the battle against white slavery. In April 1911 she had visited Constantinople and interviewed the Chief Rabbi about local conditions:

The chief rabbi knows a little, certainly not enough. I also believe he does not have the power to achieve anything. He knows, for instance, that there is a synagogue of white slavers in Constantinople. Prostitutes purchase honors for their procurers. He has enough power to close this "House of God" but does not do so. His reasons are non-existent—else, I would have to be afraid, too. The information is generally known that 90 percent of the girls on the slave market are Jewish and that nearly all the dealers are Jews also.

I put down the file. Of course it could be two different Fassnachts but I was pretty sure it was the same. Maurice Faucon who died in France was the son of Moritz Fassnacht, the grandson of? I was ready to bet it would be Franz. Moritz left Constantinople around 1905, I vaguely recalled. I could see Sam Urdell giving me the details on young Fassnacht leaving Constantinople where he was a little ashamed that his family ran a couple of "hewer" houses as Sam put it.

Faucon, born Fassnacht, and Hanan get *goel hadam* notes. Both are grandsons of major characters in the white-slavery trade around 1910 or so. Two out of eight victims or victims-to-be if you included me. This *was* a tie-up and I was ready to bet it just wasn't coincidence. It still didn't make any sense that someone or some bunch was trying to kill them because of that tie but I was sure the tie was what brought the notes. A murdering nut who believed in the staining deadliness of genetics?

When I got back to my hotel late in the afternoon there was a message to phone Elly Bricha. She said we ought to talk and I said why not at dinner. She hesitated a moment only.

At seven I walked the half-mile to the Hilton—I felt much stronger than the night before—and we took a cab to Rule's. Her suggestion. It was Edwardian and theatrical and what she had to say fitted. In the cab she told me about the Elly.

She was named after her mother's favorite stage character, Ellie Dunn, the poor but proper young lady who comes to the weekend house party in *Heartbreak House*. I said she didn't dress that way. She wore a shetland, raglan-sleeved coat that they were calling the great steamer coat that season and under it a cardigan-jacketed suit with navy wool skirt and the jacket in plum, navy, and white nubby wool.

She smiled. "You must know by now that I'm not that easily classifiable." I said that Vogelsang had called her a very private person, but not a mysterious one.

Dinner was the first time I really had a chance to appraise her leisurely and I found it wasn't easy, partly because I was taking a personal interest. The pixie face, the large gray eyes, the fact that I couldn't read her as readily as I could most women made her a challenge. Years ago there had been three categories: don't want to sleep with; can easily sleep with; and a third and much smaller group: would like to sleep with but suspect wrong chemistry. Temporarily, if I was going by the old standards, Elly would come in the third group. Except the urge was almost dormant.

She said she had hesitated a moment when I suggested dinner only because she didn't want to—she smiled briefly—"compromise me or whatever the word is for embarrassing CIA people."

She explained. "I don't know if you've actually checked out the three of us—Sam, Peter, and myself—in terms of an FBI or security check or whatever you use. If you haven't you'll probably decide sooner or later maybe it would be a good idea and then you'll find certain things about me. Might be better if you got it from me first. I am what you might call a suspicious character."

If I checked, she went on, I'd find that she was born in Geneva in

1943. Her mother was there because she was a minor functionary of the ILO, the International Labor Office, a remnant of the old League of Nations. Her father was a Swiss businessman who died in 1948. But it was her mother's activities that she wanted to talk about.

"She was an educated romantic, which in nineteen forty-three meant not a failed poet but a Communist. She belonged secretly to the 'Nichole' party of Geneva. It was headed by Léon Nichole and was not officially a Communist party but had a high component of fellow travelers. The Swiss Communist party used it as a recruiting agency for possible spies and cutouts. There were several ILO people in the network and my mother was mainly a courier. Every two weeks she'd take the train to Berne or Lucerne. She was involved in the Lucy ring—the one that got the Nazi order-of-battle information to Moscow in twenty-four hours.

"All this," Elly went on, "would have come out if you ran my name through your records. Bricha is not Smith, Jones, or Dupont. Well, you find out who my mother was and you say, aha! Let's look a little closer at this fluff who's right in on this *goel hadam* investigation. Then naturally your well-trained mind jumps to the nature of her work. Yes, yes, how curious that she's so well-traveled because of her profession. Maybe she got the Communist virus from her mother . . . a whole lot of silly maybes that have to be checked out once you find out who my mother was."

Her mother, she went on, was a silly romantic who retained fond illusions about an old love, the Soviet Union, long after an ordinarily alert adult would have realized that the love was a miserable, corrupt— and corrupting—creature.

"Once when I was a precocious twelve I came across some lines by a minor nineteenth-century French journalist, Louis Veuillot, who was also a militant Catholic:

When I am weaker than you, I ask you for freedom because that is according to your principles; when I am stronger than you, I take your freedom away, because that is according to my principles.

"At home I said what a fine Communist he would have made in the twentieth century and my mother didn't talk to me for a week.

"I was interpreting at an international health congress and I was assigned to a section considering the awful problem of children born in the nineteen-sixty-three-to-sixty-five period to mothers who had German measles; as a result the children were born deaf. Well, there were thousands and thousands of children so afflicted in that epidemic. All their lives they'll be marked as the sixty-three–sixty-five epidemic children. Sometimes I think my mother's generation had its own epidemic, a virus they could never shake off. The body absorbs vaccines like the Russo-Nazi pact, Hungary, Czechoslovakia, and still the virus persists. They're getting older so they huddle together more. Generally they're intelligent and bright on most things except communism. You talk to them about that and a glaze comes over their eyes. Viral zombies."

She was remarkably unvehement as she spoke on a subject that generally brings out progressive choler. I asked her if she had any political position as I poured more Gewürztraminer in her glass. (She is a far better eater and drinker than I've ever been.) She sipped and thought a moment. "You mean the old nonsense. Left. Right. 'I have no enemies on the Left' but also 'Every revolution evaporates and leaves behind only the slime of a new bureaucracy.' "

I said: "Maybe your mother wasn't as silly as you think she was. She named you for a Shavian heroine and you sound as if you've turned into one, after all. A self-fulfilling prophecy? All that's left to be fulfilled is for you to marry a wealthy, older, cynical Captain Shotover type. Obviously Vogelsang didn't qualify even though he was rich and elderly." She thought a moment.

"In my work I meet a lot of men. They hear my voice on the language earphones and some become curious about me and find an excuse to say hello and suggest dinner and such. It's an almost perfect job for someone who wants to meet established, reasonably successful men. Of course most of them are married, or if they're not, other disabilities become quickly apparent."

Vogelsang didn't qualify, she said, on several counts. Mostly she wasn't in love with him but there was another drawback, too.

"He's so vulnerable and vulnerable men bring out the worst in me."

The worst was? She laughed deeply. "I have a low streak in me. Do you ever look at *France Dimanche?*"

I vaguely recalled it. A purple Parisian weekly, something like our *National Enquirer.*

"Well, it's a vice with me. I never miss an issue. I love its vocabulary. A murderer is always an *assassin* or a *monstre.* Husbands are always more jealous than tigers. A mother tells her husband, 'I forgive you for killing our baby.' And the week I was toying with Peter's proposal there was a story in *Dimanche* about a woman who had killed someone. She looked like a concierge-in-training and the caption on the picture was 'The Wife with the Tranquil Face was a DEVOURER OF MEN.' I promptly got a marvelously mad image of me nibbling at Peter's finger and I knew I couldn't love, let alone marry him. The silly engines that run a woman's mind.

"There. We're really caught up now. I've been prattling about myself partly to even things up. All the material I've been seeing about you and your CIA career and your wife's death and your adventures in Europe. That gave me a big edge and since I'm fair-minded sometimes I thought I ought to balance things by filling you in on me. Even my weekly vice. I think we're caught up now."

Backing out of the dead end, I asked if she had any theories about the *goel hadam* deaths.

"I used to be filled with them. Those two weeks when I was reading murder mysteries and talking to suspense writers was a peculiar time for me. I was recovering from hepatitis, which meant I wasn't really well but not sick enough to be considered sympathetically by one and all. I was just a little miserable. Perhaps I extended my jaundiced look to the story detectives. Such fine detectives and human dolts! Especially about money. I almost abandoned one story halfway because the detective given a huge check for services rendered doesn't run down to the bank to get it certified. And sure enough when he gets around to it the check's been stopped. But I did get something out of it that might be useful. So many of the writers seem to love a plot that hinges on a crime that has its origins in the distant past, often something terrible done to children long ago. I gather from Sam and Peter that you're inclined to that solution for this thing, too."

I still thought so. She nodded and went on.

"Also, when I finished those two weeks I wanted to know if they had checked out the paper the notes were on and the maker of the rubber-block stamps. I had become an apprentice Nancy Drake. No, that wasn't her name."

She said she didn't have children's books like that but went directly from her grandmother's stories to grown-up books. "Just so you don't think I'm a birdbrain, I should add that the paper the notes were on was a very common sulphite bond and the rubber blocks were in a set made by a Tel Aviv toy company which had made thousands and thousands of them. Not very useful leads."

I said no one would ever take her for any kind of birdbrain; which she knew. She laughed a little longer than necessary. "Oh, you find me out too fast. I suppose part of my problem is that every now and then I look around, particularly when things are a little bleak as they were during my long siege with hepatitis and wonder what's to become of me, an unmarried woman on the verge of thirty, cast adrift in a highly competitive world of simultaneous interpreters. And then I think maybe I should have taken up Peter's proposal."

Surely there were others, too, I said. "There's so much travel involved in my work, it's not really conducive to steady romance. So you're faced with a series of your one-night stands or basically unsatisfactory long-term relationships with married admirers. Not for me."

She wouldn't have found favor in the eyes of Kemal Ataturk, the great Turk. He once said the quality he most admired in a woman was availability.

It was a dumb bridge which I knew as soon as the words were out. Surely a natural reaction for her would have been to marvel that I was so tolerant of Turkish male attitudes toward women after what I had been through and so on for a bad dinner close.

So, thoughtfully, she went on to say instead she had a financial cushion in two apartments she owned in Geneva on Rue Cavour, just behind the Voltaire Museum. One she had been born in and inherited on her mother's death and the other, on another floor, she bought from savings. The two apartments, furnished, gave her about $9,000 in rentals a year. "Geneva is so close to France, geographically and spiritually, that we all become property-mad, which is a sensible thing to be in an inflationary world. We're just like"—her eyes dimpled—"those simple, homespun American CIA agents who buy houses in the District and rent them out."

I said *my* house was on the market. She looked at me for a brief unvoiced colloquy whose final line surely would have been: "How thoughtful to tidy things up before dying." Instead she became curious about my charmer job with the Agency.

"I find it hard to visualize you in that role; someone so anxious to *please;* to be useful, needed; to smooth things, to anticipate the wants and needs of others."

It was a younger, different me. I had fallen in love with the world of secrecy and intelligence and would have done anything to stay in it. There was a new sudden excitement to life that hadn't existed before. Still, there was a less-friendly appraisal by someone who had once been in the business. Malcolm Muggeridge shrewdly identified a key element in many of us in the business, while commenting on the Philby case. "The ungrown-up make better husbands and kinder lovers than adults —which is, of course, why women so assiduously go after them. . . . Mrs. Philby said the four years she had been married to Philby were the happiest in her life."

Elly didn't ask the natural and impolite question: had I grown up? Which was just as well because I wasn't sure of the answer.

She recalled when an old spy book caused a lot of trouble in the Rue Cavour apartment. "I was about twelve, I think, and I had just read Conrad's *Secret Agent* and I was so impressed with Verloc—'the famous and trusty secret agent'—that I once introduced one of my mother's admirers to a girl friend as Monsieur Verloc because I thought he looked like a Verloc should. My mother went into a rage and later I found out that my Monsieur Verloc *was* having trouble with Swiss counterintelligence, who suspected him of working for the East Germans."

I said things were obviously better run in Verloc's time. Today everyone seemed to know everything about secret agents. I admitted I was impressed with the stuff on me that Urdell and Vogelsang had been able to assemble with a few foreign helpers. But, still, they hadn't made much headway in solving the *goel hadam* mystery.

I had decided during dinner not to tell her of my findings in the Solomon files. I had been involved in administrative hierarchies so long

I felt I had to give it to Urdell and Vogelsang first. We cabbed back to the Hilton. She didn't want a final drink at the bar because she had an early call for another conference the next day. In fact she'd be at it three days. We shook hands on leaving and she suddenly kissed me lightly. "I'm glad we know each other a little better now," she said and got into an elevator.

Flying back I played with scenarios. As the plane plunges into the ocean I die of cancer. Later my body is the only one recovered and a college of forensic scientists debate—for some insurance company prize —which form of death hit me first. I even had an old Southern French expression for the occasion: *"Es maï mort"*: he's double-dead.

7

February 8, 1973. New York.

I phoned Sam to arrange a meeting. I said I had some interesting material on the *goel hadam*. He said he was glad I was back but did I have to hurry so? In a day or so he would have started thinking about that $250,000 flight policy I sent him. He was touched by my thinking of him; first time anyone ever sent him an air-flight policy. "But I gotta tell you, you get one of those, you get some mixed emotions." I said I knew all about it. We arranged to meet at Vogelsang's office at eleven. They had some new stuff.

There was another victim. Number eight by our count. His *goel hadam* note bore the number (14). Vogelsang had been a friend of the victim, Jim Monash.

"This one really got to me. The others were strangers. We knew each other's troubles and I once lent him three thousand dollars when he was going through a bad time. When it's someone you know it stops being an unlikely fantasy."

It was all that and still something else. He turned to Sam, "What was that Yiddish expression you used before about Monash?" Sam nodded: *"Nur dos fehlt ihm,"* and turned to me: "Very ironic. Meaning, this was the only thing he was lacking."

Monash's body had been found in the rear of a six-story red-brick apartment house on West Twelfth Street on a Sunday morning in July 1970. He had lived on the fifth floor and his bedroom window was open and the quick assumption was suicide, even though no note was found. He was forty-seven and divorced.

"You got to understand the background to appreciate why Sam's expression was a kind of perfect obit for Monash," Peter said.

"In World War Two before I was sent overseas, I was an assistant PIO, press information officer, at a southern air base. A first looey. One night working late I met this eighteen-year-old PFC who was supposed to clean out the office. We got to talking and he seemed very bright and I was curious how come he was stuck in an office-cleaning detail. So PFC Monash told me his philosophy:

" 'Before I went in,' he said, 'I did some figuring. A lieutenant had twenty, thirty, forty men to worry about. Me, I had only myself. I had twenty-four hours a day to worry about my survival. The odds had to be with me on that basis. I did more figuring. I looked for nighttime jobs. There are fewer Caesars or Napoleons around at night. Fewer ball-breakers. At four AM people talk friendly. So I volunteer for all kinds of night jobs. Even latrine jobs, mess hall, and the motor pool. And this one.'

"Well, any eighteen-year-old who talked like that and thought like that had to be unusual and it turned out he had one year of college and had done a lot of reading and a little writing," Vogelsang went on. "So I tried him on some of our home-town releases and he could do it better than either of the two sergeants we had doing it and I finally got him to try daytime work in the office. I went overseas in a few months and didn't see him again until after the war.

"I ran into him again in nineteen forty-eight. He and a partner had a small publicity operation, mostly publicizing new products. They didn't last as a team and split. Jim got a job with a medium-sized PR outfit as an account executive but his jobs didn't last—a lot of the accounts didn't either—but mostly I found out his trouble was he came on very hot and full of brilliant ideas for each new account but he got bored with the account very quickly and it showed. He married, they had a boy who turned out a Mongoloid and had to be institutionalized, and the marriage died. Blaming each other for the boy's condition and God knows what else.

"I liked Jim and our luncheons were fascinating because he was funny and shrewd, did marvelous takeoffs on people in the advertising and PR business. And he wasn't a lush. But he couldn't hold jobs, including one I sent him to at a friend's advertising agency when they decided to open their own PR department. Then in the mid-Fifties he fell in with an agency that needed a build-up man. Man gets to be president at forty-five of a fair-sized corporation doing maybe fifty million a year. He gets dreams. Public life. Politics. Who-knows-what? After all, he got to be a big man in his field why can't he do the same outside—even as he stays CEO at the XYZ Corp. So the firm that does the corporation PR is nudged into starting the build-up. There's a whole routine I won't bore you with. Speeches before groups outside his industry. Articles about national problems. Eventually appointment to the Governor's Commission on this or that; or the President's Commission and then even working up to a minor embassy abroad. En route there are honorary degrees—paid for subtly and not so. And foreign honors, one kind or another. Everyone doing it borrows from the tricks Ben Sonnenberg used in his classic build-up of Charley Luckman years ago. Then Monash got disgusted with the great-man racket, which he defined for me as the inflation and labeling of enormous stuffed shirts, and came on really hard times. That's when I lent him three thousand dollars. And then came the apparent suicide."

The curious thing was that the week before Monash's death Vogelsang had been toying with a curious research idea. "The world was filled with lucky and unlucky people. And which side they fell on was apparent only later when you could look back on the lives. The unlucky ones, like

Monash, had clear-cut patterns of bad luck all along. But once you made the statement what could you do with it?"

We didn't get impatient with Vogelsang's digression because talking about Monash was clearly a kind of needed catharsis. It was the first time I had seen him so moved.

The *goel hadam* note had turned up thirty-one months later because the contents of Monash's apartment had been turned over to his ex-wife. She took some of the furniture to Philadelphia, where she lived, and the personal papers and things she stored in a closet. Two years later, she became curious and idly went through the stuff. Only a week ago she found the note in an envelope that Monash had intended sending to Vogelsang. Inside was a memo: "Dear Peter: A brilliant, very subtle PR campaign? What is it? Jim."

Monash came from Altoona, Pennsylvania, where his father was a moderately successful lawyer. So far they didn't have much else on the family but they were working on that.

I told them what I had found in London. I said I was certain the *goel hadam* deaths stemmed from the involvement of parents and grandparents of the victims in the white-slave trade in the last two decades of the last century and possibly the first two or three of this one. I showed them the Xerox copies I had made in Solomon's office on my grandfather and on the Faucon-Fassnacht family.

"How come I never hear of this stuff?" Vogelsang asked.

Sam Urdell cocked an eye at him.

"Hey! You think it's the kind of stuff they talk about during Jewish History Week or at temple Sunday school?"

"You just don't think of Jews in that kind of business," Peter said. "I must be pretty naïve. What do we do now?"

I suggested a brief test of my hypothesis—if they felt one was needed. Do a little further checking on the background of the first known victim, Lucksig, the California accountant. If he checks out, we could then assume fairly safely that all the rest will, too.

Vogelsang, recovering, thought it would be a fair enough test, samplingwise, and Sam said Lucksig would be comparatively easy because he had a vague recall that he and his father had been American born.

February 9, 1973.

The old bromide is polishing brass on a sinking ship, but how about tending the toothache of a terminal CA patient? The dentist says it's just a filling that needs replacement and otherwise my teeth are in good shape as he scales them with his ultrasound device. Waiting for the down elevator in 30 Central Park South is a test of patience and I'm joined in a minute by someone who looks familiar—as obviously I do to him. We make the usual approach sounds and it turns out that out of monochrome gowns it's Andresen, the surgeon. His nephew, a radiologist, has an office on the same floor as my dentist.

Andresen is understandably curious: my symptoms, pains, what have I been doing, and how many Dilaudids did I average a week. As he's asking he's also studying me intently. "Good color," he says, "no great weight loss, I'd guess. Been able to walk much?"

I said I had walked as much as ten blocks without getting too winded. He nodded, still studying me dispassionately. Then:

"Hanan, do me a little favor. Give me a few minutes in my nephew's shop. I'd like to take a few shots, front and back. We're right here and I don't have to go through the horseshit and red tape at the hospital."

When his nephew's nurse finished the X rays under Andresen's supervision, he said, "I'll compare them to the ones I have at the hospital—the ones we took before the operation. Meanwhile keep on doing just what you've been doing. It seems to agree with you." I said that what I was doing was looking for someone who was trying to kill me. I regretted it as soon as I had said it because the professionally wary look filled his eyes. His bad day: an encounter with a paranoid terminal patient. He said he'd phone in a couple of days, and couldn't wait to get me out of the office.

Feburary 13, 1973.

Hanan's Handy Sampling Technique came through.

Howard Lucksig had been born in San Francisco in 1913 and his father was listed on the birth certificate as Herman Lucksig, Commission Agent, aged forty-four, and the mother was Anna Lucksig. They checked the files of the old *San Francisco Jewish Times* and there, happily, had been a social note announcing the birth of the boy, Howard, and the fact that the family originally came from Omaha, Nebraska, where Herman Lucksig had been a real estate operator.

The bound volumes of the *Omaha Daily News*—no longer in business—yielded three pertinent items: The first, November 30, 1909, went:

JEWISH ANTI–WHITE-SLAVERY SOCIETY FORMED

JEWS ENGAGED IN TRAFFIC WILL BE
EXCOMMUNICATED AND DRIVEN OUT

In an effort to stamp out the white slave traffic among their race, prominent Jews in Omaha organized an anti–white-slavery society last week.

Evidence against Jews engaged in the traffic will be gathered and presented to the Douglas County grand jury and the offenders will be excommunicated from the church and ostracized from Jewish society.

The new society is composed of Jewish organizations, including Temple Israel, the Omaha Hebrew Club, B'nai B'rith, Order of B'rith Abraham, the Hebrew Camp of the Modern Woodmen, and the Hebrew Associated Charities. . . .

The payoff was in the January 6, 1910, paper:

Warfare against the "white slave" traffic in Omaha by united Jewish societies in the city began today.

Arrest of H. Lucksig of 1018 Douglas Street on a charge of owning properties used for immoral purposes was the opening gun of the crusade. Lucksig admits owning the place at 1018 Douglas Street and several other similar properties but denies their use for immoral purposes. Police Captain Dunn says "cribs" for women have existed there for ten or twelve years.

Lucksig offered in police court this morning to sell his houses if his prosecution was dropped.

Sam went over the copies of the clips again after I read them.

"Nothing changes," he said. "The business goes on in Omaha for years, payoffs take place all the time, and the whole town knows about it and nothing is done. But B'nai B'rith comes along, puts the finger on Lucksig, and he's got to skedaddle. Actually, it was a little surprising because Lucksig was not a small fry set up to take a fall but the area wholesaler. He'd bring in a new batch of girls every three months from Chicago and then peddle the old batch to a business partner in Montana. We got onto him by a little item in the April 1911 issue of the *B'nai B'rith News."* The story he had went:

We learn that District No. 4, Independent Order B'nai B'rith expelled from the Order a member from the state of Montana (one who is president of the Jewish Congregation) because he has a share in some buildings which are used as houses of ill fame. We cannot but commend this just decision. The morality of such an individual cannot but be of the lowest grade, and any contact with him is a disgrace. To the Jewish community where he resides he is a curse.

Sam went on: "They both got out. Herman from Omaha and his pal from Butte. Herman went on to San Francisco. In nineteen ten there had been one of the periodic investigations into the tie-ups between prostitution and the police, the older grand jury investigation, and things got tough for a time. Herman bought into a couple of houses on the seven-hundred block of Commercial Street, which was the center of the trade but he found he was still a stranger in town. Idoform Kate, a Jewish ex-whore turned madam, had a lock on the Jewish girls in town, with twenty houses. So Herman Lucksig began looking around for something else and eventually became a commission merchant in the fruit and vegetable field. But from eighteen ninety-eight to nineteen sixteen Herman was a big man in the whorehouse business so I suppose for our *goel hadam* he and his descendants were forever tainted and fair game."

They were also checking out the other victims and their possible prostitution backgrounds and Dr. Shorsh at the Seminary had been filled in on the new development. "Now that we have a motive let's see what he can come up with," Sam added in a tone that made it clear he didn't think it would be much. He went on:

"Now the real problems begin. Okay, we know *why* these characters are being killed by the *goel*. Even if we had the whole FBI in our pocket we couldn't begin to find out who are the thousands of descendants of those characters. Sure, no women descendants—as far as we know—have been knocked off. But there are still too damn many male descendants for us to check out. Even if we could—what the hell do we do with that knowledge? Send them a nice letter telling them someone may be out to kill them because of what their fathers or grandfathers did? So be on your guard, O miserable descendants! How can they be when they haven't the vaguest idea—hell, *we* haven't the vaguest idea of who or what the *goel* is."

I said I had been thinking of the problem coming back from London. Since there was no discernible pattern in the killings—it wasn't alphabetical by name; or by age; or any kind of geographical pattern—we were left with the seemingly easier problem. Never mind the thousands of potential victims: let's concentrate on the *goel* or *goels*.

"Get a psychiatrist to draw up one of those personality profiles the way the police do with a sex killer?" Vogelsang offered.

I thought of that, I said, but it would be a mistake to waste any time on it. Vogelsang broadcast a why-not look.

"Because it's a highly overrated technique. The only time it's worked with U.S. police so far was in the New York mad-bomber case where the psychological profile on George Metesky turned out to be pretty accurate. But it was a total failure in the Boston Strangler case and many others since. But even if it was more accurate a guide it probably wouldn't help us. There are plenty of sick killers and rapists of small girls; lots of killers of whores. You *might* be able to draw a reasonably accurate psychiatric profile of a *typical* one which turns out to be not very helpful, anyway. But what do we have here? Someone—or a group of someones—are killing men who are descended from certain families. We don't even have the supposedly useful factor of psychological relatedness. You might say someone raping or killing small girls has become that way because of something in his misshapen growing-up process. Any psychiatrist can start out with research in lots of papers on pedophilia and work his way onto the homicidal aspects. We don't have such a handy starting point."

Vogelsang gave me an amused look. "Okay, Hanan, you just passed your orals." Sam shook his head. "I can't believe you're telling us we can't do a goddam thing. So I gotta believe you have *something* in mind."

I said it wasn't much but it could keep us busy awhile. Let's start with the thesis that Shorsh stressed in his background papers: revenge. Let's assume that way back a girl is seduced into prostitution by a pimp. She undergoes terrible times and becomes embittered and swears revenge. Somehow she gets out of the life, becomes very rich, and then plots revenge. So now we have to switch to another fiction: Dürrenmatt's 1956 play, *The Visit*, which incidentally and more to our point was called *The Old Lady's Visit* in the original German version. Claire Zachanassian, an eccentric elderly billionairess, comes back to her hometown where she had once been seduced by a local. She had to leave town, became a whore, and then met the wealthy man, Mr. Z., who died and left her all that dough.

"Now all she wants is simple revenge: the life of her seducer, and in return she'll give the town a billion marks or whatever. Okay we don't have a one-on-one relationship here and it's terribly unlikely that one poor gal got in the successive bitter clutches of the Fassnachts in Constantinople, my grandfather in New York, and Herman Lucksig in Omaha. And even if, by some special aberration of fate, some impossible coincidence, that actually happened, we're up against the workings of time. Let's say she was only seventeen when she fell into the clutches of the Fassnachts in Constantinople in nineteen ten. That makes her eighty today."

Maybe, I continued, there are a few rich spry octogenarian ladies around but really she'd have to be in awfully good shape to have pulled off some of these deaths. In the first place she's dealing with men considerably younger—even Miguel Karir, who died at sixty-six, was a lot younger than she was—which means she'd really have to be more than just spry. If she helped two of them drown in the tub she'd need considerable strength in holding up their legs so that their faces remained under water. So for the time let's forget about eighty-year-old vitamin-vigorous traveling killers.

Which brings us to possible descendants. And here we're up against an occupational hazard: most whores didn't have children; couldn't. In San Francisco the bigger operators had a doctor on call who did hysterectomies on the new girls so that no working time was lost to menstrual periods, let alone pregnancy. Others simply sterilized the girls.

But let's assume that in this case the whore did have a child or even children and somehow gets out of the trade. Problem: is she likely to tell them what she used to do in the bad old days? Let's shift for a minute to another group of interested parties. In going through the London stuff I found a whole bunch of ardent anti–white slavers—Jews and non-Jews. Probably they're all dead by now, like Felix Solomon. But some of them had children—again, like Felix Solomon. Now I don't think that his son, William, gives a good damn about white slavers then or now. But suppose one of the others had a most impressionable child who was also on the thin edge of sanity. In his growing-up years he absorbs from papa all the horrors of the white-slave traffic and resolves to carry on the work of his father. In a more direct fashion—killing off the descendants of the traffickers.

Sure, I'm reaching out and I have to admit it's all childishly iffy. And if we had something better to go on I wouldn't want us to waste any time on this at all.

There's another possibility, Vogelsang said. "I'm sure it's occurred to you, too. All along we've been acting on the assumption that we're on the track of a cunning multiple-murderer. What if we're not?"

"Then we're wasting a lot of time and money," Sam said. "I know what you're playing with: there haven't been any *murders*. Most of these men just died of natural causes or accidents or suicides and our roving nut manages to get his notes in a little before or just after the deaths."

I said, it *is* possible. In which case we're not dealing with a crazy killer but another kind of abnormality; maybe a *farceur* who's gone over the line.

Vogelsang made a ballpark translation: "Some kind of joker?"

Not really. More, a mystifier. "He drops peculiar hints about his past and he knows more than anybody about strange cults. He works hard establishing how different and stranger he is than anyone else. I'm reaching, of course, but it is possible to visualize a character like that spraying *goel hadam* notes around. Still, it would call for a hell of a lot of digging and traveling and checking—far more than any *farceur* I've ever known would put in to keep the act going."

Vogelsang was amused: "What a footnote-dropper you turn out to be,

Harry. You and Shorsh are going to make a great odd couple. But meanwhile let's see if I can distill from all this what you think we ought to be doing:

"We've got to get all the material there is on the old white-slave trade, Jewish division, and find particularly vehement revenge-seeking victims; and check them out. If they're too old or dead we've got to see if they had children—against all the odds—and find out if they've taken over the avenger role."

He was entitled. I had punctured his Richmond hypothesis as cruelly. He read my slight grin correctly.

"I'm not trying to get even, Harry. But it reminds me a little of when I was thirteen and discovered the world of science fiction and it hit me with the force of adolescent revelation that if there were two billion people on earth why the odds were damn good that at least *one* of them was a Martian."

Sam, who had been off in a private world for the last few minutes, suddenly returned. "I don't know why I let you two high school debaters sidetrack me. I bet we got our Singapore character, ole Mickey Karir, in the net, too. Remember he left Argentina in nineteen thirty and I wondered why the hell he had to take off to Mexico instead of across the river to Montevideo. The reason he did—and I'll bet a box of cigars to a cigarette stub—was he was on the lam from the Jewish white-slavery investigation that broke out in Buenos Aires in nineteen thirty."

Vogelsang was possibly a little resentful his demolition of my thesis had been weakened by Sam's interruption.

"So what," he asked. "How the hell does that help finding out who we have to look for?"

Sam shook his head. "If you could only stop enjoying your little triumph for a second you'd see that if I'm right we've suddenly moved the action up to our time, practically. The events in Argentina are only about forty years behind us. We're no longer back in nineteen ten anymore. We suddenly moved forward twenty years. That could be a big help. If Harry's revenge idea has any merit why we're now considering the possibility of a white-slave victim who, let's say, was eighteen years old in nineteen thirty. She plots revenge carefully, gets some money, and now she starts striking out. Hell, she's only in her fifties now.

It doesn't have to be an eighty-year-old *bubbe* with a murderous intent."

I said he was a real dependable back-up man but Vogelsang was right in his own way. My idea *was* a pretty remote one.

"Who said it wasn't? But we don't have a damn thing else right now —except to wait around for the next one to be knocked off. So let's go through what's available and see if we can't pick out a few potential *goel hadams.* If we're lucky we might come up with say, three–four. It'll be a job checking out if they're still around but it won't be impossible. And even if Harry's idea is cockeyed once we start trampling the grass in this new ballpark maybe we'll get lucky and stumble on something we hadn't even thought of yet. Also, I got a bright fella in B.A. we can use."

Vogelsang agreed we had nothing better to do.

But he did get in the last word. "The one thing your theory has going for it is its falsifiability. A great philosopher named Karl Popper said the essential criterion of a scientific theory is its falsifiability; there have to be ways of *disproving* the theory. No problem: the way to disprove your theory is to work on it."

February 16, 1973.

One of the standard rules for survival in the Agency when you were in the field was to have a friend in Personnel or Finance back home. Someone who could let you know what's happened to your petty cash vouchers and who's coming over for a visit; or if your income tax return is working out right. For many years my home-base friend had been Al McCready, a wheelchair case. He lost the use of both legs in Korea and he was one of a surprising number of handicapped the Agency now employs. While I had been in Turkey we had been corresponding on a biweekly basis and I suspect that he lived the life of a field man vicariously through them. In turn he was my unofficial eyes and ears at Langley. I got the better part of the bargain.

Al phoned today. A doctor named Andresen contacted an Agency

medic named Stanley Bally. They had gone to P&S together. The reason
he was fishing around was to see if a Harry Hanan was working for the
Agency and was operational. Bally said he didn't know and naturally
wanted to know what all this was in aid of. Andresen said something very
peculiar had come up and he had to know. Bally talked about old times
and only promised that he's ask around. He passed the information to
CI and a character there remembered McCready had been my Langley
hand-holder. So what's up?

I told him Andresen had operated on me. Al said he knew that, of
course, because they had checked him out when they knew he was going
to cut. In fact the Agency also had an extra anesthetist on hand in the
OR that morning just in case I babbled anything before going under.
I'd be happy to know all I said was GAAAH.

He added that I had been seen in London and they knew I was there
to see some cancer quack or someone and no cause for alarm. How was
I feeling?

February 17, 1973.

Urdell was calling him Shorsh the Source and his latest compilation
was in the mail. Now that Shorsh had a motive he was able to narrow
his searches. Still, he couldn't resist a lot of fascinating peripherals like
these:

I don't want to sound like—let alone look like—a Father Brown with
a *tallis*. But I find myself toying with the idea that one of the overlooked
possibilities here is divine retribution. Until the mid-nineteenth century
British coroners often gave verdicts of death such as "by visitation of
God." An old idea. In the Talmud (Sanhedrin 37b) you'll find: "Divine
justice steps in where a human court is powerless to convict a criminal
because of lack of witnesses and the inadequacy of their evidence. He
who should be stoned meets his death by falling from a roof or being
trodden by a wild beast; he who should be burned dies by fire or by the
bite of the snake; he who should be hanged dies either by drowning or
suffocation."

But I'm dealing with nonbelievers and I won't press on.

The reason Vogelsang never heard about it even though he had a proper *bar mitzvah* is the whole subject is very embarrassing. Back in 1908 the *Jewish Daily Forward* acknowledged that letters from "victims of white slavery come to our attention quite often but we do not publish them. We are disgusted by this plague on society, and dislike bringing it to the attention of our readers."

The *Forward* wasn't the only silent hypocrite around. For example, you would have to search awfully hard in Arab sources to find that even during the last decades of the nineteenth century the Moslem slave trade captured 80,000 African blacks a year. At least the Jews had the decency—indecency?—to confine themselves to preying on Jews only. And the figures were probably in the hundreds per year instead of tens of thousands. Also: a fair portion of the women involved were probably not that unwitting or unwilling.

Still, someone looking hard *will* find references to this *chillul ha-shem*, this disgrace to good Jews everywhere. Even the *Universal Jewish Encyclopedia* of 1939, brought out during the height of Nazi anti-Semitism, included this paragraph in its long article on Argentina:

About 1900 the Jews of Argentina began a vigorous campaign against the Jewish white-slave traders in the country who were considered outcasts and branded as Tmanyini ("unclean ones"). It was customary to see signs posted on doors, theatres, clubs and synagogues, reading Tmanyini Verboten ("unclean ones not allowed"). The Ezras Noshim organization was founded to aid the victims of white slavers. After a struggle of more than 20 years the campaign came to a successful conclusion with the fall of the Migdol brothers, notorious Jewish white-slave traders, and the breaking up of other white-slavery rings.

The current *Encyclopaedia Judaica* is slightly more forthcoming but Chaim Rafael, a noted critic of the sixteen large volumes, recently commented:

Perhaps we should be grateful—or complain?—that while the editors thought it right . . . to include a list of Jews in criminology they do not give us a list of Jews in crime. To be fair, the encyclopedia is not mealy-mouthed on this subject. Among some disturbing features (often related to the abnormal situation of the Jews) it acknowledges their heavy role some years ago in the white-slave trade in Argentina (with links to Eastern Europe), showing also the strenuous and successful efforts of Jewish welfare organizations to remove this blot.

Actually the body of Yiddish literature has several works dealing with the white-slave trade. The most famous is probably Sholem Asch's fascinating play *The God of Vengeance*, written in 1907. It was produced in Yiddish theaters all over the world for many years. The central character is Yankel, a brothel owner in a provincial Russian town around 1900. The whores in it are Jewish and so is the pimp. The dénouement comes when Yankel, who tried to be a good believing Jew in spite of his occupation, makes the shattering discovery his seventeen-year-old daughter is in love with one of the prostitutes in his house.

Another popular play on the subject was written in Buenos Aires in 1927 by a Yiddish playwright named Malach. It was called *Ibergus* and played in New York, Warsaw, and Buenos Aires. Very melodramatic. Act One opens in a brothel in Rio where the madam and the whores are closing shop in honor of Yom Kippur eve. The heroine, Rayzl, refuses to join in the ceremonies or to accompany her colleagues to the synagogue for Kol Nidre services. Instead she's about to take on two sailors when in walks an old customer of hers, the distinguished mulatto Member of Parliament, Dr. Silva. He asks Rayzl to come live with him and abandon this life. She accepts. The sailors are left in the lurch. Eventually she marries Dr. Silva, gets pregnant, and gets exposed as a former whore. And on and on.

More recently Isaac Bashevis Singer has had several fleeting references to the trade in his *New Yorker* short stories.

Yiddish scholars have begun resurrecting materials on the Jewish underworlds of the prewar Polish cities. The pimps, prostitutes, pickpockets, smugglers, and gangsters had a life-style all their own, as they do the world over. For example, on Yom Kippur the entire Jewish underworld would gather in the famous Gesia cemetery in Warsaw to hear Kol Nidre. The story was that most of them prayed in stolen *tallisim*. The wardens used to allow the condemned prisoners to be brought there in chains, just to hear Kol Nidre.

Of course, the original historian of the local Jewish Mafias was Isaac Babel whose stories about the Jewish gangsters, murderers, pimps, procurers, and thieves of Moldavanka, an Odessa suburb, have had international readership.

Perspective: so far we know of only eight Jewish deaths at the hand of the *goel* over a period of seven years. Hardly anything. *Every year* at least two hundred Indian untouchables are killed by higher-class Indians who thought the outcasts were getting uppity by trying to get educated or assert their rights in other ways.

From the Talmud (Sanhedrin): The following are strangled: he who strikes his father or mother; or kidnaps a Jew (to sell as a slave). . . . Surely applicable in the case of the girls seduced and transported to work in bordellos. According to Maimonides the procedure of strangulation was: the condemned is lowered knee-deep in dung, then a hard cloth placed in a soft one is wound around his neck, the two witnesses pull the ends of the cloth in opposite directions until the culprit dies. Obviously our *goel* is not following the classical method.

If we consider some of these Jewish prostitutes to be "white slaves" we might look at Maimonides' comments in his *Book of Acquisition:*

A Hebrew female slave is a minor whom her father has sold into slavery. After she has become twelve years old and shown signs of puberty, the father *cannot* sell her into slavery, though he still has power over her and can marry her to whomever he wishes.

A father may not sell his daughter into servitude unless he is reduced to poverty and does not have anything left, land or movables, or even the garment upon his body. And yet we may compel the father to redeem his daughter after he has sold her in order not to disgrace the family. If the father flees or dies and does not have the means to redeem his daughter she must serve until she becomes free (after six years).

"The Hebrew female slave is more privileged than a male slave in that she becomes free with the appearance of her signs of puberty. . . . Even if she shows signs of puberty a day after she is bought she goes out free."

I am rambling but clearly even with the crueler standard of other millennia there is nothing in the Talmud that could even remotely justify the seduction and keeping of women in a life of prostitution. But there is in Sanhedrin 4:5, this motivation for belated vengeance: "He who kills an innocent person is responsible for the blood of all the victim's potential descendants to the end of time."

What we really need here is a good, old-fashioned *mosur*. In Czarist Russia every Jewish community had its miserable informer, the *mosur*. He got pleasure—and some reward, too—from getting his fellow Jews in hot water with Czarist officials by telling them of local violations. No, our *goel* is too clever to tell anyone but the fact that he does leave the saffron note around would indicate some pathology here. A pathological killer surely deserves a pathological *mosur*. If we're lucky. . . .

February 19, 1973.

Andresen phoned. We got to get together and have a little talk and he wanted to apologize for being nosy about my background. We arranged to meet at the hospital at 11:30.

The problem, he said, is that something is out of whack and it might not be me. This called for some background and he proceeded to give it to me.

"For the past couple of days I've been phoning friends of mine in the business, other thoracic surgeons around the country. And there's pretty solid agreement. The relative five-year survival rates for lung cancer is lousy. Particularly for your type, squamous cell carcinoma. Less than one percent survive five years regardless of treatment and when it has metastasized as much as yours had it's probably one percent of one percent, or practically nil. I gave you some nobody-knows estimates on how long you had, but actually the median life expectancy in cases like yours is two months from the time of diagnosis."

He saw my puzzled look. "Yeah, why am I telling you this *now?* I gave you the dismal figure when I saw you in the hospital and nothing has changed since then, about six weeks ago. So what is all this about and why the hell did I phone my old classmate to find out if you worked for the CIA?"

I said it was thoughtful of him to save me these questions.

"Thoughtful? Forget it. I ran out of thoughts after my first one, which was a little stupid. You know, outside their specialties, most doctors are not the smartest people in the world. They're also among the most gullible. They fall for every con game out. Well, my first thought was maybe this is like that James Bond picture. The one where he's supposed to be dead at the start of the film and it turns out, no, he's only playing possum because they want the enemy to think he's dead and out of the game. So when I guessed this Hanan fellow might not be State Department but some kind of CIA character I began following the plot. Everyone's supposed to think he's dying and he's going to emerge someplace with some new identity and all that kind of movie razz-matazz.

"But then I told myself this is crazy: nobody could have faked those metastases, that orange-sized tumor. I *saw* them. It wasn't anybody's doctored X rays. I had the biopsy. I had the X rays I took in my nephew's office. If I was still being hoked after all that, well I ought to turn in my union card. So the only alternative was I wasn't being conned in some kind of brilliant spy drama, which meant I was up against a different kind of problem.

"I play golf with a lawyer who does only criminal work. He once told me that the worst possible thing that could happen was if a really innocent client came to him. He almost wouldn't know what to do. Crooks he can and does handle well, getting them out on bail—so they can pull more jobs so that they can pay his fat fee—and then getting them the best possible negotiated deal with the DA in plea bargaining. But the innocent . . ."

He interrupted himself. "You get tempted by any those unproven-methods sheets I sent you? You know, Krebiozen, Laetrile, and the other stuff?"

I *had* made a quick trip to London but it wasn't to see any cancer quack there. And could he come to the point: what the hell was bothering him about my case?

What it came down to, he said, was two possibilities. The first was a sensitive one for him: he may have performed an unnecessary operation on me. I said I promised not to sue him for malpractice. Obviously he hadn't even entertained that possibility because he went right on to the second: "And everything considered I'd settle right now for the first possibility. That would cause a hell of a lot fewer headaches."

I said that for a tough, laconic surgeon he was turning into a wind-baggy family GP. What was he *trying* to say? I didn't have cancer in the first place? (Why didn't I feel a sudden rush of elation, a last-minute reprieve for the condemned man, a medical miracle stemming out of human error?)

"What I've been trying to say, Hanan, is that the X rays say you don't have cancer *now*. And if you don't have cancer now that's great for you, and a great big pain in the ass for me."

An attitude like that would explain much about the profession's public-relations image, I said. If I didn't have cancer now why wasn't he pounding me on the back; why weren't we breaking out champagne and why wasn't he rushing off to tell his colleagues? What's the catch?

"You're right, Hanan, I'm handling this badly. My only excuse is that this has never happened to me before. In fact there's only one other doctor in the entire country to whom this has ever happened. Also I was thrown a little by your being a CIA man and that bit you threw at me in my nephew's office about spending your time trying to find someone who was out to kill you. I figured you'd gone over the edge and that made it harder for me to add up all the evidence coolly.

"What has happened in your case," he went on, "is what we call a spontaneous remission. For no good or known reason your cancer has disappeared. It happens. Not often. About two hundred verified, well-documented cases in the medical literature since nineteen hundred. In that time about eleven and a half million persons have died of cancer. So the odds work out to about one chance in fifty-seven thousand. Which isn't good but not beyond imagination. Actually the odds in your case were much, much worse because most of the spontaneous remissions or regressions were in rarer forms of cancers such as neuroblastoma, which afflicts kids mainly; malignant melanoma, a cancer that starts in the pigment-forming cells of the skin; and choriocarcinoma, a rare cancer of the uterus.

"What you almost never, never hear about is a spontaneous remission on a verified lung cancer such as yours. You could jump out the window and fly Superman-style to your apartment from here and I could almost believe *that* sooner.

"And because it is so goddam rare the typical surgeon or clinician is going to insist on other possibilities before he's ready to admit that one of those once-in-a-millennium miracles took place. And all the other possibilities somehow come down to some error of omission or commission on the part of the surgeon or he didn't read this plate right; he didn't do that properly; he didn't biopsy adequately enough. In short, some kind of human error. Well, there isn't a doctor or a surgeon who hasn't made a mistake, some worse than others, which is why the malpractice business is one of our growth industries. Doctors are very uneasy with medical miracles, real ones, I mean. I'm a so-so Lutheran and I gather you're a so-so Jew. What we should have been are ardent Catholics who believe in prayer. Preferably praying to St. Peregrine, the patron saint of cancer and malignant diseases. Then we have a possibility. According to church legends St. Peregrine suffered from a leg cancer and his surgeons advised amputation. The night before his operation he faithfully prayed to be saved from cancer surgery. In his dreams he imagined he was being cured. Upon awakening he was miraculously and spontaneously cured. He lived a long life, dying at eighty with both legs intact and no cancer."

Besides our being nonpraying types, he went on, there's another peculiar problem here which is why we aren't breaking out champagne and I don't rush to the typewriter to get out a fast and fascinating case report for the *American Journal of Surgery*.

"I'm ready to stake my reputation that you no longer have lung cancer. You might have housemaid's knee or Japanese crud but I'll bet anything you don't have lung CA. Fine. Will you get lung cancer again next week, next month, next year? God knows. You could still be one of the seventy-two thousand Americans to die of lung cancer this year. Because we have so little to go on in this kind of incredibly rare spontaneous remission, my opinion here is worth about as much as an eighteenth-century London barber-surgeon."

What he did have to go on was the only other case known in surgical annals.

Early in 1959 a thirty-seven-year-old ex-bartender named Joseph

Mayerle walked out of the Seattle Veterans' Hospital with the same word I had: go home and die. They had opened him up after the X rays had found an orange-sized tumor in his left lung. He was opened up, as I was, and found inoperable because the cancer had spread so far. The thoracic surgeon was Dr. J. W. Bell.

"The only difference in your case and Mayerle's was that he got some minimal radiation, a tumor dose of twelve hundred Roentgen units, hardly anything really, and he had fever during most of the time he was getting the radiation.

"Three months after he leaves the hospital Mayerle walks into Bell's office rosy-cheeked and bubbling with health. Bell went white as a sheet —as white as I did when I looked at the X rays I took of you at my nephew's office." Bell, of course, promptly put him in front of the X-ray machine and took a series, but they were superfluous; one look at Mayerle and he knew this fellow was not about to die of lung cancer.

"So he questions Mayerle as I did you. What quack medicines and routines and so on? Mayerle knew some doctor or other said people never died with cancer but died of starvation because they couldn't eat. So Mayerle decided he'd force himself to eat, to keep his stomach full.

"But eating is no cure for cancer, believe me, so his opinion on what did it is worth about as much as yours. Funny thing is that Mayerle is back smoking cigarettes. They checked his blood and found lots of plasma cells and lymphocytes which would indicate that he's probably immune to lung cancer now and can smoke until he's ninety."

I recalled my fevers probably running up to 104 or 105.

Andresen nodded. "That *could* have triggered the regression except that fever is a fairly normal aftermath in these cases."

I was trying to recall other similarities in the cases. I told how I had slurped down a huge Cranshaw melon after one of the fever bouts. He smirked: "*That* did it."

He took some blood samples and got me to aspirate some sputum for testing. "I'm just going through the motions," he said. "When I write this up for the *American Journal of Surgery* I'll have to show them I did all the right things because most of the readers are still going to think, oh boy, Andresen blew that one. Bet the poor sonofabitch never had cancer in the first place. Surgeons can be pretty rough on each other in private."

I asked how long it would be before any report he did on my case appeared. He said several months at the earliest and he assured me the report would only discuss the case of a forty-year-old white male. Ordinarily they would give the patient's initials but if that was a problem here he'd omit them. I said I'd think about that and let him know.

He said congratulations and with my luck I should hurry out and buy sweepstakes tickets or stock or something. And he was sorry he had put me through a period of unpleasant questioning and doubt. "It was like I had to be the devil's advocate in a precanonization rite." I said I didn't feel very saintly and invited him to lunch with me at the Oak Room.

A celebration was in order, he said, but as far as the profession was concerned unless I survived at least five years they wouldn't consider it a cure. He wondered if I was going to go back to smoking like Mayerle did. I said I didn't think so. I hadn't had a cigarette in nearly two months and maybe it was as good a way as any to stop.

At lunch after several drinks and wine we were on a very friendly Harry-and-Art basis and I told him some old CIA stories and he poured out some funny operation stories and we didn't break up until 3:30. It was the first time I'd had a load on in months.

Before we broke up I asked Art not to broadcast the news. I'd just as soon it wasn't known, even to his old classmate at the Agency. He naturally wanted to know why not and I said it was very involved: someone *was* trying to kill me and I hadn't figured out yet how to handle the situation. Also, I'd just as soon stay on leave from the Agency for a while until the thing is cleared up, one way or the other.

"Harry, ole buddy, you get yourself killed and I have a very tough kind of report to write for the *American Journal of Surgery.* Do me this one favor: don't complicate my life any further and keep yourself alive. The hell with five years; I'll settle for just one. Fair enough? Who the hell's trying to kill you? The Russians?"

I said it was very involved and didn't have anything to do with my Agency work and he let it go at that although his curiosity was at the bursting point. When he left he reminded me that he had urged me to get something vital to do after I left the hospital, to keep busy somehow. "So let's put it down that whoever's trying to kill you also had some kind of role in this spontaneous regression. It kept you busy and active and on the alert. Maybe we got a new explanation for these mysterious spontaneous regressions."

On the way out I picked up a *Times* at the newsstand. For the past few weeks I had reversed an old custom. In preparation for a new overseas assignment you always read in on a country, particularly local newspapers. For some time I had, in effect, been reading myself out of the world by avoiding newspapers. Now that I had been adjudged a viable part of the world again surely it was proper for me to take on the load of woes and cares you bought for twenty cents.

Having reassured myself I promptly uncovered the real reason when I turned to the obituary page. When I was much younger, I knew if someone who was supposed to die didn't, someone else would have to die in his place. So I scanned the obits and the death-page announcements to see what forty-year-old had replaced me. I couldn't find any.

February 20, 1973.

I awake with a fogged memory of a passage I once used in an English Lit. course at Columbia. It was from Dickens' *Hard Times* and it went something like this:

"Are you in pain, dear mother?"

"I think there's a pain somewhere in the room," said Mrs. Gradgrind, "but I couldn't positively say that I have got it."

Move over, Mrs. G. There's a pain around here somewhere, too.

What's bothering me? I should be ecstatic, gloriously drunk. Born again. Hanan Rises! But I'm sure Lazarus after his resurrection was really a great embarrassment all around. Why don't I phone Langley and say I'm ready for duty, as any physical will prove—if Andresen isn't lying. Why aren't I thinking of handling the challenges of deputy director of plans? Why no rousing celebrations and feasts? I shall live and drink and fuck and enjoy well beyond a mere forty and mine enemies shall be confounded as never before. Surely the time has come to pay much more attention to Elly Bricha—no longer a pleasure regretfully forgone. Yes, yes and more.

What's bothering me? The pattern of chance. First the one-in-ten-million chance of the ricochet death in Turkey; now the one-in-God-knows-how-many-millions chance of a spontaneous regression. There's a hidden pattern and meaning and I can't discern it. *That* scares me. What's the frightening old line? I am being toyed with? No. *Fished for.* Who? Why?

February 21, 1973.

"I've been talking to a few old-timers and I've been running through the forgotten garbage I got stored away up here," Sam said tapping his right temple. "So I come up with some names we might follow up on on the whorehouse scene in New York from nineteen hundred to nineteen fifteen."

I suggested visiting the spots in my car but he waved that away. "What the hell would you see? Most of the places are gone. On West Fortieth and Eighth Avenue there was a whole row of whorehouses from two hundred West to two twenty-two and it's all the Port Authority Bus Terminal now. One of the houses was owned by a character named Kartofles, which means potatoes. He had a Frenchie, Carrie de la Marr, run the house for him. West Twenty-third Street, off Fifth, had a string of houses owned by a Mrs. Hyman. In all these houses if a gal wore a red rose in her hair she'd do anything, which meant she'd go down on you or take it in the *tuchus* which a lot of the girls wouldn't do. The most expensive houses were on West Forty-fifth, Forty-sixth, and Forty-seventh streets—the ten- and twenty-dollar houses. For twenty dollars you'd get a circus, two whores going down on each other.

"Let me ramble a little. We'll come to something. Sadie the Chink ran thirty joints. She had a son in college and he played the violin. There were about ten thousand whores in New York in nineteen fourteen. Hardly anything. London is supposed to have had eighty-five thousand then. Most of the Jewish whores entered the business voluntarily. It was a terrible life. Anyone surviving two or three years in it had gonorrhea.

If she lasted five years she had syph at least once and that was long, long before you could say, quick Doc, a big penicillin shot in the ass.

"Most of the houses were dollar houses. A buck meant something when good jobs paid only ninety dollars a month and the average worker got maybe twenty dollars a week. You couldn't afford a buck, you got a colored whore for twenty-five cents. The biggest earners were the good-looking Jewish whores with red hair. They were supposed to drive the boys crazy.

"Two blocks from here, West Fifty-eighth Street between Eighth and Ninth avenues was filled with brothel flats. Hearst owned some of them. So did Trinity Church. A Supreme Court Justice named Weeks owned three whorehouses on Second Street. Everybody was in the business. WASPs, wops, Chinks, Frogs, *Yidlach*. The Jews controlled about twenty-five percent of the vice in New York. Yes, Sadie the Chink. I can see her now: ugly, short, fat, slovenly. She was Shmier Litzig's girl friend.

"We gotta find out what happened to Charlie Dubillier. He had a house on Twenty-fourth Street between Sixth and Seventh avenues in nineteen ten. Ike the Blood was shaking down whorehouses and he tried it on Charlie, who killed him. Someone I know ran into Charlie in Phoenix around nineteen forty-four. He was still pimping and gambling then.

"Some of the whorehouse operators had a crazy sideline: machinkas. Those stupid little money-making machines. An old con. You put in a paper blank and out comes a genuine five-dollar bill. Sure. They sold the machines for five hundred dollars. Once they sold one to a couple of very sharp operators, Sam and Meyer Boston, bookies whose wives were leading shoplifters. Meyer and Sam were also cocaine traffickers. And those guys fell for the machinka!

"Your grandpa, I remember, used to hang out a lot in the Orpheum Restaurant, which used to be on Second Avenue and Eighth Street, and a block away was Abe Rebele's restaurant, which used to be a mail drop for the United Benevolent Association. One of your grandpa's business pals had a son but he was a *fagele* so they managed to get him married to some woman. They adopted a child and every Sunday the boy had to push the kid in a baby carriage up and down Second Avenue to show he was a man. We gotta find out what happened to *that* kid.

"Wait a minute. Another kid we've got to check out on your theory. There used to be a delicatessen at Seventh Avenue and Twenty-ninth Street. Barinstain's. It was a curb exchange for the pimps and house owners where they bought and sold houses and girls. A couple of politicos had sidelines: they were *mecklers* or agents for the house owners." He mentioned one. "Now his grandson is a big shot in the state legislature." Well, anyway, the Barinstains lived above the store. They had a daughter who used to mingle freely with the pimps, procurers, and house owners. Barinstain made it clear he'd cut to pieces anyone who tried to defile his daughter. I'd love to find out what happened to her.

"Another name. Mucha Goldberg. He was the collector for Police Inspector Lahey, who protected the houses. He also had a house he operated with the Savina brothers, who operated a whole string. Mucha was short, stocky, and very smart. When the big investigation got underway here in nineteen thirteen Mucha saw the direction and lit out for Buenos Aires. I bet we come across him again when the stuff starts coming in from there. In nineteen thirteen there was an estimate that the business in New York was taking in seventy million a year, which would be like five hundred million today. Real dough."

He took time out to catch his breath and pee.

"I'm like an old broken clock," he laughed when he came back. "One tap and all the wheels and pins and works come tumbling out. I got another lead. I remember a case of a daughter of a rabbi. She was just hauled off the sidewalk and placed in a house by a 'cadet,' a roving pimp. There was a big outcry in the papers, not just the Jewish papers but *The World*, too. How could a respectable girl be abducted in broad daylight? But the funny thing is even with the publicity and everything she stayed in that Bowery brothel and like all the other afflicted families, the rabbi's simply turned her picture to the wall. Everybody knew once a girl went into the life she could never come out. We look for a possible granddaughter out to avenge poor grandma?"

I said a few more leads like that and we'd be launched on the most hopeless search since perpetual motion.

He wanted to know if I had ever been in a house? Only professionally, I said. "Yours or hers?" Mine. We used some houses for meetings with my border-crossers.

He was asking, not to exchange cat-house confidences, but because there was a line by some writer that always filled him with sadness. "A man has missed something if he has never left a brothel at dawn feeling like jumping off a bridge into the river."

February 22, 1973.

The stuff is starting to come in from Buenos Aires.

The 1930 investigation got underway because of a combination of circumstances. Ordinarily the citizens of Buenos Aires, the *porteños*, couldn't care less about the evils of prostitution. The city was wide open and most citizens probably thought that was the best way to handle the problem. The only prohibition was against exploiting minors—those under twenty-two. But if the young whore had an identity card establishing her as over twenty-two she was free to carry on her trade, as was the house she lived in, the pimp she worked for, and the trafficker who brought her into the country. Naturally, there was a big market in counterfeit identity cards.

Argentina was always liberal about the houses because they had so many unattached men floating around. They had come to Argentina from Italy, Spain, Yugoslavia, France, Turkey, Germany, and almost every other country in the world because there was opportunity and jobs and it was easy to get in. So they left their wives and families to earn enough to bring their families over. It took quite a while for most of them. Meanwhile a man had to eat and drink and get laid once in a while.

Bringing in the whores and exploiting them were a number of different-nationality gangs. There were the French, the English, the Italians, and the Jews. The last were in turn divided into two gangs: the Russians and the Galicians, who worked together; and the Rumanians.

The first sizable batch of Jewish immigrants were French and Alsatian. Businessmen, doctors, dentists, bankers, and all were fairly comfortable. But from 1888 onward large numbers came from Eastern Europe, mostly Russia and Galicia, many of them sponsored by Jewish agricultural groups such as the Baron de Hirsch Fund. The idea was to show that the Jew wasn't just a city mouse; he could be a useful denizen of the farm and the pampas. But most of the colonies weren't too successful, and worse, some of them were just flimsy con games. So in the end most of the colonists drifted back to the cities, especially Buenos Aires.

The newcomers had little or no money and when they found that the land they were supposed to settle didn't exist or had poor soil, they got tempted by the whoremasters. Urdell's representative in Buenos Aires sent along a translation from the Yiddish autobiography of one of those early settlers, Mordecai Alterson: *Thirty Years in Argentina.*

Early in the book Alterson described his first encounter with the "Unclean." He had just arrived in Buenos Aires in 1891 with a group of other Polish Jews who were supposed to become part of a Baron de Hirsch colony. They had just been processed at the Immigrants' Building:

At the iron green gates, near the fence, we met about ten well-dressed ladies and several fat-bellied men in top hats. Through the bars they spoke with our women, gave our children candies and chocolate, and one by one, meanwhile came closer to the guard. They kept whispering something to him but he kept shaking his head and refused to let them inside the gate.

Now a young man appeared, blond and freckled, and introduced himself as a representative of Baron de Hirsch's office. He told us that we would be sent to the country in a few days, the land that the Baron bought for us. . . . He also advised us to avoid any business with the men and women who were standing on the other side of the gate. They were the "unclean." Then he continued: "There are no honest Jews here. Only these unclean, the scum of humanity."

The guard was bribed and some of the unclean entered the courtyard. They described the horrors facing the colonists and urged them to take "jobs" right in Buenos Aires.

The result was that a few good Polish Jews, their wives, and their children, all went to the place from which there is no return.

The 1930 cleanup got underway because one of the two local Yiddish dailies, *Die Presse,* had been running a long series on the activities of the "unclean" and the efforts of Señora Helene R. de Oslan, head of

Esras Nashim, the Association for Aid to Women. She had been after the local government since 1927 with documents proving that the *Sociedad Israelita de Socorros Mutuos, Cementerio y Sinagoga Zvi Migdal*, although posing as a mutual-aid and burial society and synagogue, was the central headquarters of the pimps, importers, and whorehouse owners.

Still, nothing might have happened—the payoffs went all the way up and they were very solid—until a minor case came before Judge Rodriguez Ocampo. Not only was he smart but he was honest, a strange and dangerous condition in Argentina then. In May 1929 Rachel Lieberman appeared before him and swore that she had been brought to Buenos Aires from Warsaw by Solomon Joseph Korn, who had promised to marry her but instead forced her to become a whore. Rachel had been a good listener and she had acquired a lot of information about Korn's superiors in the *Zvi Migdal* organization.

Actually, Rachel had been in the business more than twelve years and was now managing a house. She gave Korn 30,000 pesos (about $12,000 then) to get two more houses to run. Instead he kept the money and kept stalling her. So she went to Judge Ocampo to get Korn arrested for swindling.

As it happened, Judge Ocampo was one of the many Argentinians who were ashamed of the invidious role their country played as one of the largest importers of women for prostitution, as detailed in the 1927 report of the League of Nations on the "Traffic in Women and Children."

Sam Urdell came in while I was reading some of the Argentinian items.

"We're gonna get a lot of stuff from B.A., mostly clips from the Yiddish daily and some from the English-language *Buenos Aires Herald* and translations from a book about the case done by a police inspector on the case. But we're up against the fact that we have no live sources. Everyone connected with the investigation is dead. Judge Ocampo, Police Inspector Alsogarray, Señora Oslan, Felix Solomon's local representative, the man who had headed B'nai B'rith down there at the time. So is Bascom Johnson, an American who was in charge of the League of Nations' investigation. I'm pretty sure most of the officers of the *Zvi Migdal*, which means big power by the way, are probably dead. They were in their late forties or fifties back in nineteen thirty. Most of them ran away to Brazil or Europe but they'd now be in their late eighties or nineties if they were still around, which I'd bet they're not. Those characters did not lead quiet natural-food lives. The editor of the Yiddish daily, *Die Presse*, which led the campaign for years, was Finie Katz. He's dead, too."

As he talked a tiny tendril of remembrance fluttered through. "Don't give up, Sam," I said. "We just might have a living witness."

My brother Warren married in 1952 when I was a junior at Columbia. He was assistant to the president of a regional Chrysler distributor and his bride, Selma Averbuch, worked for the advertising agency handling the account. Her mother was dead and her father lived on the West Coast. The wedding reception was held in our apartment at the Beresford on Central Park West. Her father, Mike, came in for the wedding. He was six foot two, weighed about 240, and had black curly hair, deep-set blue eyes—and the facial remnants of an ancient acne battle.

A *bullvon*, someone called him, which meant a kind of mindless strongman. Actually he was a former Immigration and Naturalization Department inspector who became a lawyer handling immigration cases in Los Angeles. He had been a genuine hero in World War I, winning a Silver Star for rescuing his captain at Château-Thierry, and after the war the latter had gotten Mike a job in Immigration even though he had never finished high school. Mike later got his law degree at some third-rate California night school. He also was a big man in the Jewish War Veterans.

My brother liked him—even before Mike invested $35,000 in Warren's VW distributorship in 1954. I had put in $6,000 a year later. Now that the operation was being sold, Mike and I were having a lot of correspondence. His latest letter had arrived that morning from Mexico, where he had been living for the past eight years.

The crinkly hotel sheet was headed

Hotel y Apartamientos
"PRINCE"
Mazatlan, Sinaloa, Mexico
Facing the Ocean 70 Rooms—70 Baths, The Best in Mazatlan
Wonderful Ocean Views

The letter began, typically:

> Dear Relative,
> What the fuck hell is now holding up the works? I know my brother
> lawyers love to drag things out because time is money for them but Feisen,
> Conrad etc. is overdoing it. It's not the principle of the thing. It's the
> goddam money and I can use it now. Give them a *shtup.*

At the wedding, I remember, he had been the hardest drinker around
but he didn't get drunk. He had made a couple of smiling passes at one
of my mother's divorced friends and I later heard the pass became more
that evening and most of the next day at his room in the Essex. But there
was something else that stayed with me. Someone had said something
about the UN and he said it was the same old League of Nations
runaround. A friend of my parents', a broker who was also active in
One-World circles, said there was nothing wrong with the League of
Nations except it didn't go far enough. Mike looked at him and his
bantering tone changed suddenly: "There was a lot wrong, mister. I
worked for them."

The broker was naturally skeptical. Mike just didn't look like any
League of Nations–UN type. It was hard enough accepting him as a
fairly respectable lawyer. He had the look and temperament of a born
gangster, the kind who gets muscle jobs.

The broker couldn't let it drop. This phony had to be shown up.
"That's very interesting. What you do for them?"

Mike laughed. "Listen, pal, you wouldn't believe me if I told you."
Obviously just a stall so the broker persisted. Mike put his bear paws on
the much shorter broker's shoulders so that he was talking to a receding
hairline. "I'll tell you what I did for the League. I tried to buy whorehouses for them." The broker drew back, headed for the bar, away from
a nutty drunk.

I was curious but I couldn't get to talk to Mike that evening. He was
hot for my mother's friend and in an hour the two of them left for his
hotel room. I had not seen him again.

It was a long shot but with the way my luck was running, it was worth
a call to Mazatlan. It was a little past noon here so I thought with the
three-hour time difference I had a good chance to catch him in his room.

I did. His voice had grown gravelly and he was still coming out of sleep. When the operator told him it was a call from New York several sleep layers vanished.

I brought him up-to-date on the state of the final negotiations and gave him the latest word: we should be out of the woods with final checks within two weeks and it would help if he could sign some papers and get them back to us quickly.

We got onto family stuff—what little there was, and he said how's Harry the Boy Spook doing. By now most of the family knew I was CIA. I was tired of appreciating the old joke: "Oh you mean Goldberg, the *spy*. He's in apartment six-E."

I kidded him as everybody had for years how he left his daughter's wedding before it broke up. He laughed. "Her name was Hortense Fleischacker and she was a marvelous piece of ass, God bless her wherever the hell she is now." I was fishing around in the memory pool. What hotel had he stayed in for the wedding? No um, ah, lemme think. "The Essex and the bed clicked like a madam's store teeth." Clearly his memory was in great shape, which was getting at number 2 before I had established the all-important number 1.

I got back to the wedding—he interrupted with a rusty laugh, "I hope the government's paying for this"—and I asked if he remembered the talk with the broker on the League of Nations.

"Sure, a dumb One-World type. He worked for Bache and he wore a single-breasted navy blue suit with a thin red stripe and if he had a little more Old Spice on him I could have had a drink out of him. What is this? You testing my memory? When I was Commander California Department Jewish War Veterans I knew more than five hundred members by name."

I said he passed the test. Now we had to see if he was eligible for the grand prize. What had he really done for the League of Nations?

"Lemme test *your* remembery, spook. You remember what *I* said to him when he asked me at the reception, the broker who was so pissed off because he didn't like the tone I used about the UN?"

"You said you were trying to buy whorehouses for the League of Nations."

Okay, he said, I passed and what the hell was I getting at because it hurt him when even someone else was paying these crazy phone rates. I asked what had he really done for the League—and when.

He hesitated a moment. This is strictly family?

"Strictly family. I've been on leave from the job for the past couple of months."

What he had done was become an undercover investigator for the Special Body of Experts on the Traffic in Women and Children. He was asked to take on a job with them by Bascom Johnson, the American director of investigations. Most of the money for the investigation came from the American Social Hygiene Association, which in turn got it from the Rockefellers. Mike was asked to come in by Johnson, who heard about him from Mike's sponsor in Immigration and Naturalization, the man whose life he had saved at Château-Thierry. Mike had several qualifications they needed: he had done undercover work before; he spoke Yiddish and kitchen Spanish; and although no one said it, he looked like he belonged in the underworld. Mike was assigned to work on the South American traffic and its European origins. He got leave from Immigration and Naturalization and reported to Johnson in September 1924.

I asked him would it be okay if I came out to Mazatlan for a few days? I could bring the papers for him to sign and I'd like to hear more about this League of Nations work.

"Why?" He naturally dismissed the idea that I was making the trip to save a few days in getting the papers signed.

I said it was a little complicated—and perhaps indiscreet—to discuss over the phone. He said okay, come on out, and to let him know the day I was arriving. Meanwhile he'd try to reorder the jumbled memories of his League work.

Since he'd have to be made "witting," to use that awkward trade term, I'd have to clear this with Sam and Vogelsang.

February 23, 1973.

At Vogelsang's office I fill them in on my Mazatlan connection. Not to introduce any bureaucratic entanglements I quickly make it clear that the expenses would be borne by me—or my brother's estate.

Vogelsang nodded. "That'll help. Otherwise I'd have to explain to the Committee why we didn't use our man in Mexico."

Sam was way ahead. "That's the easy one. The tough one is Harry will have to tell his relative about the *goel hadam.*"

How do you give a man an instant security check? You can't. And what do you want him to be secure about? I said Mike was out of the mainstream down in Mazatlan and he had been in jobs where he had to keep his mouth shut. A better-than-average risk and the fact that he had been active in the Jewish War Veterans would probably make him even less likely to talk about this unsavory aspect of Jewish history to anyone.

"If it gets out through him, we'll be blamed," Vogelsang said. Okay, they can blame me, too, Sam chipped in. "Listen, if Harry's size-up of his relative is right he could be a helluva source of information we might never be able to tap. He was actually on the scene down there. We don't have anyone else like that around. Let's take a chance on him."

I phoned Mike in Mazatlan and got him after a lot of *holas* up and down the line. I said I'd like to come out as soon as possible, say tomorrow, a Saturday. I assumed that I could get on a Mexico City flight.

He said wait a minute and looked up something.

"Shit. We're coming up to Carnival time down here. Starts February twenty-sixth and it's the biggest thing in Mazatlan all year. The place jumps with tourists. Can it wait until after March third when it's over?"

I said it was important to get it done quickly. Anyway I thought that what I needed from him could be gotten in a day or two at most so that I could be leaving there on the twenty-sixth at latest. I'd call him from

Mexico City on my connecting plane. He said he'd meet me at the Mazatlan airport. And he'd try to get me a hotel room but I might have to end up sleeping on his couch. Carnival was the time when no motel or hotel would let anyone come in for less than a week.

8

February 24, 1973. Mazatlan.

His hair is almost milky white now and he has pouchy dewlaps but he's recognizable even after twenty years. His weight is about the same but distributed a little differently. He has the forward lean of the old and from the way he positions his head I'd guess the hearing in his left ear was shot. There are remarkably few liver marks on his arms or face.

He has a 2 1/2-room apartment at the Prince, which is near the Yacht Club on Paseo Clausen, paralleling the waterfront. He's on the sixth floor and we were sitting on the balcony facing the Pacific. He has been living there since he came down to Mazatlan in 1965.

"How could I live so far away from my daughter and grandchildren?" I didn't ask but obviously it was a question he expected from anyone remotely related to him.

"Very simple. I can't stand my daughter and the girls come down once a year for a few days and that does it for me—and for them."

His daughter—my ex-sister-in-law—he went on, has become a kook, a new paranoid.

"Your brother was not one of nature's saints so he got fed up with her a little sooner, maybe, but she's become impossible to live with. Or talk to. She's become one of the big mommas of the conspiracy business. They're supposed to have started with the Kennedy assassination and it's become an industry since. They got newsletters and annual get-togethers. She knows we're sitting here, a CIA fella and her old man who used to be big in the Jewish War Veterans, in ten minutes she *proves* not only we give Hitler his start, we're financing the Nazis hiding out in South America. Some fathers have all the luck: their nice kids turn red-hot commies in high school or college and they turn their back on middle-class outlook and morality. Then in a few years or so most of them come to their senses. They got a tough inoculation. Not me. My only child has to get infected when she's in her forties. And what a dose. Right now I'd settle if she'd only take on something quiet and respectable like Maoism or Trotskyism."

Fortunately, the girls—his granddaughters—seemed to be immune. Anyway they were away at school—this had been part of the divorce agreement—and they seemed to have developed an amused tolerance of their mother and her circle of conspiracy explicators.

Since this was clearly the time for getting the preliminaries out of the way I got him to sign the various forms I had been given by Feisen, Conrad, and explained that when the deal was finally closed his share would come to nearly $700,000.

He had known it would be in the area so that was no great surprise. "That was some little thirty-five-thousand-dollar investment I made in your brother. I couldn't even talk about it at first because a big JWV man like me investing in a Volkswagen distributorship back in nineteen fifty-three—boy, that would have practically called for excommunication. *Herem* is the Hebrew word. We had a rabbi in L.A. who bought a Mercedes in the late Fifties and you should have heard what a tumult *that* caused. Another reason I didn't talk about it was because what I put in was dirty money."

I looked a few questions.

"Where the hell would I get thirty-five thousand back in the Fifties? Sure there was a government pension and I had saved a few bucks but thirty-five thousand to piss away on some blue-sky investment in a crazy little car *Germans* were making! Let it go for a while. First tell me what the hell *really* brought you down here apart from the pleasure of talking to an old fart."

I gave him a thirty-minute version—one I had rehearsed while waiting for the connecting flight in Mexico City. Only in this one I eliminated the cancer aspects. I said I got the *goel hadam* note in the hospital where I was spending a couple of days for a checkup. I finished the account and my second margarita at the same time.

He went to his small kitchen for another batch of macadamia nuts. He munched a few, patted me on the head, and broke out:

"Now *that's* a story. Only I suppose I can't tell anybody, huh?"

I nodded. "Nobody. It's kapok." I explained that was an old agency code designation for top, top secret.

He marveled: "So secret even your old firm doesn't even know about it. Okay, I'm complimented on being let in on it but I guess the price is you want stuff from me in return. You know, my wacky daughter hears a plot like this, could keep her going five years. Like having multiple orgasms every day. That's only the start. She's got a solid few months of stuff for their conspiracy newsletter just on how she was conned into marrying a descendant of one of the most evil families on earth, the horrible Hanans."

To reassure me, he said it would be a pleasure to deny her such pleasures. "Before I go into my story let's settle the quartermaster details. There's not a room to be had in town, as I figured, but I got you the loan of an apartment on the fifth floor here. Belongs to an American who also lives here the year-round but scoots out before Carnival. Says he always gets ripped off then. Once they lifted his wallet and another time his camera so he runs back and stays with a sister in Laguna. You can use his place for a few nights."

He took me down to the one-room apartment with a kitchenette. I changed after a shower and we went back to his balcony. We'd have dinner about nine at a place called Mamucas which he said had the best seafood in Mexico.

"I keep thinking of this *goel hadam* bunch and I think what a waste.

A smart killing operation like this avoiding all the really juicy targets! Some of those Nazis still hiding out in South America. Yasir Arafat and the killers in the Palestine Liberation movement, the ones who got the Israeli athletes.

"Even if your specialty is the prostitution and profiteers, why not gun down some of those Eighth Avenue pimps in their pimp-mobiles, or the respectable suburban *momzers* making two thousand percent on their crummy hotels where the whores bring the johns. Why go back all those years we got so much of it around now? Since it doesn't add up you got to . . ." He broke off. "Your outfit assumes they're nuts some kind?" I said we hadn't any agreement on what kind of nuts they were. We'd worry about what bothered them really after we caught them.

"Before they catch you. . . . Okay, let's see what I got for you."

When he took the job he knew it could be dangerous but the offer was irresistible. "I'd be doing a lot of travel. Great. All expenses paid. Oh boy! And I'd be getting six thousand dollars a year, about double what I was making working for Mr. Whiskers. Also they provided a twenty-five-thousand-dollar insurance policy which had my mother as my beneficiary. All this, you understand, was coming not from the American Social Hygiene Association, which was really in charge of the world-wide investigation, or the League of Nations, which fronted it, but from Mr. John D. Rockefeller, Jr.

"They sent me to New York to talk to Bascom Johnson who had been in charge of battling prostitution near army camps in World War One. Then he went to the League of Nations on loan. When I met him he was about forty-five and he knew enough about the scene to know that the only way they could get real stuff on the international traffic was to get inside it. There were two other guys who'd be going undercover but my job, he admitted, was the toughest because I had to concentrate on the South American–European traffic and that's where the big money was. Which meant, naturally, where the big risk was. Later, when it was over, Johnson sent me a letter of commendation." He quoted from memory:

. . . information of such a nature could only have been obtained by a skilled investigator, full of resource, able to extricate himself from difficult situations, and prepared to risk the dangerous consequences which would follow detection.

"My cover wasn't too hard to make up. I was Mike Averbuch of L.A. working with a bunch worried about the stopping of immigration to the U.S. from Europe which meant we might be having trouble getting talent for our houses on the border and the West Coast. I had some characters who owed me favors and I had a few names who would testify that I was who I said I was if they were questioned. Don't forget, those were the days when overseas phone calls weren't that easy to make so most of the checking, if any, would probably be done by mail—not even airmail because there wasn't much of that around either."

On the boat trip down to Buenos Aires he spent a couple of hours a day conversing with some Argentinian Jews who had visited relatives in New York. He polished his Yiddish and Spanish with them.

He got connected in less than a week.

"Easy. These characters really couldn't care less who the hell I was. Sure, they accepted me because I had the lingo and looked like I was in the business and I mentioned a few names they heard about. But what they had going for them was the solidest arrangement any underworld ever had. To start with there was no law against prostitution or even solicitation—providing it was done indoors. And they had lots of facilities for indoor solicitation. First there were dozens of so-called cabarets with dance-hall privileges. You paid the city ten thousand dollars to get that privilege, which meant the girls could circulate freely. You paid ten bucks for a bottle of lousy Mendoza wine and that gave you the right to dance with the girl and make your arrangement. B-girl stuff. The girls would also circulate in the balconies of the movies. Some of the movies were owned by the bigger operators. The only thing you had to watch out was to make sure the whores you controlled were over twenty-two —or had papers saying that. Beyond that, you were home free."

Still the mobs made sure that the payoffs were handled right and on time. The payoffs went right on up to the top bosses of the major political parties, as well, of course, to the police and a few judges.

"B.A. was the noisiest goddam city I ever been in. They were still building their subway and everybody tried to talk over the racket. You didn't talk. You yelled. Also, one thing scared the shit out of me. At the time there were twenty-five hundred lepers walking the streets of B.A., like they were waiting to be called up by Central Casting for a *Ben Hur* spectacular. Well, today the disease doesn't have the fear it had then but it was scary. Of course, the *porteños* should have been more scared of the ten thousand whores among them in the population of two million because at least half those girls were knocked up one way or another with syph or clap."

Most of the trade was designed for visiting sailors, the yokels from the interior, and city yobbos, but there were also a lot of high-class houses all over the country. "I was in one in Rosario, the country's second city. Madame Safo's joint. It was a large chalet with marble staircases, silk sheets, red velvet curtains, and it was up in the Sphinx category in Paris. The girls were almost all high-class French and good-looking Polish-Jewish."

He spent most of his time in B.A., the center of the trade.

"My second week there they knew I was a serious buyer and I got invited to look in on the headquarters of the Warsovia, which ran the works, in a way, for the Polish-Galician operators. On the surface it was a benevolent fraternal with its own cemetery and synagogue. The Polish consul who was being pushed by the various Jewish anti–white-slavery groups finally got them to change the name from Warsovia, which meant 'of Warsaw,' to *Zvi Migdal*, which in Hebrew means 'big power.' I heard two versions of the new name. Once they told me it was named after Luis Migdal who started the whole thing back in eighteen eighty-four and another time I heard 'big power' meant just that and nothing else. They *were* a big power."

The headquarters was a "wedding cake" building, on Calle Cordoba. "It was an elaborate three-story mansion the group bought in nineteen fifteen. It had a large ballroom which was, in effect, a miniature stock exchange where they bought and sold girls instead of shares."

It was also diplomatic headquarters. They maintained liaisons with the other nationality prostitution groups in the province—the French, the English, the Italians, and the Rumanians. They even had a kind of arbitration setup for disputes but still a lot of the *Zvi Migdal* members carried guns. In fact that was one of the commonest reasons for their getting busted occasionally. It would only mean a fine, usually.

The Calle Cordoba building was also where payoffs and smuggling strategy was devised. Some of the incoming women made it roundabout through Uruguay if they were under twenty-two and maybe their phony passports might not stand up under any kind of check. So they landed in Montevideo, took a train upriver to Salto and then crossed at night in river launches to Concordia in Argentina. The frontier guards were paid off.

In the official League of Nations report on white-slave traffic into Argentina the *Zvi Migdal* is described thus:

The entrance to the underworld of traffickers, *souteneurs,* and prostitutes was effected at Buenos Aires by establishing relations with the owners of a number of premises. These men had organized themselves into a club for offensive and defensive purposes. The members of this club deal in women as merchandise. They also find suitable houses and trustworthy housekeepers, agents, commissionaires, and notaries.

The girls were of three types. First were the "greenies." They were recruited in Poland by handsome traveling pimps who usually posed as an Argentine businessman who had come back to Poland to find a nice Jewish bride. After he met the girl he wined and dined the family and showed them photos of his store or factory. He had to rush back to Argentina on business but his fiancée should follow on the next boat—he gave her a ticket—and they'd be married in Argentina where his parents lived. Some of the recruiters set up a phony matchmaker—*shadchan*—service in Warsaw. They ran ads in a couple of dailies. Sometimes the recruiter, if he had to, would marry the girl in Poland. He couldn't care less. If he worked it right he could marry two or three in the same month and have them come to Argentina on separate boats.

Another group were the apprentice whores. Generally they had menial jobs and did a little polite hustling on the side for "gifts." Inevitably, they heard stories of how well the professionals were doing in Argentina and they didn't need much persuasion. And finally, there were the professionals who weren't doing too well in Warsaw because there was so much competition. With them, the pimps were choosy. They wanted them young, clean, and willing. Mike recalled a conversation with a returned pimp.

"A lot of those Warsaw whores are orthodox: you gotta do it their way or you don't. And their way was the old way. The cock goes into the cunt. Only. If they didn't want to learn, fuck 'em. Let 'em starve in Warsaw."

It wasn't just a Warsaw problem. Mike also talked to a French pimp who skipped bail on a vice charge in New York and brought down with him a Philadelphia whore. The pimp said: "She wouldn't suck so she couldn't make a living. I had to send her back to Philadelphia. If she had done as I told her she would have made twenty thousand in three years. I have girls in some of my houses who make five hundred a week —even if they only get two dollars from a customer."

Occasionally, the recruiter would undergo a "religious" marriage ceremony with a greenie he brought over from Poland. All it involved was the exchange of symbolic gifts between the man and woman in the presence of an adult witness. Usually it would be held in the phony synagogue run by the *Zvi Migdal.*

The second week Mike was there his friendliest contact, Eduardo Zisman, said that an *Amerikaner* wanted to meet Mike. This was his introduction to Mucha Goldberg.

Goldberg scooted out of New York during the 1913 investigation while out on $15,000 bail and now he was a kind of wise international counselor to the *Zvi Migdal.* They also let him own a few houses even though he wasn't an Argentinian.

Goldberg was short, fat, and pockmarked, Mike went on. "But this little sonofabitch had been for years the Number Two man in the New York vice setup. He was smart and reasonable, so when Number One up there told him he had to get out of the country—or get killed—he got out of the country and came to B.A. He came down with forty-five thousand dollars."

Mike interrupted himself with a gurgled laugh. "It just hit me who the hell he was talking about. He was telling me stories about the *Numero Uno* in the New York setup, *his* boss. Max this, Max that, and you know it just hit me for the first time he was talking about your grandfather, Max Hanan."

My grandfather wanted Goldberg out of the country because little Mucha was the only one who could tie him into the racket; and sooner or later, Max Hanan felt little Mucha would crack under the pressure of the continuing investigation.

"The first time Goldberg took me into the headquarters building he showed me the bulletin board where the day's prices for the new girls were posted. The range was from eight hundred to two thousand dollars, depending on their looks, their age, and what they were willing to do for clients."

The society had four hundred members and nearly all of them had cover trades. They ran movie houses, drugstores, real estate businesses, owned apartment houses and import-export setups. One of them, Simon Rubinstein, owned a condom factory. Another ran a profitable sideline: male whores, *guapos*. Most of them had money-lending businesses: they'd help newer or less well-financed members bring over girls from Europe.

Generally they got 10 percent a month.

From Goldberg and others in the society, Mike got a picture of the mixed relationships the *Zvi Migdal* had with the rest of the Jewish community. Some Jews said the business wasn't illegal and the whores and *rufians*, the procurers, were good spenders so what the hell. But most of the organized Jewish community kept on battling the trade in many ways.

"They're worse than anti-Semites," Mucha Goldberg once told Mike. "They don't let us in their synagogues or burial grounds. So *Zvi Migdal* had to get its own cemetery in Avellaneda. In Rosario a woman who owned a couple of houses wanted to be buried in consecrated ground so she offered to contribute two hundred thousand pesos—which was around eighty thousand dollars then—to Jewish charities if they'd let her be buried there. They turned her down so she had to make do with Avellaneda when she died six months later. A lot of stores, synagogues, theaters, and clubs here have signs, 'Unclean ones forbidden.' They have two Yiddish dailies down here. One of them is a live-and-let-live kind. It keeps quiet and takes ads from one and all. The other one, *Die Presse*, is a bitch. It runs exposés on us, runs our names and the businesses we run and the houses we own and we can't buy them off. What do you expect? A socialist paper."

Mucha admitted he wasn't a good Jew but still he felt that Jews were too stiff-necked, too unforgiving. He once told Mike "Catholics maybe had the right idea about forgiving and forgetting. There had recently been a great local murder case in B.A. A chauffeur named Benelli murdered his mistress and cut her up into several sections. He was sentenced to life and while inside got permission to marry his other mistress in prison. A big monsignor came to the prison and married them and it was with the full works like it was being done in a cathedral or something. Now can you see a rabbi doing that in a penitentiary?"

Mike broke off so we could have an early dinner at Mamucas since I was still on New York time. Huge succulent shrimp, turtle soup, grilled lobster, and several bottles of Dos Equis. I ate more than I expected but I was getting tired simply because it had been a long day. Mike sensed this and instead of filling me with Buenos Aires detail which might be crucial he rumbled through dinner about himself and Mazatlan gossip.

"I first heard about Mazatlan and its miracles from some old-timers in Immigration and Naturalization who retired down here. It was comparatively cheap to live here—this was back in the early Sixties—but so was most of Mexico. That is, if you didn't have to live on one hundred percent U.S. meat and groceries. And the fishing was great. But there are a lot of places where that's true. No, the thing that really brought them down here in droves, as one of them told me: 'The place gets your balls moving again.' A lot of them said when they came down here— and most of them were bachelors or widowers or divorced men in their mid- or late sixties—they started getting hard-ons again. No goat glands, no hormone shots. Some of them said it was the air, the climate, the thirty kinds of shrimp. They had lots of reasons and none of them made much sense to me. So eight years ago I came down for a two-week visit. I was sixty-five and anything that would revive my sex life was worth a try. As you probably know fucking had been one of my lifetime hobbies. When you have to quit it's not like giving up handball. It's more like dying a little.

"Yeah, the air was okay and I loved the local shrimp and I got in a few days of great deep-sea fishing but still the old urge was missing. Then two nights before I was supposed to go back to L.A., I found the secret."

He became acquainted with a local *abogado*, sounding him out on legal problems connected with a possible long stay in Mexico for an alien, on local investments.

"We're sitting in his office and he gets a call from a client. He invites me to go out with him for a ride outside Mazatlan, where the client ran two houses. Technically, prostitution is outlawed in Mexico. In fact, it is tolerated as long as it is done discreetly. Occasionally when a local *fiscal*—the DA—got mad or there had been an uproar with some unhappy customer or maybe a killing—Mexico has one of the highest murder rates in the world—the place would be closed down for a while. But closing down would cost the operator a few hundred a day and he didn't like that so he had the *abogado* on permanent retainer. The lawyer was able to earn his fee because Mexico has one of those great legal gimmicks crooks love.

"They call it an *amparo* and it means literally 'protection.' I bet the Mafia would chip in ten million if it could be lobbied into law in the U.S. What it is, anybody who has been *or is about to be* the victim of unjust police or court action can apply to a local judge for an *amparo*. You get the *amparo* and the police can't arrest you and the court can't order the fine paid or the prison sentence served until the *amparo* is lifted. Great stuff. But it became such a racket that the Mexican Supreme Court had to modify it in nineteen fifty-five to cover only lesser offenses—crimes carrying sentences of less than five years. So it covers prostitution and running a house and my lawyer friend comes running out with an *amparo* as soon as his client gets the word that a police raid is coming. The *amparo* is flashed and the cops leave. Of course, the owner has to pay his cop friend for the warning."

When they got to the house the lawyer introduced Mike to the owner and then had a private talk with his client. A few minutes later he took Mike aside and said, "He'd like to have you be a guest in his house. Something very special. All the Americans in Mazatlan come to his house for the specialty."

Mike was a little reluctant. "First, I haven't had to pay for the stuff since I was a kid in Boyle Heights and then I figure who needs a dose at my age. But the lawyer, who knows what I'm thinking, says not to worry, the girls are clean and besides it's different. And he himself gets the specialty once a week and he's okay. So I said okay and he introduced me to Rosita who was maybe eighteen and cuddly, a kind of darker Shirley Temple in the old days. She assured me 'You luff it.' "

He did.

"She strips me very professionally and then has me lie face down on her bed, which had fairly clean but slightly damp sheets. Then she brings out her bottle of tequila and some absorbent cotton and starts sponging down my asshole gently. She gets in some very professional slow, long licks and in less than a minute she has my cock as erect as it's ever been and then she goes down on me and I tell you that was one of the best I ever had. That girl was *trained*. Of course, it was the old round-the-world technique which the Havana girls used to specialize in back when. She set me up for a week, felt twenty years younger. So I go back once or twice a week and Rosita and her sister Stella have become old friends. Of course, I pay for it now. So that's how I discovered the local fountain of youth. I wasn't Joe Schenck so I couldn't get Marilyn Monroe to go down on me once a week in his Hollywood office but I bet our local girls do a better job. What the hell—it also keeps me seven hundred miles away from my crazy daughter."

February 25, 1973. Mazatlan.

We had breakfast in the coffee shop of the Prince and then went back to his balcony.

"I could talk for hours on how things were in B.A. and how things worked from the European end but that's not gonna help you much. The details you can get from the League of Nations report of the Special Body of Experts on Traffic in Women and Children which came out in nineteen twenty-seven. In the report, incidentally, there are no names. Everyone—investigators and the pimps, procurers, whores, and *Zvi Migdal* members I talked to all have code designations like Six-T, Four-X, or One-oh-one–P. I'm just listed as 'the investigator' on the South American stuff. I forget what the code was. I think we used T mostly for Argentinian sources. All the original stuff I turned in which has the real names of my sources is under lock and key at the League Archives in Geneva. Can't be released for sixty years from the time the stuff was filed so that makes it nineteen eighty-six or so."

What it added up to was that young women and girls were and still are a valuable commodity in international trade. Whether they sent them out singly—with phony promises of marriage—or in groups of dancers for a cabaret engagement in Tangier or Rio—with phony promises of employment—didn't matter. Sure there were more amateurs in the field and today it is a whole lot easier to lay your classmate, your neighbor's wife, or any other attached or unattached female but still there was a demand for whores—go down Eighth Avenue in New York any evening—and there does seem to be an endless supply of them. Which meant that there is still a hell of a lot of money to be made out of them by pimps, procurers, landlords, cops and politicians on the take, and the lot. In effect, the League investigation—and all subsequent ones —probably didn't make the least bit of difference. No, he corrected himself, there was a difference. "There are now whores' unions in the U.S. and France. They insist they have the *right* to be whores."

But all this big-picture crap, he continued, is no help to you.

"I've been thinking last night on your idea. Someone, maybe second or third generation, is looking for revenge. Incidentally, I just remembered. That guy in Singapore, Miguel Karir. He *was* in the *Zvi Migdal.* I think I even met him once. He became treasurer of the organization."

The trouble is, we're geared only to think of revenge as a one-to-one proposition, he went on. "In the late Forties a lot of Germans and Austrians were killed by Jews who were out to get even with the men who tortured them in the camps. That we can grab hold of. But what the hell can you do with the proposition someone or someones out there is getting even for something that happened to their grandmothers or mothers. Maybe it's a Sicilian Jew. That might fit. How about a Chinese Jew? Listen, I once believed in Fu Manchu and his pledge to avenge the indignities the West had visited on the Chinese."

He answered the phone.

"Great idea, but I got company. . . . Wait a minute. Lemme call you right back."

It was a fellow Californian who'd been living here for a year, he said. "His name is Brand Hixon and he's here because the State Bar put him on two years' suspension for fiddling around with the estates of some Agua Caliente Mission Indians for whom he was court-appointed guardian. They're land-rich—in Palm Springs. When he came down here to sit out his suspension—and just in case some of the victimized Indians decided on their own vengeance—he was pretty well fixed and brought down his four-seater Cessna one-eighty-two. So he flies around a bit and he bought a piece of the local English-language tourist weekly. Well, once a month he flies out to the Islas Marias about one hundred miles from here and he always asks me to go along. I know the governor of the islands. Hixon wants to go out today and my first reaction as you heard was to pass it up this time but I remembered there's somebody on the island you might want to talk to. How about it? It's only a forty-minute flight and there might be some pay dirt."

I said, sure. He called and said if he could bring a guest it was on. We'd be picked up in the lobby in thirty minutes.

Mike filled me in while we waited. "He looks like a Greek god, the son of the old Arrow-collar man of my time, but he's a kind of sad piece of shit. No, it wasn't diddling the Indians. What the hell, a lot of lawyers couldn't have resisted that temptation. Those Indians own millions of dollars worth of some of the highest-priced land in the country."

When he came to Mazatlan he took an apartment in the Prince and Mike met him. He seemed mysterious and never talked about where he came from or what he was doing in town. Pretty soon the idea got around—and the Californian didn't discourage it—that somehow he was working for the CIA. Mike shot that down privately because he had once used some legal term talking to Hixon and that naturally led to, Are you a lawyer, Mike? And Mike said yeah, but retired, and Hixon had to know which law school and Mike told him.

"Okay, I went to one of those crappy night schools which are accredited only in California. A lot of lawyers did and I had to pass the bar exam like the other law students. But when I mentioned my school I could see the sour curl on his lips and I figured only another California lawyer would react that way. So I made a few calls and sure enough Hixon is out of Stanford Law and a rough bout with the state bar disciplinary committee. Well, an item like that you don't give away so I'm holding it in reserve. As far as he's concerned he's still our mysterious stranger who has dough and a plane and probably works for the CIA. At first some of us figured he's queer, part of the normal reaction of us ugly heterosexuals when we come across a man who's too good-looking, but he isn't."

You run a private plane, Mike went on, and you're not using it for business regularly you got a real problem: where do you *go* with it? You got to find places, reasons why you should take your toy up. So when I first suggested a visit to Islas Marias, Hixon grabbed it. He'd heard about the islands but as far as he knew outsiders weren't allowed to visit. I told him I had an in: I had known the governor of the islands when he was working for the Mexican border police in Tijuana.

I could tell from the beginnings of a millimeter-wide grin starting to form on his lips Mike was waiting for me to ask the obvious: what the hell was so special about these islands that you needed permission to visit them?

"You need it, pal, because it's Mexico's great prison island—with a little do-good garnish. It's ninety-seven miles due west from Mazatlan and it was started as a prison by the dictator Porfirio Díaz in nineteen oh five to keep his political enemies. He had a lot. When they knocked him over in nineteen twelve they continued using it for some prisoners but the big event was in nineteen thirty-one when Mexico abolished capital punishment. Well the country had—and still has—a hell of a lot of murderers, particularly in DF, Distrito Federal, or Mexico City. Sure, they could have shoved the convicted murderers into their big old penitentiary, Lecumberri, but they figured, correctly, a lot of murderers in that joint would lead to a lot more murders committed on behalf of the men and women who had been killed in the first place. So they shipped them out to Islas Marias. Actually, there are four islands but only one is used for the penal colony. In the Thirties, Mexico was moving to the Left fast and very liberal in some things and gradually someone decided it would be a good idea to let long-term prisoners bring their families out to live with them. Well, they have about five hundred male prisoners there and about forty have been allowed to bring their wives and families with them. Also about twenty women prisoners."

The arrangement, he went on, was that the prisoner could build a hut for his family and he would work four hours a day for the prison community and four hours a day to support his family. Some of them make leather novelties, domino sets, wooden toys for sale on the mainland. Some catch lizards and make the skins into shoes and belts and wallets. A few, illegally, make tequila out of the maguey plant. One enterprising naturalist catches specimens for museums. Others operate a barber shop or tailor shop. When they work for the prison they're in the salt ponds or do building repairs or in the hemp factory.

The prisoner he thought it might be worth talking to was a Jean Gâtebourse. "Since you're the family's French expert you know the name means 'spoil purse' or maybe 'wallet-walloper,' but it fits this character more or less because one time he is a top engraver on counterfeit plates. That's neither here nor there. Why I think you ought to talk to him is between nineteen twenty-seven and nineteen thirty in his pretty hectic life he is the chief doctor and manufacturer of passports for an outfit in Paris that worked very close with the *Zvi Migdal* in B.A. That's not what he's in the islands for. He killed someone in Mexico City in nineteen forty-one. Nothing to do with our bunch, by the way. But I'll let him tell you the story of his Paris tie-up."

We still had a few minutes before Hixon picked us up—he now lived in a rented house outside town—and Mike was clearly enjoying this new tactical line he was developing in Handling the Sensitive Situation.

"I introduce you as CIA, we put Hixon in a jam, we blow his imaginary cover like that. He doesn't have the secret handshake or what the hell you guys have and that would embarrass the shit out of him. So we can't do that because he and his fly-machine are a nice convenience every now and then."

I would be introduced as a relative and business partner of Mike's—from New York. And while I was at it, Mike smiled, I should also drop the word quietly about how Mike ought to think what he's going to do with the million he's getting out of the VW deal.

"A little exaggeration but I wanna lay it on him. He never believed me on the VW deal but didn't say anything about it. Just as I never took up his CIA-involvement hints. Also I love the envy bit with a schmuck like him."

I told Mike our pilot sounded like a perfect recruit for Manny's proposed operation, which I outlined. Mike was pretty skeptical. "There enough other characters like him around, *with dough?*" I said Manny was pretty shrewd and if he thought the idea had a good chance, there probably were enough prospects. I was ready to ask Mike to invest in it when our pilot came into the lobby just then and I knew all Mike's preparation was down the drain. Hixon recognized me about the same time I did him.

Louise Bertolotti's stepbrother, the Stanford tennis bum. I met him once in Washington, before the mess began, the one with her old involvement with someone from the other side. I vaguely recalled he had been interviewed for one of the then-new JOT—Junior Officer Training —programs but nothing came of it. When Louise was ten her mother had married a California supermarket operator named Hixon. He was a widower with an eight-year-old boy. Hixon was the Americanization of some Armenian name.

Hixon seemed glad to see me again. He still had the over-developed right forearm of a heavy tennis player and at forty or so he seemed in good shape. What was added was contact lenses, which give old myopic eyes a slightly unfocused element. And vanity, of course. A forty-year-old male learning to wear the lenses had to have that in abundance.

Mike was naturally bewildered at our greeting each other—and surely put out. Only at the airport while Hixon took a couple of minutes to file a flight plan was I able to fill Mike in, even though by then he had been able to put together most of the pieces from the talk Hixon and I had during the ride out.

"So he did have some CIA connection," Mike said a little sourly. I said it was pretty remote and if it made Mike feel any better he didn't have any now since even his stepsister was out of the business.

On the way out Hixon told me how well Louise was doing now as a partner in the ad agency and I told him I had run into her in the Plaza a few weeks ago.

"Oh, she told me about that and she added she was glad you were dying or she would have acted on her old impulse to kill you because you were the one who should have stood up for her and you didn't."

A stupid situation: now I was the one who held out on the truth and Mike would be wondering what was I supposed to be dying of; and worse, why hadn't I said anything so that the news had to come from an acquaintance he despised.

Fortunately, speech in a Cessna aloft is not easy and since I sat in the back row it was even harder to cross-talk but I heard that it cost Hixon about $10,000 a year to maintain the plane and that he was multi-engined licensed also. But all wasn't one-sided: I got in an aside to Mike that he ought to let me know soon how he wanted his one million handled. And my dying was highly exaggerated. I had some exploratory surgery but was okay now.

9

February 24, 1973. Islas Marias.

Hixon radioed for permission to come in and it came quickly from the island's radio operator, a civilian, who had standing orders from the governor to admit the plane when his old *compadre,* Señor Averbuch, was aboard.

When we landed on the unpaved landing strip the governor's jeep was there and the driver-trusty explained while he drove us to the main center of Balleto that the governor was with an inspection party from the department of *Prevención Social* of the Mexican Department of the Interior, which runs the island prison. They were at the island's fifty-bed Maria Madre Hospital.

Balleto has the island's only pier. The navy cutter comes twice a month with supplies and new prisoners and occasionally takes prisoners back to the mainland and greater freedom.

Mike explained to Hixon that I had to talk to one of the prisoners on private business and that Mike was needed as a translator. Hixon was very curious and annoyed he was being left out. He walked over to the Lazy Tree, the island's main social gathering spot, a general store and soft drink and ice cream emporium near the hall where movies were shown twice a week. Men play dominoes and gossip. The store is owned by a former prisoner who received permission to remain on the island after his sentence expired.

Mike walked me to a hut on Benito Juarez Street and he explained how Gâtebourse built it. He had to make dozens of trips to the mountains to bring back thin poles of hard Margarita wood. Then more trips to the public water tap a block away so that he had enough water to make the mud and clay that filled in the chinks between the poles. At first he had covered the roof with wooden boards but later got permission to substitute red tiles. The patio was covered with dried palm leaves, and surrounded by fragrant jacaranda and bougainvillea.

He was able to afford to bring over the red tiles, Mike explained, because Gâtebourse had several sidelines. He did engraving on silver buckles; he taught engraving in the local school; he caught turtles in a cove nearby; and from time to time he and another prisoner would start up a secret still in the interior to make tequila. Also Mike would leave him a hundred pesos or so on every visit.

"I like the bastard," Mike explained. "Also he's born the same day I was, March fourteenth, so I figure we're birthday brothers, even if he is a little younger. He's a great yarn spinner and I know most of it is true because so much of it is on public record. But when you get right down to it the few bucks I slip him is like an offering to the gods. He got the bad luck I might have had. One or two things when I was younger turn out differently, it wouldn't take much for me to end up an old con today. Okay, a little exaggeration but I hate to tell you how little."

Gâtebourse came in about a half-hour later, greeted Mike with an *abrazo* and shook hands with me when Mike introduced me as a *primo*, a cousin. He added something I couldn't catch in gravelly Spanish. I was a nosy bastard, Mike said, but he would be grateful if Gâtebourse could help me. Mike now opened the red plastic insulated picnic bag he had been carrying and brought out two dozen Dos Equis cans, still fairly cold.

Our host had told his story many times and like a jazz musician loved rearranging the chronological riffs, tones, emphases, beginnings, and endings. He tells it in a home-made Esperanto composed of French, Spanish, and a Chicano-English which he acquired from the island's only U.S. prisoner, a Mexican-born car thief from Los Angeles. I would be thrown off occasionally when he'd pop up with French slang of the '20s and '30s. A woman was a *gonzesse;* bank notes were still *faffes* in his sleeping-beauty vocabulary. A man didn't have balls, he had *olives,* and a vagina was still *un étau,* a vise.

He's about five-foot-ten with heavy shoulders and a bulbous, heavily veined nose and has the darkened complexion of a Marseillais. His obligatory prologue to my questions went roughly like this:

His real name was not Gâtebourse but Popaul and he was born near the Gare Saint-Charles in Marseilles, *la Marsiale.* He got the name Gâtebourse because he had once made himself a French passport with that name, which he chose as a kind of trade joke because Giraud de Gâtebourse had been the classic French counterfeiter of the nineteenth century. He was so clever the Bank of France invited him to make suggestions on how to improve their bank notes. But finally he was caught and sent to Devil's Island and tried to escape. The authorities said he died in the attempt but folklore had it the Bank of France rescued him and for a year he worked quietly in a remote vault of the bank—looking for counterfeit notes.

His modern counterpart had gotten into counterfeiting from an apprenticeship in engraving. He "drifted" into political work for Italian counterintelligence, *Fasci all'Èstero* (Fasces Abroad), which kept tabs on—and often eliminated—the many enemies of Italian fascism abroad. What he did for the despised *Ritals,* wops, was forge passports, letters, documents, and so forth. He was allowed to do work on the side and in 1927 he began a connection with a Parisian group headed by an Englishwoman, Celina Ricks. Mike nodded when her name was mentioned and I assumed this was what we had come for but there was no way Gâtebourse would deviate from his eccentric narration.

The Celina Ricks operation—he didn't make clear what it was except it was criminal—was ended by a police raid in June 1930, and Gâtebourse got away in time and went to Spain. There he tied up with a gang working on U.S. twenty- and fifty-dollar bills, designed to be sold to credulous Europeans who would hoard the bills against the time they could wangle their way into the golden land. The gang was caught in 1933 and Gâtebourse got a five-year sentence, but was amnestied in 1937 just in time to be taken on—forcibly—by a new secret-police operation called SIM *(Servicio de Investigación Militar)*, a Communist-run operation designed ostensibly to find right-wing spies—Franco and monarchist.

Originally he was supposed to work on altering the many passports the Communists seized from the foreign volunteers who came to Spain to defeat the Fascist forces. Then the SIM was called upon to surrender all the seized passports to Moscow where the facilities were better for altering passports that would be used later by Soviet agents abroad.

SIM now devolved into an NKVD-like operation for the interrogation and torture of Republican Army soldiers who were unwilling to follow the orders of Communist commanders. Mainly, Gâtebourse became involved in a clever, brutal scheme concocted by one of the SIM bosses. It first involved the spreading of rumors around Madrid that a tunnel had been dug to run from a suburban house in Usera to the Franco lines. There were a lot of Nationalist-Franco sympathizers hiding out in Madrid and in several foreign embassies. Gâtebourse was one of several men who negotiated with them to get into the tunnel and freedom. With all their transportable valuables they were led secretly to the mouth of the tunnel and shot. After the war the Franco investigating commission said at least sixty-seven were killed this way. Gâtebourse had been able to pocket a few of the passports the victims grasped and used one of them to make his way out of Spain to Mexico.

There, in late 1938 he got in with a counterfeiting mob working on U.S. hundred-dollar bills to be peddled in border towns but he and his companions were arrested in 1939 and sentenced to Lecumberri Penitentiary in Mexico City. Inside he became friendly with a couple of Cristeros.

In the '30s the Cristeros were Mexico's main underground movement. Their aim was to overthrow the Left-leaning Cárdenas government, which was continuing a state policy of nationalizing all Catholic Church property and deporting foreign priests, nuns, and monks. In the summer of 1939 the Cristeros mounted a clever escape operation—

aided by two prison guards who were secret Cristeros—and Gâtebourse and his two prison friends got out. The Cristeros wanted him to counterfeit Mexican currency so they could buy arms and munitions abroad for a new revolution.

He worked for the Cristeros for ten years and in that time he made about seven different sets of plates but difficulties in printing and getting the right paper limited the whole operation to a dollar value of less than $100,000. Gâtebourse would be moved every few weeks from one "safe" house to another. Then in 1950 he was arrested while disguised as a Mexican army officer. He shot and killed one of the arresting officers and was sentenced to life imprisonment on Islas Marias. In 1970 his sentence was commuted and he talked the authorities into letting him spend the rest of his life on the island as a free man. He convinced them that his life outside—in Mexico, Spain, or France—would be hazardous. He was sure there were still any number of his victims intent on revenge. Ordinarily, they wouldn't let anyone stay on but they made one of their rare exceptions. He had proved himself a useful island citizen.

Orwell, who must have been in Madrid when Gâtebourse was working his murderous scheme, once wrote that autobiography was only to be trusted when it reveals something disgraceful. Of course, with someone like Gâtebourse the question always had to be: does *he* consider it disgraceful, too?

It wasn't easy to tell from Gâtebourse's tone. He certainly wasn't the self-abasing, contrite sinner relating a terrible catalogue of crimes. Really, it was more like: what a strange life I've led; how oddly fate has dealt with me—with the bare implication that happily he had been one of those chosen not to lead a humdrum, uneventful life. Another writer once said we can be divided into the sane, who *know* they are acting, and the mad, who do not. I think Gâtebourse *once* knew he was acting.

The beer was half-gone and so were the tacos, sunflower seeds, and coconut strips. Now that this athlete of life had completed the obligatory exercises I could get him on the voluntary. Celina Ricks, of course.

When he met her in 1928 she had a very nice house in Ozoir-la-Ferrière, Seine-et-Marne, about a mile from the American Country Club. He had begun looking around for other work because he was starting to worry about the *Fasci all'Èstero* characters he was associating with. Publicly, the despised *Ritals* were making a lot of anti-French noises and Gâtebourse's very latent patriotism may have been plinked. One day a visitor from Rome came into the Paris office—in the Italian Embassy—and introduced himself to Gâtebourse and his boss after giving the Fascist salute: "My name is Castellani. Nineteen assassinations."

When Gâtebourse met Celina she was in her early or mid-thirties and very businesslike. She was attractive but had an icy English don't-touch look which would vanish when she was in a rage. Then, he said, she sounded like a Cockney whore. But that was later.

She had heard of his reputation, she said, and he came well recommended. She needed a steady supply of certain official papers—passports, birth certificates, visas, and so on. On the average she would need him perhaps two days a week now and she was ready to pay top wages for a skilled artisan.

It didn't take long for Gâtebourse to realize Celina was the important continental end of a long chain of prostitution and seduction that started in Central Europe and Poland and ended in Argentina and Brazil. Gradually he began acquiring more information about her from the servants.

He was naturally curious, of course, but there was a more pressing reason. Once, alone in her office for a few minutes, he rummaged a closed desk drawer and found an alarming dossier on him which, in the hands of a French examining magistrate, let alone the counterintelligence service, would get him a stretch in Fresnes prison. He replaced the dossier carefully and a minute later Celina returned.

"She smiled at me. 'So, m'sieu, now you know.'

"For the first time I was really afraid of her. To have planned the incident so carefully, to have led me to that drawer and the dossier, one had to have respect for such a mind. Of course, she had another copy in a more secure place so even if I had foolishly let myself take what was in the drawer . . ."

Celina made it clear that it was merely insurance. But Gâtebourse knew that life insurance was worth something only when someone died.

Gradually he started acquiring his own insurance in the form of bits and pieces about Celina. She had come to Paris in 1913 from Darwen, a small town in Lancashire, twenty-five miles from Manchester. Originally she came over as the secretary of an executive of a British tobacco firm with a branch office in Paris. In fact, she had been the executive's little friend. But she did work in the office as one of the newly emerging *dactylos.* In 1915 her friend went to work for the British Embassy's passport-control office and she went along.

There are certain phrases that get automatically underlined and "passport control" is one of them. For decades it was the local designation for Britain's secret service, MI-6. The passport-control officer was generally MI-6's man in the embassy or consulate. But questioning Gâtebourse brought out only that Celina worked *with* passports; he really wasn't sure of the section's proper name.

In 1919 in Paris she met Mauricio Haro, an Argentinian on a business visit. At first it was strictly business. He paid her what was then the equivalent of $3,500 for certain forms the British used, duplicate rubber stamps, and the key data on hidden marks the British used in their passports. Also, Celina introduced him to a Frenchwoman who did similar work for the French passport office. After a few months Mauricio and Celina's business relationship "blossomed and deepened"—I'm quoting Gâtebourse—and in 1920 Celina had a child, a boy he thinks was named Listare. We assumed he meant Lester—or Leicester. In 1928 when he went to work for Celina the boy was in a British school. He wasn't sure of the name but it sounded like Bat-fort.

Celina became Haro's Paris partner in what Gâtebourse called "the *bidochard* business." *Bidoche* is low-quality meat and *bidochard* is a slaughterhouse worker, but in the argot *bidochard,* of course, referred strictly to human cattle, the whores and the whores-to-be who were exported from France to foreign markets.

She was one of the main suppliers and routing-agents for the *Zvi Migdal* of which Mauricio Haro was then treasurer. She was ingenious, Gâtebourse recalled. Girls being shipped out of Paris or Marseilles would be accompanied by Celina's female aides dressed as Salvation Army members or Sisters of Mercy. The girls supposedly were destined for a special branch of Salvation Army work abroad.

Gâtebourse had a number of boyhood friends who had become powers in the *Marsiale* (Marseilles) underworld. And one or two who had become bent members of the *Police Judiciare*. So he had good sources of information on Celina's all-around operations. She had also built up a sideline of blackmail because she had invented—or someone had invented for her—a handy little gimmick known as the two-way mirror. Mike interrupted. "Jean and I have been over this a lot. I told him I've talked to five U.S. madams who claimed they invented the two-way mirror but he thinks Celina really did. In any case I bet the damn thing was invented by someone in the trade."

The device naturally made surreptitious picture-taking easier and Celina and her staff used the pictures profitably. Mostly it was used at another country house Celina ran. There, she sent her choicest material for rendezvous with what Gâtebourse called "*dignitaires*," French, British, and Spanish. Not just dignitaries; ones with money and families.

Gâtebourse never saw Celina's child but he did see Haro, who came through on a business trip in 1929.

"He proudly showed her a gold medal the *Zvi Migdal* had given to its 'great and honorable member,' Mauricio Haro. He said they should give Celina a medal, too, but she wasn't a member and she wasn't Jewish."

What did Haro look like? "Like a *caid*, a chief of a prostitution racket. They all look alike. Dark-haired, tight eyes, broad face, the beginning of a paunch, silk shirt, an expensive diamond ring and a way of hunching their shoulders forward when they're going to bawl someone out."

In May 1930, Gâtebourse was in a fix. Celina wanted him to work full-time for her. He had been supervising the passport and visa and birth-certificate work of two assistants but she felt that he ought to be there all the time. That would mean leaving the Italians, which he had long wanted to do but was afraid to. Castellani, "Nineteen Assassinations," would come through the Paris office every few months—to knock off another exiled Italian anti-Fascist. Including a dubious Frenchman wouldn't bother him.

That month the problem got solved. French counterintelligence had begun shadowing Gâtebourse and he stopped visiting the *Fasci all'Estero* office but deliberately kept up his twice-a-week trips to Celina's house in Ozoir-la-Ferrière. He says he didn't do it to bring the law down on Celina's operation—there was no profit in it for him—but rather as a test for fate. If the counterintelligence people didn't follow up the lead, didn't investigate Celina's passport factory—which would ordinarily interest them—well, he'd stay on even if he was getting restless. And a bit nervous. He had found where Celina kept a "petty cash" cache of about 50,000 francs for emergency expenses and every now and then he'd dip into it for a few thousand, assuming that it wouldn't be missed.

Gâtebourse's problem was solved in mid-June because Celina tried to blackmail the wrong man. This official had originally been in the Finance Department but in a shakeup was moved over to Interior, which meant that he was now a power in the *Sûreté Nationale*. Celina's payoffs had been to someone in the *Police Judiciare*, which was often at odds with the *Sûreté* and the two of them with the *Gendarmerie Nationale*.

The official arranged a raid on Celina's place by *Sûreté* men. They took every picture, every negative in the place as well as the whole passport works. She was arrested, held incommunicado forty-eight hours and then another eleven months before the examining magistrate decided there wasn't a good case against her.

Gâtebourse got a warning of the raid because he worked out a little *condé* with a *Sûreté* inspector. He would be an informer and the *Sûreté* would turn a blind eye if his crimes stayed small. Gâtebourse fled to Spain—taking with him most of Celina's petty cash and several passport blanks and other useful equipment.

"Not very gallant, was it?" he shrugged. "But I was getting very afraid of her. She knew I was fiddling around. She'd look in the workroom and say, 'Something has a bad smell here' and that was a warning."

What really frightened him was the discovery that the petty cash he was dipping into was all counterfeit. He had never really looked at the bills and he hadn't had any trouble using them.

"It was a woman's trick. The money was there for me to find. If I took it I was an ordinary thief. Then if I'm caught with counterfeit money—me with my background, my *casier judiciaire*, I'm finished. I was very lucky. I hadn't spent many of the bills but I realized Celina didn't need me very much anymore or maybe she had found out about my little *condé* with the *Sûreté*."

When Celina was seized during the raid, Gâtebourse was on his way to Barcelona and on the train ride down he mused on what the police would be putting her through during the forty-eight hours, the *passages à tabac*, because tobacco leaves are also pounded in processing.

"The Interior official must have said don't worry about her being a woman. Trying to blackmail *him!* Their best one was banging your kidneys—but only through a wet towel so that there were no marks. They also loved to handcuff your hands behind you and make you kneel on a bicycle wheel for several hours. The thin wheel spokes sink deeply into the bare flesh and hurt like hell."

The images of Celina being put through those tortures comforted him because he realized that he had really been afraid of her all along. "Yes, I could have killed her with two blows—she was no Amazon—but I was afraid of her because nothing added up. She has an affair with one of the biggest whoremasters in Argentina but doesn't become a whore, working for him. She has a child by him, deliberately—because in nineteen twenty you could easily arrange a private hospital abortion in Paris. She has the child and then sends him away to an English school so she sees him only on her visits to England. Everyone knows the English are very strange but that such a woman could become a respected and feared chief among the *bidochards*, the human-cattle dealers . . ."

Clearly, by now envy had also entered the hate complex against Celina. Not only had she done far better than he financially but she was able to give orders that were carried out and he was still a so-so free lance in the criminal world with uncertain prospects and no power.

In any case he never saw Celina again but once in Mexico he ran across a Paris acquaintance from the *bidochard* business. He heard Celina retired somewhere with a lot of money and left the business completely after she was released by the examining magistrate in 1931. Haro, he heard, scooted out of B.A. in 1930 just before the police could take him and after a stay in Europe for a year he went to São Paulo, Brazil—along with several other B.A. whoremasters—and started business all over again.

Mike closed that road quickly. "In nineteen thirty Haro was about forty-five and that would make him, say, eighty-eight today so let's forget him. . . . I wonder if the son's name was Lester Haro or Lester Ricks?"

He added some confirmatory details on Celina. "She was one of the

Paris leads I got in B.A. in nineteen twenty-five. When I got to Paris I contacted her and even gave her a letter Mauricio had given me. He said I was interested in girls and prices and deliveries. She was skeptical almost from the start. Why should my group be bothering with Europe when there were hundreds of girls available for the asking in Quebec? And did my group know the inordinate difficulties the new U.S. immigration quotas had placed in shipping merchandise? New York was not Buenos Aires. After fifteen minutes she got up suddenly and said, 'Averbuch, not only don't you make sense but you suddenly don't smell right either.' And that was the last time I saw her. I think she was the only one who ever questioned my identity in that eighteen months I was underground. Oh, I got what I needed in Paris from other *bidochards,* who took me for what I appeared to be."

He remembered some personal details. "Attractive but a little hard-looking. You know who she looked like a little? A kind of tougher-looking Mary Astor. Remember her? Celina was obviously English but the accent wasn't pronounced. She had hazel eyes, dark-brown hair, and at a time when most women were flattening their breasts she wasn't. Maybe because hers were worth looking at. At the time I figured she must be clearing about a hundred thousand a year which was a hell of a lot of dough in the mid- and late Twenties. When I saw her she was about thirty-one, thirty-two, which would make her about eighty today if she's still around. After the Paris mess she's supposed to have moved on to Alexandria."

Before we left I bought a silver buckle from Gâtebourse and a beautiful hand-made domino set in an intricately carved wooden container. Sam Urdell would appreciate it. Mike took Jean aside and presumably slipped him the customary hundred pesos. We both thanked him for his time and information.

We were back at the Lazy Tree by four when we were supposed to meet Hixon. I was nice to him in an offhand way. I said he was obviously doing a whole lot better than if he had ever taken on as an Agency JOT trainee and was probably a lot happier. The late thirties were a rough age for most Agency men. By then they know just how far they're going with the Agency and for most of them the distance is pretty short. They generally have a family and only a barely adequate income and there's a lot of temptation to leave and start elsewhere. I said he had wisely avoided all those problems.

He said, well, it might have been fun for a few years but he had developed expensive tastes and he probably would have left after five or six years, but still . . .

In short, he wished he'd been *asked.*

We were back in Mike's apartment by 5:30. We had a drink on the balcony. He assured me with a smile that he had taken care of the security details. I looked blank.

"I figure nosy Hixon sooner or later is going to get hold of Gâtebourse and try to pump him on what we were talking about so before we left I told Jean I'd appreciate it if he kept quiet about our talk on Celina and her operation. I slipped him an extra hundred pesos this time." I said that was good thinking and I was further in his debt. But the fleeting frown, the unconscious giveaway, must have been caught.

"Not SOP?"

I said it was an old argument in the business. If you paid for silence —or for information—you put a money value on it and inevitably a lot of people assumed that if it was worth X to one man, maybe it was worth at least 2X to another. Which led to problems and diamond-cut-diamond nonsense, like deliberately paying to keep silent when you really want him to sell the stuff to another side. Endless wheels-within-wheels. But I thought Gâtebourse was fairly safe. He looked like he stopped being hungry some time ago. And he wouldn't want to rile someone like Mike who was such an old friend of the island governor. No, he was a pretty good risk.

Mike said, a little sourly, I sounded off a little like someone just trying to keep a franchise.

I said I tried to sound like someone trying to forget a memorable college experience. Once, at Columbia, I thought I wanted to be an *actor.* So I got a little part in a college production of an old English classic, *School for Scandal.* I was Mr. Snake and my most memorable lines were, "You paid me extremely liberally for propagating the lie, but unfortunately I have been offered double to speak the truth."

Mike grinned to show he was over his pique. "So you became an actor after all." I said, yes, that was a big part of my business.

How did he know Celina moved on to Alexandria, Egypt, after 1931? He laughed. "Come on. There must be something else nagging you." I joined him in a giggle. We were playing a kind of wise-kid game. "Now that you mention it, Mike, and only if you think it's any of my business: what was that about your putting dirty money into my brother's VW distributorship?"

In 1945 he got a letter at his Los Angeles law office from Havana. It was signed by Simon Hartshtein, one of the *Zvi Migdal* officers Mike had met in Buenos Aires. Hartshtein, like several of the other *Zvi Migdal* people, had read the League of Nations report and its tantalizing bits of conversation the mysterious investigator had had with them in B.A. It didn't take long for them to figure out that it must have been the American visitor, Mike Averbuch. Since he said he had come from Los Angeles, they checked him out and found he was a lawyer there and had once worked for the Immigration and Naturalization Bureau.

Now Hartshtein desperately needed the help of an American immigration lawyer and the only one he knew was Mike. So he wrote. He was in Havana on a three-month tourist visa. He had left Montevideo when things got hot there; in fact, there had been an attempt on his life by a rival gang. He was now sixty-three and anxious to lead a quiet life. He wasn't poor and could afford excellent legal and *other* help.

Mike phoned him in Havana and got a few more details and they fixed a price. Mike said it would cost $40,000 to get Hartshtein legally into the U.S. Hartshtein must have really been desperate and in a week he agreed. Mike went to Havana, got various details and a $20,000 advance on his fee.

"He was a first-class bastard," Mike said. "He ran the largest condom factory in B.A., which he got control of by knocking off a man named Baron who owned it. Simon and Baron's wife got together and then he moved into white slavery and the *Zvi Migdal*. He was the bagman for most of the police payoffs and naturally a lot of it stuck to his fingers.

"So why let a son of a bitch like that into the U.S.? Well, I figured at sixty-three he's ready to quiet down and in the U.S., without any organization or real contacts, he wasn't going back in the old racket. Our own locals didn't need him. So if he was going to be a fairly harmless immigrant why not shake him down a bit. I had to spend five thousand in one or two places to see to it that his rap sheet never figured in his immigration hearings and I got him in. He paid off the other twenty thousand without a whimper and he bought a house in Sarasota. He died there late in the Sixties, I heard.

"I wasn't as tough as I thought. The whole thing bothered me— even if it was the easiest thirty-five thousand dollars I was ever going to earn. So I bought some bearer bonds and put them in the vault and forgot it. Dirty money. Then when your brother came along with his VW proposition I put it in. I think unconsciously I was hoping the whole thing would flop and I'd be rid of the dirty money. Now you know."

A man opens himself that wide you don't fob him off with a story about an exploratory operation. I knew Mike was still curious about the fast line I let out in the plane going over so I told him my cancer story. He shook his head.

"There's an old Hebrew expression, means miracles and wonders, and as you're finishing the story I'm thinking: how come Harry Hanan rates that kind of miracle? Then I remembered something your father let slip at the wedding. You were born one of the anointed of the race, you know that?"

He had me. "My father told you that?" He didn't believe in God, fate, luck, or any kind of anointments.

"Yep. A couple of hours after you're born at the American Hospital in Paris the obstetrician, a *goy*, takes your father aside and says, 'Mr. Hanan, I don't want to intrude on what might be a religious matter. I know you plan to have your son circumcised but I think you ought to know that it won't be necessary. He was *born* circumcised.' Turns out it happens very, very rarely. So rarely that in some primitive Jewish communities they believe that anyone born that way is not only going to bring good fortune upon his family but that from such naturally circumcised lads will come the Messiah—when he comes."

I couldn't resist an adolescent shot: "Over the years, Mike, I had lots of witnesses who swore I had a blessed cock. Little did they know."

He grinned, patted my head as one might a grandson leering prematurely: "It's not such a big thing anymore. Since women started taking the pill a lot of these natural circumcised *momzers* are turning up all over the place. Happens now about once every few hundred births. A whole generation of kids who can now say, well, if I'm a big circumcised prick, by God, I got that way naturally."

10

February 27, 1973. New York.

On the flight back to New York I tried to sort out the useful from the merely fascinating. Celina Ricks would now be in her eighties if she was still alive. Her son, born in 1920, is now fifty-three. Where is he and what is he doing—and why should we be interested? Why on earth should Celina's son be knocking off descendants of some of his mother's terrible associates in the late '20s? No sense.

Suddenly, there was a whole lot more that made no sense in New York. The morning after my return I visited Sam and Vogelsang to give them a condensed report of my Mexican visit. Sam came forward a little grimly. I said he looked like someone died while I was away.

"Someone," he said, "and something."

The something was my theory about the *goel hadam* deaths. While

174

I was away another *goel hadam* death became known and this one just didn't fit. The latest victim was a Tampa insurance man named Harald —no O—Christy, who was forty-nine. He had walked into a moving car on East Columbus Drive. The coroner found a dose of LSD in him and the car driver wasn't held. They checked his office in Belmont Heights and found remnants of the LSD in the remains of a glass of Scotch he had taken before leaving the office. Quite fancy. Christy had a black marble desk with a red suede wall behind him and there was a seven-foot white suede sofa. Clearly he wasn't dependent on some occasional life insurance commissions or homeowner comprehensives.

About a week before he was killed Christy had received a *goel hadam* note—numbered (15)—which he took to a friend named Wentworth who occasionally did some work for Christy. Wentworth had once been a member of the Commandment Keepers Congregation of the Living God, a New York sect of blacks who considered themselves Jews. After Christy died Wentworth worried about the note and finally took it to a Jewish lawyer and asked for advice on whether or not to show it to the police. The lawyer didn't think it was a good idea and told Wentworth to forget it. In turn, he gave the note—and the details—to his rabbi, who mentioned it to Shorsh when they met at a rabbinical assembly.

The police did some investigation into Christy's death but their hearts weren't in it. They figured Christy was long, long overdue. They had been trying to get him for years. For Harald Christy, a black, had been the brains of one of the meanest prostitution rackets in the South. The working details were handled by his three nephews—Clinton, James, and Herbert—who ran thirty whores very profitably. The girls—black and white—were transported to migrant farm-worker camps in Pennsylvania and Georgia and to Tampa-docked merchant vessels. Several girls had been kidnapped off the Tampa streets; one had been forced into doing ten-dollar tricks because her infant daughter was held by the pimps. All of them had been beaten with pointed steel rods several times. A federal strike force finally got the three brothers indicted, tried, and convicted. Each got eight years but their uncle, Harald, wasn't included because none of the three would talk. Harald paid for their very expensive defense—and appeals—but after his nephews went off to prison Christy continued his insurance business undisturbed—until his death.

Vogelsang took it up: "The Black Jew thing intrigued us right away, of course, and we checked it out. Christy had been born a Baptist and still went to church for business reasons. His connections with Wentworth, the Black Jew, were pretty distant and they certainly weren't related. Then we checked with the Black Jewish congregation in Harlem. Wentworth had been a member until about six years ago when he moved to Tampa, which doesn't have a Black Jewish congregation.

The Black Jews of Harlem, he went on, are self-elected Jews. They're *not* descended from the Falashas of Ethiopa who claim descent from the affair of Solomon and the Queen of Sheba. Actually, there are no Falasha Jews in the U.S. because they're just too poor to have gotten out of Ethiopa. Black-Jew cults started appearing in New York and Philadelphia and Washington, D.C., around 1915. Between 1919 and 1931 there were at least eight Black Jewish cults in Harlem. Now there was one major group in Harlem, the Commandment Keepers Congregation of the Living God, or the Royal Order of Ethiopian Jews. It had about a thousand members, most of them West Indian in origin.

"What we got here," Sam interrupted, "is the first real non-Jew—Faucon had converted from Judaism—who is a victim. But he's now very much in the prostitution racket, even if they couldn't prove it. So where does it leave your theory, Harry? Yeah, it's possible he got some tainted Jewish blood in him someplace but that's reaching. His family comes from Georgia and he's the grandson of slaves. I know there's some white blood in many blacks because their slave grandmothers and great-grandmothers were laid by white overseers or slave-owners. But when we gotta reach that far to hold up a theory I think it's easier to drop the theory."

I said there was another possibility here. One of the toughest problems I had in Turkey had nothing to do with the Russians or defectors or the rest of the normal worries of an intelligence service. It was sickness. Real, not Aesopian.

"We had an agent come down with typhoid so we had to send him to Frankfurt for top-level hospitalization. Then we had to work out who he had seen and contacted and who else in our group might have been infected. We didn't even think of the possibility that one of us was a carrier. Well, the man's wife is anxious to be by his side in Frankfurt so she flies out. The kids are left with the family of another agent and then one of the children comes down with typhoid. Total disaster. One of the secretaries who is studying Turkish goes around with a new Turkish proverb she's learned: 'Oh sorrow, I give thanks, if you are alone.'

"Naturally, we couldn't let the locals know because they might have wanted to kick us all out before half of Ankara had typhoid. Public health there is not very high on the list of national priorities. So we had to figure out what to do with the eleven-year-old boy who had typhoid. Obviously we had to get him out of the country and to Frankfurt, too, but he couldn't go out as a typhoid patient. We figured the only way was to get him out safely was as a mental patient. Which meant we had to concoct a series of reported incidents to show the kid was a dangerous psychotic and that we'd have to send him to Frankfurt for confinement and treatment. It took us two days and we finally had enough to convince the Turks it would be better for the poor kid to be out of the way. We bundled him in a straitjacket to the airport and then into a special plane for the flight to Germany. We took him out of the straitjacket aboard and the doctor was there to administer liquids and whatever they were using then.

"It was an innocent deception and we were lucky no one else on the staff or members of their families came down with typhoid and eventually the stricken man and his son recovered completely but we had to reassign the agent.

"All right. Now what the hell has this got to do with my theory being shot to hell because a black non-Jew in the prostitution racket is killed in Tampa? Well, we had to get the Turks to stop thinking of typhoid for a while; so we gave them something else to think about—a crazy eleven-year-old. Maybe a black non-Jew is put into the picture just to divert *our* thinking."

Sam said, "Possible. But it means . . ."

I nodded. "It means one of two things. The first is that our *goel hadam* somehow gets to know that we're now working on the Hanan theory and he or they or it is out to show us the theory is just a crock.

How many knew we were working on the Hanan theory? Between us here in New York and Sam's little helpers out in the field and maybe one or a few people on the American Hebrew Leadership Council or whatever it's called, say we have twenty, at least. Maybe thirty, if we count on the fact that some of them have nosy wives. The other possibility is that we're dealing with a smart *goel* and it knows sooner or later we got to tie the ends together and come up with a coherent theory. Well, why not anticipate and throw in a monkey wrench, a victim who doesn't fit the pattern?"

Vogelsang came in a little disconsolately: "If it doesn't matter which theory is the valid one the big problem is what the hell do we do now? We're at a standstill. The *goel* is still calling the shots and we're just reacting."

I said. "Let's forget the dead black in Tampa—unless you think there's some profit for us in trying to get more details on who might have planted the LSD in his Scotch glass. But I don't think that's too live a lead, even if this death is the most recent we have. Also, I'm running out of time."

This brought on the sympathetically quizzical looks and Sam's: "Hey, I thought you were looking better every day."

So I gave them the whole spontaneous regression marvel in abbreviated form. They congratulated me and Vogelsang brought out a bottle of cognac and insisted we drink a toast to my miraculous recovery and to the confounding of the *goel.*

When we quieted down Sam asked: "So why are you running out of time on this if your lung is okay now?"

I said sooner or later—long before he does his medical note for the *American Journal of Surgery*—Doc Andresen is going to be spreading the story. It's too rare an occurrence, too incredible. He'll be mentioning it to other surgeons and residents at the hospital and I figure I have a month before, one way or another, it gets back to Langley. If I'm okay now why don't I end my leave and report back?

"A month is also what I probably need for the final details on my brother's estate, which is what I got the leave for in the first place. Here's what I think we should be doing in the next thirty days."

There were four jobs, I thought. Five, if we wanted to include the dubious Tampa task of trying to find out *who* Christy had been drinking with before he got the LSD dose and went out in the street to be killed by a passing car.

First, I thought, we ought to find out a whole lot more about the missing-heir business. I had gotten a letter from Dave Quittle in London listing the six top missing-heir hunters in the U.S. I said I thought this might be useful because it struck me that using the missing-heir hunting cover might be a good one for running down the genealogies of some of the families involved. You tell them there's a possible inheritance, people open up.

Second. We should find out what happened to Celina Ricks and her son. The English school the boy was sent to, Bat-fort, sounded like Bedford. There couldn't be too many with that name.

Third. We needed a fix on Mauricio Haro. When and where did he die and did he leave anything to his—and Celina's—son?

Fourth. There were certain other aspects, mixed odds and ends, I wanted to look into myself.

Vogelsang volunteered on the missing-heir investigators. "I know a fellow used to be doing it. Now spends all his time locating missing stockholders for large corporations. He'll know who's worth talking to."

Sam said the Celina Ricks details would have to be checked out, probably in London's Somerset House and maybe Paris police records, and he'd get people after it. On Haro, he'd try to get some stuff out of a contact in São Paulo.

"Harry, tell me again why I feel like all this is just a WPA make-work project."

I said he was only partly right. "But even when you're making work about half the time you stumble on something that really has to be done. We're due."

Sam said, "So far the only real luck we've had has been yours. God bless you and your medical miracle. But where the hell are we after all these months? Listen, maybe Shorsh with his hand-of-God possibility has something."

Vogelsang rumbled: "Let's have Him call a press conference and we'll ask Him."

February 28, 1973.

I was in the throes of a curiously complicated emotion. I was ready to admit perhaps I had made a bad mistake, that I caused others to waste a lot of time and throw the investigation off its true path. In short, I was a big man, ready to confess egregious error. But for tactical reasons it was better the troops didn't know of my doubts. Besides, men have gotten killed for smaller errors.

For the first time I had to rethink some basic assumptions—and omissions. Was I still certain the whole *goel hadam* business had no serious tie-up with some unknown international intelligence operation? To begin with, I had never followed up with Vogelsang on how he *knew* the first six known *goel hadam* victims were not in intelligence work.

Next bit: Had Celina Ricks been involved with British intelligence in the early '20s? The passport-control connection could simply have been Gâtebourse's own language gargling. But he also said she had come over with a British tobacco executive to Paris. For many years British intelligence in Paris had used a British tobacco company as cover.

More: Elly's mother is involved in the Lucy ring in Switzerland. The ring and its participants had been studied as a textbook case by at least one generation of apprentice spies in the '50s. And it had been written about considerably. In the library I found at least seven books—three in English, two in French, and two in German—on the case, which continued to fascinate readers because the mystery still existed. Where had this strangely assorted ring—an Englishman named Alexander Foote, several Swiss, some expatriate Germans, one former Hungarian —gotten the incredibly detailed and very current information on German military movements that was radioed daily in voluminous detail to the Soviet Army intelligence center in Moscow? The arguments still went on: The information came from some high-ranking German army officers who had befriended Soviet counterparts when the Germans— outcasts after the Treaty of Versailles—and the Russians conducted secret training sessions together. Others said that the information really came from British intelligence, which had penetrated the Nazi code and took this elaborate and intricate bypass because the Soviets would never believe the information if it came directly from the British. It was an old argument among professionals but there was no doubt that the information was an important, perhaps a major, contribution to the Red Army success in sweeping back the Nazi divisions.

One of the books had a bit more on Elly's mother, a minor player in the Lucy ring. She had been brought into the ring by Christian Schneider, a Communist.

The first "cutout" was to be Schneider himself, and the second a woman friend of his; if anything happened to him she was to take his place as the first intermediary [in getting the secret data to the radio operator]. She was called Helena Bricha and like himself she was employed by the International Labour Office. She lived in Geneva. Although of foreign origin she had a Swiss passport. During the war she had gone through a "white marriage" with a Swiss. This was a fairly common practice at the time and one that was highly profitable to a number of Swiss citizens who sold their names—and the security that they brought with them.

Schneider's code name was "Taylor"; Helena was known as "Leslie" and Rudolf Roessler, the German Protestant who actually got the incredibly valuable information, was "Lucy." He also supplied the Swiss intelligence office, the Bureau Ha, with the same information. When the ring was broken up by the Swiss in November 1943, Helena Bricha had been arrested, put in Saint-Antoine, the Geneva prison, but released after two weeks because she was very pregnant. Elly was born in December. There was nothing on Elly's father.

And finally: if you really wanted to reach, why not include the Zelkowicz *goel hadam* death? The man killed in Berlin while he was trying to locate a Swiss safe deposit box supposed to contain a dangerous dossier on Lenin, Russia's permanent God. Surely the NKVD had also been interested in locating that box.

What a rich choking stew if you threw all these mysterious morsels in the pot! I spent some time trying to work out some kind of recipe but it was hopeless. At one point I worked up an inner laugh: I call Mike in Mazatlan and ask him for his daughter's phone number in California. He says, what the hell you wanna talk to her? You don't have enough troubles? I say, Mike, I need a free-swinging conspiracy mind. Here are the pieces and I'd like her to work out a deep, dark, incredible plot for me. The wilder, the better.

11

March 2, 1973. New York.

I'm getting restless so I've started fixing time limits. I called the Washington broker and took my house off the market. Whether or not the *goel hadam* thing is solved by March 20, I report back to Langley. As Mike would put it, I'm trying to give fate a *shtup*, a push, to hurry up and resolve matters.

So far a lot of nothings. The General Register Office at St. Catherine's House in London has no marriage or death record for a Celina Ricks. And no recorded birth of a Lester Ricks around 1920. Sure he was probably born in Paris but Celina probably would have had the birth recorded with the British Consul.

The news on Mauricio Haro isn't worth much. He died in 1968 in São Paulo when he was eighty-three. In an *asilo dos velhos,* a home for the aged, in the Vila Mariana section run by the Jewish community of the city. For the last ten years of his life he suffered from Parkinson tremors. He left no will, mainly because there was no money to speak of. None of the other residents of the home had ever heard him speak of a son and he hadn't had any visitors in more than five years.

Celina's son, Lester, drew another blank. There was an English public school, the Bedford School for Boys in Bedford, but their Old Boys office had no record of anyone named Lester Ricks attending back in the late '20s.

Vogelsang has some stuff on missing-heir hunters. Most of them are small one- or two-man operations. The ones that got bigger went in for finding missing stockholders for corporations. But the ones who stayed on finding missing heirs for a percentage sometimes took on assistants on a purely expenses-and-commission basis. They might give someone a tough case to work on. If he got lucky and unearthed the second cousin of the dead miser and got him to sign the agreement to pay 25 or 30 percent or even 50 percent of the inheritance he was entitled to because of his remote blood kinship, why the apprentice might end up with half of the percentage—and sufficiently encouraged to stay in the business. But few of them did and there was a considerable turnover. A lot of them were floaters by nature. Some of the missing-heir hunters in the New York metropolitan area estimated for Vogelsang that in the past five years they probably had more than twenty people float in and out of their offices trying their hand at the peculiar business. Of these, only three stayed on to become partners in the firm.

The apprentices were on their own pretty much and encouraged to use the long-distance phone. If one of them was really there to find out who were the sons and grandsons of some of the prostitution racketeers, instead of the potential heirs of some female recluse in Washington Heights who died with $82,000 in bank accounts and no known kin, well, he could get away with it for quite a while.

It would take a lot of work, Vogelsang concluded, to try to run down those twenty or so ex-apprentices in the business to see if they had any connection with the *goel hadam.* He didn't think it was a "fruitful area" for us.

What's left? Someone was poking around in the Tampa case but no one there was really interested. As far as the police were concerned Harald Christy's was one of the happier deaths of the year. If someone really helped kill him he deserved a medal of some kind.

More from Paris. Nothing on Celina Ricks in the dead files of the *Sûreté*. Sam's local man suggested that it might have simply gotten lost in the bureaucratic maze but just as likely was the fact that in the '20s and '30s for a surprisingly modest price embarrassing dossiers could be made to disappear from the files.

Again, back to nowhere. Maybe I ought to find out what happened to Sue Vecera, who used to work at the Agency until the recent firings. Her only job was to read every spy novel published in English, French, and German. She used to do brief summaries of the plots but mostly she was looking for gimmicks invented by the author that might be of some use to us. Some novelists are surprisingly inventive and every now and then one imagined a dodge, a gimmick, an approach that *might* be useful in one situation or another. But most of the time they simply reinvented the wheel.

Look, Sue, here's my problem. Given the following elements give me a plot a spy or suspense novelist might come up with. But of course if she could do that she wouldn't be looking for just a *reader's* job in a publishing firm.

Try this. Say around 1912 all the leading Jewish whoremasters of the world gather at a self-defense conference. Perhaps to plan strategy against the vigorous Jewish anti–white-slavery groups or maybe to prepare a common defense against the stronger and more numerous French, Spanish, and Italian whoremasters. When they finish they have a big windup dinner and several toasts later someone proposes a tontine. Everyone puts in a few thousand bucks and the money gets invested in whorehouses; profits are reinvested and held until, say, 1975, when the third generation—the grandsons or granddaughters of the original investors—divide the kitty. *If they're around.* So, if some of the survivors are knocked off one by one, why there's less to divvy. . . . No, it was turning into a Richard Condon plot.

Face it: the old-timers didn't give a good damn about their grandchildren and who would they trust to control the tontine money? This wasn't going to be one of my better days.

Elly Bricha called. She had been back from Brussels a couple of days and Vogelsang had filled her in on the developments. She wanted to congratulate me on the incredible news of the cancer disappearance. I said I was glad she reminded me of important things because I was getting depressed by our almost total lack of progress on the *goel hadam* research; so much so that I had been spending a couple of hours constructing juvenile scenarios to explain it all.

She said perhaps I would be cheered by a small victory dinner in her apartment. It was surely time she repaid my hospitality in London. Great; why didn't I bring some champagne and caviar? A lovely idea, she said, but I should be prepared for a somewhat jumbled apartment. She had only moved in a couple of months ago.

She lived on East Seventy-fourth Street near Madison, a brownstone. Top floor. There was a zebra-design rug on the floor, a large Italian mirror over a deep sofa, an all-wool V'Soske rug on one wall. Japanese dinner plates, Bohemian wine glasses, and a tablecloth based on some Javanese design. On another wall a copy of a turn-of-the-century painting by someone called Steinlen. A young woman in a blue mohair shawl is in the foreground. Dusk in Paris. She has soft reddish hair and piercing hazel eyes. You didn't fool with her. She was counterpoint to a poster next door. It was done in red, yellow, green, brown, black and was apparently designed to sell a book called *La Traité des Blanches*, "Grand Roman Inédit par Début de La Forest." Presumably, the four figures in the poster, three whores and a pimp, represented the world of the white-slave trade, around 1900. In the foreground is the blonde, crying girl, face concealed in her arms. In the middle is the still-battling brunette not quite ready to accept the life. Next to her is the smirking red-haired professional with an uncovered bosom. The pimp is plump, watch-chained, and has a gold-knobbed walking stick. He has small black eyes and he's obviously impervious to the shrieker and the weeper.

Steinlen, Théophile-Alexandre Steinlen, was an old favorite of hers. She discovered him during her first visit to the Petit Palais Museum in Geneva. Steinlen was born in Lausanne and even though he did most of his work in Paris the Swiss regarded him as one of their own. His favorite subjects were cats and the outcast and oppressed. His favorite expression was "The poor are always right."

The white-slave book poster had been suppressed until he agreed to paint black lace over the naked bosom. The original poster was now a rarity and she got a copy for $250 recently in Paris.

"I've come into some money," she explained. "So I decided it was time I left the apartment house I was living in on East Seventy-fourth near First. Too many drug peddlers, pimps, and prostitutes—and airline stewardesses. And finally a shooting. The *Daily News* loved the building."

I opened the iced champagne and she had chopped eggs, onions, and thin squares of toast ready. We drank to my miraculous recovery, to the money she just came into, to solving the *goel hadam* mystery.

She looked at me across her glass. "It's pretty ridiculous, isn't it? We've been circling each other like wary cats for several weeks. It's almost as if there's a line down the middle between us and if either steps over it there's no getting back." She laughed lightly. "Or am I doing away with too many introductory comments too soon?"

I said she had no idea of how she probably struck many men: very attractive, sexy, smart, but a kind of challenge that a lot of men would rather not take up.

"Any one of those qualities most men can handle; maybe any two, but you put the three together and most of them are going to say: Yeah, but she's not for me. But what they really mean is: what if I don't measure up; this one will cut me down. Big-league play or nothing. Which means you've got to be on your guard all the time for the natural bush-league inclinations most of us live by."

She smiled archly: "That's not what held off the self-assured, very experienced Mr. Harry Hanan, the master charmer?"

What held me off, I said, was a different kind of problem. She reminded me in some ways of one of the most satisfying affairs I had, the one with a fellow agent, Joan, an attractive, clever woman who for several years used the cover of a Riviera call girl. "She almost knew me too well; she'd cut through crap quickly and wouldn't go for posturing such as making believe we were in love with one another when we weren't. Yet she was loving, warm, and funny. If I'd had the courage I'd have married her instead of the Agency employee I did but when I looked back I realized that I was a little unsure I could handle Joan on a long stretch. So I copped out and she married a rich German."

She poured more champagne. "This is known as getting naked before taking your clothes off, no?" The laugh led to an embrace and more and we were in bed in a few minutes.

She has a luxurious, tawny body with firm, dark-nippled breasts and a marvelously active sense of sex play. I think it was Henry Miller who once divided women into those with laughing cunts and those with crying ones. Hers laughs. And like me she likes to talk after. Happily, she's not an instructor. Tall women, I've found, sometimes feel they've got to tell you how to work their machinery just so: press A, nibble B, caress C, pinch D. Elly, the love, was willing to trust my instincts. At least the first two times.

By then she had christened my prick "Schublig," which turns out to be a giant Swiss sausage. She said one of her fellow interpreters had once suggested a great test while sucking: could you suck and also say: "She glugged a glut of glottals"? She tried but I settled for glug, glug, and a heavenly suck without sound. I told her of my strange incident at birth: little Harry born with a natural circumcision and if I played my cards right I was destined for messiahdom somewhere. She rose to her knees for a deferential bow: "You are too kind, master, to permit me this honor." When we got over our silly laughs she told me about Countess Castiglione, one of the great nineteenth-century "horizontals," who was given a sugar candy at a banquet. A reporter asked her: "Does madame like to suck?" "Yes," she replied prettily, "but nothing sweet."

After our extended romp—unhurried, deliberate, extended, touching all bases—in-out, up-down, and hardly a "hey, what have we overlooked here," she confessed that I had been enticed to her premises with false promises. I had been seduced with lies: there was no *dinner.* She's a terrible cook so she ordered some epicurean dishes from one of the casserole-kitchen places on Madison but they phoned about five minutes before I got there to say they'd had a fire and there would be no deliveries that night.

"I won't tell you what splendid dishes you've been denied as a result," she teased, "because that would be unnecessarily cruel and besides I really don't remember what I ordered." I said in that case she would have to make the ultimate sacrifice: cannibalism. I ate her again. Delightful wet, warm nourishment. Later, she said she was courageously ready to make more fleshly sacrifices to my overweening hunger. I devoured her very firm nipples and aureoles.

We slept until about 6:30 AM. She was up, brushed her teeth, made some coffee, and roused me. "Wake up. I'm up." She did a takeoff on a small child's peremptoriness and there was no resisting her when she went to work again on Herr Schublig, the roused vanguard of messiahdom. Slow, leisurely, with a few "let's try this and that" and it was 9:30 and I was hungry and she was sleepy again and she confessed that her airy-fairy housekeeping habits had reduced her to only one egg in the refrigerator and only scraps of bread. She was asleep a minute later.

I showered, dressed, rummaged through her purse for the keys, and went down for a little shopping. Eggs, hard rolls, brioches, several cheeses, and bacon. On the way back I passed a hole-in-the-wall locksmith and had him make me a copy of Elly's house-key, which also opened the front door.

We ate—she really wasn't *that* unhandy in the kitchen—and on our new levels began taking stock of each other all over again.

When she was in college, she said, she knew she was never going to marry and naturally began to investigate where it was best to end her days as a spinster. She did quite a lot of research and decided the best place was Denmark. Why?

Well, Denmark had six so-called lay convents where a small number of elderly unmarried women of the right social class could live in great pomp in their own apartments rent-free. But they take no more than twelve women. "You have to be entered for the convents at birth or baptism, when your parents paid a registration fee of five hundred dollars and the girl gets the interest until she marries. She gets insignia and ribbons of the order but she has to give them back when she marries. If she stays single she keeps the ribbons and in later years can live in a moated castle with peacocks on the lawn and a six-room apartment and a coach-and-pair and a liveried coachman to take her shopping."

I said it sounded like Sleeping Beauty without the intervention of the bramble-cutting prince. "I used to love the image," she said dreamily. "A great old lady, honored by all, surrounded by the last trappings of royalty." I said it all had a girlish-dream charm but I just couldn't see her in those surroundings. She raised herself on an elbow and half-smiled: "Just because you've had your way with me, wayward sir, doesn't mean you really know me." It was nicely balanced: not too much serious strain in it. Just enough. I said I really didn't, and this was a good time to learn more.

"More, more, sir?" We were now in our own little Restoration comedy. "More, sir? You devour me. I yield, I vanish. Oh, kind sir . . ." And we started afresh all over again. But I never got more detail.

She was doing a conference in Toronto and at about three Saturday afternoon she started making parting noises. There was some study she had to do, some packing, phoning, and things. We kissed lightly when I left about 3:30.

I walked back to Central Park South gaily, a little light-headed, seeing her translucent image on store windows, on oily patches on the wet street. I even whistled, which I hadn't done since my teens. I played with the wording of the Agency rule on marriages to foreign nationals. You had to resign and then wait forty-five days, during which the alien was checked out thoroughly. *If* she passed you were invited to reapply for your old position.

At the apartment I remembered I had to do something about my suits. I had lost about twelve pounds during the cancer bout. Some of it was coming back but my suits still hung on me a little awkwardly. Several times I had passed a tailor on West Fifty-eighth Street who advertised "Intelligent Alterations." Looking for suits to take down I fingered a pinstripe I had made in London years ago and tried to remember when I had last worn it.

I entered a fugue state for a few seconds and in that subconscious wandering, neurons and synapses connected unexpectedly and the pinstripe became an old French adage you get in school. "If you see a pin and let it lie, you may yet want it before you die."

I came out of it, gazed blankly at the suit and nothing connected. I went to the phone book to get the tailor's name—perhaps a little phone consultation was in order—and while my fingers walked the white pages it bounded through.

Christian Schneider got the code name Taylor. Obvious enough. A *Schneider* is a tailor. And Alexander Rado's code name, Dora, was a simple anagram. But why did Helena become "Leslie"? If you want to stick to the obvious, why wasn't she, say, "Troy" or, anagrammatically, "Leah"? It bothered me enough to start along paths I hadn't explored before.

March 5, 1973. New York.

At the British Information Service Library on Third Avenue they had just what I wanted: a directory of private schools for girls in Britain. There were photos of most of the schools and, happily, an *alphabetical* index, instead of what I feared—listing in descending order from year of founding.

The closest approaches to Gâtebourse's assumed mispronounciation "Bat-fort" were Bedgebury Park School in Goudhurst, Kent, and the Bedferry School in Hampton, Middlesex. And both had been operating in the '20s.

Bedgebury Park was an independent school for girls aged eleven to eighteen, which wasn't good. Gâtebourse recalled the child was away at the school in 1928 when it was only eight at most. Still, the age-admission policy might have changed over the years.

Bedferry School was "founded in 1920 and there are at present 230 places at the school for girls aged seven to eighteen." Much better. "The school is set in its own magnificent 180-acre Park and a very substantial redevelopment program is just being completed. . . . The school offers the accepted academic curriculum to the O and A levels of G.C.E. (Cambridge) and for University entry. . . ." Fees were £425 per term.

I put in a call to one of the numbers Dave Quittle had given me in London. I got him at the second. After the preliminaries—I simply said I was feeling better and doing some personal research—I asked if he was available for a private assignment. In a way, a missing-heir case. But I didn't expect him to do it on a percentage basis because I doubted if anyone was going to come into money. He deciphered me quickly:

"What you need is a private detective, Harry."

Not really, I said. Besides I'd rather pay him the $150 a day and expenses than pay it to a stranger in London. If he was available, he was the ideal man for the job. Better still, there was a $1,000 minimum fee involved even if he did the whole thing in two days.

I hated having to get down to money right away. I owed him too much to ever repay that way, but the transatlantic phone is not made for subtleties.

Finally I said, "Dave, I *need* this help. I hate to ask you for another favor after all you did for me but . . ."

He grunted. "You and the thousand have charmed me."

There were two girls' schools in England. One, Bedgebury Park in Goudhurst, Kent, and the other, Bedferry, in Hampton, Middlesex. He was to call the alumnae offices, the Old Girls Department, and try to find if back in the late '20s they had a student named Leslie Ricks or Leslie Haro. Probably from Paris. If so, do they know what happened to her after she left the school and when was the last time they heard from her.

"If that's all, it's not worth a grand."

"Not all. If either school works out right there will be more. Just phone me collect if you hit pay dirt and I'll give you the next step."

March 6, 1973. New York.

He called at 7 AM. Noon in London.

"Bedferry. She enters in nineteen twenty-eight at eight and stays on until nineteen thirty-seven when she's seventeen. She does fine at school and then goes on to the London School of Economics as a special student. I called the LSE and they had her down okay. She was a student there until nineteen thirty-nine when she wangled a job with the International Labor Office in Geneva."

I said, "Dave, we're onto a winner and we can't quit now. Please fly down to Geneva for me and find out what you can about her at the ILO plus any other personal details."

I added, "Gneigi is still in Berne, isn't he?" He was an Agency friend, which meant he was on the payroll for discreet help in Switzerland.

Dave didn't think *he'd* need our old friend. Why did *I*? "Well, there might be a World War Two intelligence tie-up with our Leslie Ricks."

The expected pause. "Harry, this *is* private business?"

No Agency connection at all; and I was still on sick leave. He'd phone from Geneva. I asked if he needed any upfront money. He said I was good for it.

March 7, 1973. New York.

Dave got me at 7 PM this time, midnight in Geneva.

"Turned out I needed Gneigi after all. Some of his old Bureau Ha friends were helpful."

In 1941 Leslie Ricks, a provisional ILO employee, began an affair with Yves Gameau, whose real name was Ewald Schildkraut. He was a French-German writer. In 1942 when she was already active in the Lucy spy ring she became pregnant. She didn't marry Gameau.

"Why didn't she marry Gameau?" Dave asked. "I was very old-fashioned and curious. Some of Gneigi's friends were helpful. She didn't marry Gameau because when she was six months pregnant she and other members of the Lucy ring suddenly discovered that Gameau, the German Jew, was working for the Nazi *Sicherheitsdienst,* the security service of the SS. He had gone to work for them because they were holding his parents and sister hostage in Germany. Gameau's job was to penetrate the Lucy ring through Leslie Ricks.

"It was too late for an abortion. Instead Leslie arranged a so-called white marriage with a Swiss character named Pierre Bricha who had been through this route before. It cost her three hundred dollars."

He had some trouble running down the marriage certificate because for some reason she married under the name of Helena Ricks and she had been known as Helena at the ILO job. Apparently she stopped using the name Leslie about 1940 when she became active in the Lucy ring.

The ring was broken up in November 1943, when Helena was seven months pregnant. She and the others were jailed but she was released after three weeks and gave birth in December. The child was named Elly.

It should have been a great, terrible surprise but it wasn't. Intuitively, I had been prepared for it. Too many minor tracks were suddenly running into one road.

I could see Dave sporting a crooked smile in Geneva. "That was the nice piece you met in Scott's that night in London?"

He went on. Swiss counterintelligence decided to let her alone even though the others in the ring got several months in prison before they were released. In any case Helena Bricha, née Leslie Ricks, got her old job back in the ILO and took an apartment in Rue Cavour. Gameau disappears, and the best dope the Swiss have is he's killed by the Germans. The little girl is brought up by her mother until 1955 when Helena Bricha dies in an auto accident near Pilatus.

"Okay, now what happens to the motherless twelve-year-old Elly?" Dave asks.

I said I hoped he was about to give me one of the most useful pieces he'd dug up.

"Well, she goes to live with grandma, who is a rich old lady in Nyon, a summer resort on Lac Léman, above Geneva."

Since it almost certainly couldn't be Yves Gameau's mother there was only one possibility. She drops out of sight until 1931 and now after twenty-four years she's the good old grandma in Nyon. Why not?

"Her name is Celina Ricks and she's very proper English. She belongs to the English Genevese Society at two Rue Athénée. She lives in a fine house on the hillside overlooking Lac Léman. She's a great collector of Nyon chinaware, which has had a boom market among collectors in the last ten years. She's also one of those rare Swiss who own Hoffman-La Roche stock, which is now worth about forty-five thousand a share. She bought it back in the mid-thirties apparently and it's almost as good as IBM as an investment."

He anticipated me. "I don't talk to Celina Ricks because she died in Nyon on Christmas Day, nineteen seventy-two, of a coronary embolism. The word around Nyon is that she left about two-and-a-half million Swiss francs—about a million bucks U.S. Her sole heir is her granddaughter, Elly Bricha. So you did have me hunting an heiress after all."

I said this was an heiress with some very peculiar problems. The house, he went on, had already been sold through the *notaire* handling the estate.

Were any of the servants still around Nyon? There had been a *femme de charge*, a housekeeper, who had been with the old lady for the past eighteen years or so. She was now living near Zurich. Her name was Christine Solca and she lived in a suburban section called Dreispitz with a son, who was a coffee-shop manager. The *notaire* paid her off and got her out of the house because she felt Madame Ricks hadn't been generous enough: she's only left her 5,000 Swiss francs, about $2,000, for her many years of service.

Disgruntled servants are traditionally a great source of spiteful gossip and sordid intelligence on the household.

"Want me to talk to her, Harry? You still got a couple days coming on your thousand bucks. I'm starting to get interested in this one."

I said anything he could get on the years Elly was living with her grandmother would be particularly useful. I'd wire him $500 on account care of American Express in Zurich.

March 8, 1973. New York.

I phoned Elly, got her answering service. She was still in Canada but they expected to hear from her in a day or two. I left no message.

The duplicate key was a good fit.

What was I really looking for? Mainly I was trying to construct a profile. A kind of Identi-kit process but instead of using the impressions of witnesses as to what the person *looked* like I would have to depend on the impressions of her belongings, books, stray items, the contents of the closets, drawers. What's she like when she's at home, alone?

And not the nonsense of the differences in women who favor Hermès scarves over Liberty's; the characteristics of those who prefer Joy to Sortilège, Jourdan shoes over Gucci. James Bond could probably tell you but as all the new people at the Farm learn quickly, Bond is a lousy agent; his cover gets broken in the first five minutes of the film. Incidentally, she had no Vuitton bags or Gucci shoes on the premises.

I didn't think concealment wasn't really going to be a problem here.

Still, I went through the motions. The underside of the dropleaf table for papers taped out of sight; the ice-cube compartment; the hollows of two table lamps; the bottom of the Yuban coffee can. All the traditional places of concealment, including, of course, the back of the pictures on the wall, under the area rug, and so on. And just as a tribute to some old training I unscrewed the phone mouthpiece but I really couldn't imagine who would be hot-miking her.

In one of the closets was a rectangular thick package that felt like a framed picture. I opened it and found a very good copy of Pierre-Paul Prud'hon's "Head of Vengeance," from a study of his allegory *Vengeance and Justice Pursuing Crime.* Vengeance didn't look at all like Elly. Also in the closet was a carton tied with twine. In it was a considerable assortment of local guidebooks and Esso maps. Caracas, Los Angeles, Berlin, Tampa, eastern France, Westchester County. And lots of Michelin guides with dog-eared pages. Interspersed were clippings and pages from magazines, a very eclectic mixture. There was a clip from what looked like the *Sunday Times* of London:

George Gissing, who was to contribute generously to the literature of women's rights, actually married a young prostitute with whom he had fallen in love. Gissing regarded her as a victim of society, and he undertook the job of redeeming her but she proved to be crude, unsympathetic and unruly.

A page from an old *Reader's Digest.* An article on spiders, with a section underlined:

Because of the danger, the tarantula male uses caution. He approaches his mate. She rears in hostility. He jumps and pets her. She opens her fangs to bite and poison him; but in a quick maneuver he grabs her fangs with hooks on his front legs and hangs onto them while he deposits the sperm in a pocket in her abdomen. Now he can walk away safely.

A page pulled out of an old issue of *Commentary.* A Jewish scholar named Setzer is speaking:

I have come to the conclusion lately that something which is almost completely evil, or almost without any mixture of good, can exist with a strong will to life. For example, a complete murderer or evil genius can have a powerful drive for life. But I don't think this is the case with a good person. He must have an admixture of evil to live and want to live strongly. If he loses it, he is finished. I know myself that much of my striving and accomplishment and power come from my *yetzer hara,* my evil impulse.

An article from the *Annals of Internal Medicine,* 1971, called "Sudden and Rapid Death During Psychological Stress: Folklore or Folk Wisdom?" The author concluded that a pretty good case could be made for the phenomenon.

A clip from some unidentified paper, probably British:

Brecht's fathers are always corrupt; Galileo, for example, prevents his daughter from marrying and turns her into a spy and informer. Brecht male protagonists are usually drunks, cynics or compromisers; his heroines, such as St. Joan of the stockyards, and Simone Machard, are mostly instruments of salvation.

(I was tempted to phone Professor Shorsh. The stuff would have made his week.)

There were issues of several professional journals. A 1965 issue of the *British Journal of Psychiatry* with an analysis of sixty-six Glasgow murderers. A 1956 copy of the *American Journal of Clinical Pathology* with a heavily underlined article, "Classical Mistakes in Forensic Pathology." From the London *Spectator,* a photostat of a 1937 article, "The Crux of a Murder," which told, with donnish chuckles, how to get rid of a body, chemically. A page pulled out of a May 1965 copy of *Fortune.* It was a whimsical ad by a minor electronics firm which called it a non-ad, a "humorous essay by Alexander King, 'Advice to a Young Woman Who is About to Commit a Murder.'" What was underlined was:

If nothing can deter you it is best for you to proceed in such a manner that your crime will seem justified in the eyes of the community and will be sympathetically condoned by the jury . . . under no circumstances have the assistance of a male accomplice. This always has a bad effect in a courtroom. . . . Think it over. Consider that even if you are acquitted, you might have difficulty in persuading some rather desirable men to spend an evening alone with you. I really think you had better not.

There was another tied carton, labeled "Books." Several were books by and about British coroners, such as the biography of Sir Bentley Purchase; "The Detection of Secret Homicide" by J. D. J. Havard. The dog-eared pages in it were very much to the point: "Killing by obstruction of the air passages may easily leave no signs of violence. This was the method used by the notorious Burke and Hare."

Several old annual reports for the Hebrew Association for the Defense of Girls and Women. A 1906 Emma Goldman pamphlet on "The White Slave Traffic." The proceedings of the International Congress for the Suppression of Traffic in Women, London, 1913. *The American Metropolis*, by Frank Moss, which told about the New York prostitution rackets at the turn of the century.

Diaries, lists, address books? None. It was now about noon and I should be getting a call from Dave in Zurich soon. I put everything back, tied the cartons. I didn't bother wiping prints; I even thought of leaving signs of a nosy presence to give her a warning. Too many variables involved for quick decisions on that so I walked down the stairs and took a cab back to my apartment.

While I was fiddling with the key I heard the phone ring. By the time I got to it the ringing ended and all I got was a dial tone. Thirty minutes later it rang again. This time it was the London operator. Would I take a collect call from a Mr. Samuel Garrett? Dave's cousin, the missing-heir hunter. I said, sure.

He was agitated, querulous, rambling. He knew Sam was doing some work for me in Switzerland. He got a call two hours ago from the Zurich police. Dave had been having a bite in a place called the Silver Kettle, in the arcade tunnel leading to the Hauptbahnhof in Zurich. After a couple of minutes he keeled over. The manager called an ambulance but he was dead on arrival. The hospital he was taken to said he died of a coronary infarction. They found Sam's business card in his brother's wallet and phoned him, as well as the U.S. Consul.

"Listen, Hanan, you didn't do him any favors with that assignment." Why not? "Didn't you know he'd had two minor coronaries before?" I hadn't known. Turned out that was the real reason he left the Inspection Corps, not the RIF-ing instituted by Schlesinger.

Garrett turned a little less hostile. "I guess he didn't like to tell anybody so maybe you couldn't have known." He was trying to reach Dave's divorced wife and daughter in the States to see if they wanted the body shipped home, which would be expensive, or just to London, where he could have it cremated at Golders Green much less expensively. I said he should tell Dave's ex-wife that the funeral expenses would be on me. He had been working for me when he died.

Was the stuff he was working on "sensitive?" Meaning, the kind of thing to induce murdering anybody nosing around? I said I was pretty sure it wasn't that. Besides, a coronary infarction, particularly with a previous history, wasn't to be overlooked just because it was the obvious cause of death. I said Dave was one of the best and I owed him a great deal. I wish I had known about his previous coronaries; I certainly wouldn't have asked him to go to Switzerland for me. "You couldn't have known. He was pretty down hanging around my office here. He didn't know what the hell to do with himself. Your assignment gave him a little excitement and maybe that's the way he would have wanted to go." I asked how his ex-wife and daughter were fixed. He said things weren't too bad. He left a $75,000 policy and his niece was finishing college in June and planned to get married. I said Dave would be missed by a lot of people in the Agency. For a moment I could visualize the little obit notice going up on a lot of the open halves of Agency bulletin boards, the side not hidden by the locked stiff metal shade hiding the covert announcements of current operations and assigned duties.

The notes were still on the pad near the phone. Celina Ricks' housekeeper was a woman named Christine Solca who lived near Zurich in a section called Dreispitz. There was the *notaire* in Nyon, of course, but he'd be damn close-mouthed. Handling the estate would give him a fine $30,000-to-40,000 windfall. No, the disgruntled ex-housekeeper was the best source. The international operator couldn't find a phone number listed for a Christine Solca in or near Zurich so it couldn't be done the easy way. Besides it wasn't the kind of information you could get by phone from a suspicious Swiss in Zurich.

A reservation for the night flight to Zurich was easy but much more difficult was Sam and Vogelsang. Do I tell them now or when I return? Half the world's suspense stories would collapse if only A told B in time; if only X had known *before* what Y knew all the time. Sure, I had a working hypothesis but without any solid evidence; only several wobbly pointing fingers. Still, they *should* know.

Sam's apartment phone didn't answer; neither did the one in Vogelsang's office. Sam's daughter said her father was in Washington for a couple days checking some old files at B'nai B'rith national headquarters but she didn't know where he was staying. Vogelsang's phone on Sutton Place was answered by their housekeeper who said the family was in Baltimore for a niece's wedding that weekend. Clearly, fate didn't intend them to know *yet*. But I had been in the bureaucratic maze too long to disregard the old CYAWP rule: Cover Your Ass With Paper. I wrote a very condensed account of my suspicions and findings in Elly's apartment, put it in a sealed envelope addressed: SAM URDELL, and left it with Patsy, the house doorman. If fate sent Sam by while I was gone he'd get it. Presumably, he'd also get it if I didn't come back.

Much tougher was the problem of very-sick-leave Hanan suddenly popping up in Zurich a day or two after another former employee, David Quittle, dies of a heart attack. It might possibly come out the same David Quittle had been making inquiries of an Agency friend, Alois Gneigi, of a World War II spy ring in Switzerland. Still, Quittle was retired and I couldn't see them pursuing it very energetically. *They* knew he'd had two coronaries before. Some surface cover work could be done. At the Swiss consulate on Madison Avenue they gave me a list of Swiss sanitaria, *Cliniques privées en Suisse*. I introduced myself to the receptionist and then one of the clerks and I managed to leave one of my State Department cards around. At the Swiss Tourist Office on Fifth Avenue I talked to one of the travel experts and asked for driving instructions to two of the clinics I found listed in the booklet. I tried carrying a pale and anxious look. I pestered the clerk at Swissair at Kennedy for superfluous directions of how I would get to the Klinik Notkerianum in St. Gallen, which I simply picked at random. Not much but something. Hanan was Going to a Swiss Clinic. Obviously, he was ready to try anything. I hoped surgeon Andresen could keep his big news to himself for at least another week.

I phoned my lawyer, Russ Conrad, for a little help.

"Where can I get a very brief version of Swiss inheritance law?" He made some interoffice calls and came back: "We have a smart new associate from Harvard Law and he knew that at the back of the *Martindale-Hubbell Law Directory* they run digests of the law of many foreign countries. He's running off a Xerox set on Swiss law for you. You can pick it up in ten minutes if you want or we can send it over." I said I'd come by and there was one other little favor. Could I have a couple of his calling cards? I was going to Switzerland and I might need to have a Swiss lawyer talk to my lawyer. I promised not to use the cards carelessly. "That's okay," he said. "I could always say you took the cards without permission." Only with very well-paying clients did he permit himself such flippancies. I mused a moment on the size of the legal bill the estate would get.

12

March 9, 1973. Zurich.

I'd have three, four hours before jet lag knocked me out in Zurich. I managed to stretch out on several seats in the half-empty plane for about a three-hour snooze. But not before I got in about thirty minutes of the "Switzerland Law Digest" on inheritance. The Swiss have a system of compulsory heirs who cannot be disinherited—parents, brothers, sisters. Most of the work is done by a *notaire* acting as executor for the estate. Illegitimate children inherit on the side of the mother just like legitimate children. I had enough patter if I needed it.

Fortunately, the correct and careful Swiss know there should be a directory for *everyone*, not just owners of telephones, so they have a fine fat volume called *Addressbuch Stadt Zürich*, which lists every street in town with *all* the residents and their occupations on it. Rather like the reverse phone books newspapers and politicians use in the States. Christine Solca, *wwe*, lived at Dreispitz 171. From my primitive German I assumed *wwe* was short for *Witwe,* or widow.

Someone in the tourist desk at Kloten Airport showed me where Dreispitz was on the Zurich map, up in the northeast corner. And it was better if instead of taking the airport bus to the main railway station in town I would simply take a taxi to Dreispitz. Much shorter.

Dreispitz 171 is part of a garden-apartment complex, two-story gray stucco homes built around gardens and walks. Widow Solca lived on the ground floor. She held me at the door while I explained in French that I was from an American law firm representing a potential heir to the estate of Madame Celina Ricks. I flashed one of Russ Conrad's cards. She grudgingly admitted me to a respectably dim living-dining room done mostly in Swedish modern of about thirty years ago.

She was stubby-short, brown-gray-haired, about sixty. Several facial moles. Grim-lipped. The lips made me decide to use Russ' card rather than my State Department one. Money was the lip-opener here; not officialdom.

I explained that Madame Ricks had a half-sister in America who possibly was entitled to a share in the estate under Swiss law even though she wasn't mentioned in the will. I was in Zurich on some other business and thought it might be useful for us to have a talk. Naturally, I'd want to recompense Madame Solca for her time. The lips opened a bit.

"You know how I was treated by Madame Ricks? After eighteen years of faithful service I am left only five thousand francs, less than two hundred seventy-eight francs a year." She had obviously used the figure many times before. "From a Swiss I would not have expected more; but from a wealthy foreigner?"

She'd never heard about a half-sister in America but then Madame Ricks never talked much about her past. And what information could she give me? Naturally, if I was paying her for her time she wanted to feel that she was giving money's worth. I said, yes, I thought she could be helpful. I'd need perhaps sixty minutes or so and in return I'd be happy to pay her 60 francs. It sounded like a very professional rate.

On behalf of our client, I went on, we felt we'd have to make some kind of settlement with the main heir, Mademoiselle Elly Bricha, the granddaughter. It would be useful to learn all about her so that we could negotiate more intelligently when the time came.

I now rated coffee. She had gone to work for Madame Ricks in 1955 shortly after Elly had come to live with her grandmother, following her mother's tragic death. The house in Nyon wasn't small and it required a lot of work. Madame Solca as housekeeper and cook was helped by a part-time handyman and gardener who also did a little chauffeuring from time to time. Later in 1955 the even life in the house was disturbed again when Elly went off to the clinique, the Maison de Santé de la Rochelle.

Such tragedy for a twelve-year-old. But surely it was for the best. The child was filled with such strange fears. Dark, swarthy men were coming to kidnap her and take her abroad. Once she announced over the dinner table that there was a big floating purple ball in the room and soon men would come out of it and drug her and take her away. Once when Madame Solca was walking with the child on the Promenade des Vielles Murailles she insisted that two men were following them and they were going to kill her because she knew their real identity. Nyon, like most Swiss towns and cities, had its permanent corps of professional prostitutes, duly registered with the tax authorities. Little Elly would seek them out and tell them they shouldn't worry. She and Ullalla-Bassissi would be there to help them so they wouldn't be beaten. Madame Solca explained that the permanent Children's Circus in Zurich was called by those nonsense syllables. And of course the teachers at the school complained to Madame Ricks that the child paid no attention in school. There were other incidents. The private clinic was the best answer.

Elly was there nearly two years. There was in the clinic a young foreign doctor—she wasn't sure if he was English or American—but he spoke good French and he was able to help the child recover. Madame would visit the child every week after the first six months. The psychiatrist had recommended that she not visit at all during the first six months.

Did she remember the doctor's name? Oh yes, Dr. Hug. Dr. Ernest Hug. I was taking lots of notes, mainly to assure Madame Solca that her information was indeed worthwhile.

Did Madame Ricks have many visitors from abroad, perhaps? Occasionally. Some French-speaking; some English. People of Madame's age. Also someone may have been a French dealer who discussed Madame's valuable collection of Nyon chinaware which was displayed in fine cases in the living room and dining room.

When the child came home from the clinic permanently—she had been coming home for weekends about two months before that—she seemed changed. Quite subdued but no more fantasies. And she didn't have to be reminded to take her two pills every day. She was behind in her studies but caught up very quickly. She had no friends but read greatly. Then at eighteen she went off to Geneva University and lived at a student dormitory. She'd come back to Nyon perhaps once every two weeks. Madame had been proud of Elly's achievements as a much-in-demand simultaneous translator.

Was Madame disappointed that Mademoiselle Elly hadn't married? No great-grandchildren for her sunset years? Madame long ago made it clear she didn't really like children.

Did Madame Solca know by some chance if Dr. Hug was still at the clinic? Oh, no. He left about six months after Elly was discharged. She remembered because Madame Ricks gave him a small farewell dinner. She didn't know where he had gone.

Where he had gone was another clinic, this one near Clarens. A call to the Society of Swiss Psychiatrists located him quickly. I didn't want to phone him to set up an appointment. Psychiatrists are professionally reluctant to talk of ex-patients by name, even those of eighteen years ago. Surprise might work for me. I went back to the airport, retrieved my bag, and got on a Geneva flight.

Clinique Lac Léman, said the gilt letters on the ironwork arcade leading to the two-story light gray stone chalet. It looked like a second-class Swiss hotel. Inside, two white-jacketed young women were busy in the front office. As I came in, a duffle-coated middle-aged Englishman was mildly protesting the size of his bill. While I was being led to a pale-green waiting room I heard an American voice coming from one of the private rooms opposite: "Say, nurse, I get one needle or three today?"

I sent one of my State Department cards to Dr. Hug. He came into the waiting room after ten minutes and asked what he could do for me. About six foot, pear-shaped, huge. Hooded eyes, flapping ears. Late forties, early fifties. The voice was friendly. It was also, after all these years, still American.

He took me to his fairly large office. I explained that a former patient of his was being considered for a sensitive job by the U.S. State Department and we were anxious to know more of a psychotic episode she had as an adolescent. Her name was Elly Bricha and she had been a patient of his at the de la Rochelle Clinic about eighteen years ago.

He was routinely suspicious. Wasn't that the kind of thing the FBI did? Yes, but this was a special case for various reasons. The government would be grateful for his cooperation.

He considered my card a few seconds and then broke into a weak smile. "I'm stalling because I got a bad conscience on that case. I kept notes on it for years and I kept telling myself that I ought to do a paper on it but I never did and then I got into this"—he hand-described an arc above his head—"and I just forgot about it. How is she now?"

She was fine, and living mainly in New York. She traveled a lot, doing simultaneous translating at international conferences. No, she wasn't married.

Since the case had personally affected him and his professional career he thought I ought to be filled in a little. I sensed talking about himself was a form of revving-up for a more difficult talk about Elly Bricha.

He came from southern Wisconsin, which was still a Swiss enclave of sorts. His father was a Swiss engineer. Young Hug went to the University at Madison but wasn't much of a student until his senior year when he decided he was going to be a doctor, a psychiatrist.

"In the Thirties a lot of kids decided to become doctors because they got inspired by Sinclair Lewis's *Arrowsmith* or de Kruif's *Microbe Hunters.* Me, I was motivated by *The Snake Pit,* read while I was in college. I'd become an enlightened psychiatrist and clear up those terrible conditions in mental hospitals. Not likely. I was a college jock and not the smartest kid in the Deke house and I couldn't get into med school—not with a C-plus average and low boards. So I was shipped off to my father's sister in Lausanne and I got into their med school. While I was there I became friendly with a Swiss and I ended up marrying his sister when I graduated. I brought her over with me when I did a residency in Central Islip State Hospital on the Island—half the psychiatrists in the world probably did time there—and we hung around long enough for me to pass my American boards. But my wife was getting restless for Switzerland. I kept telling her two hundred thousand Swiss were happy *outside* Switzerland, they must know something. That in Switzerland I'd always be a *frömde Fötzel,* a bloody foreigner. But she wanted back and my brother-in-law kept writing me of opportunity lying around there for a French-speaking American-boards psychiatrist and all about the great psychiatrists who had come out of Switzerland like Forel, Bleuler, Jung, Rorschach, and von Monakow. Why was I being so stubborn? Well, by then I knew the cleanup of the snake pits wasn't something I really had the stomach for. So when my brother-in-law asked me to come back to join him in operating a small mental clinic, La Rochelle, I took him up. We came back and stayed."

Their present clinic was a busy competitor of the Niehans operation a few miles up the road. "We're in the youth business here. We inject living cells prepared from the unborn offspring of freshly slaughtered sheep. It revitalizes a lot of people and it also makes a lot of money. As far as I can tell it doesn't do anyone any harm and there's a chance it does them some good. Sure I still practice a little psychiatry around here; these people have lots of other problems that led up to why he can't get it up and why she's dry and why they have flashes and miseries and so on."

He decided to get out of straight psychiatry and into what he called placebo psychiatry—"a third of all patients will react favorably no matter what if you tell them it's a new magic cure"—partly as a result of his experience with Elly Bricha.

"Actually, she was one of my first big successes. She came along just at the right time so I was a hero. Her grandmother brought her in, if I remember, early in nineteen fifty-five. A year before, Jean Delay and Pierre Deniker, two French psychiatrists, reported great results using chlorpromazine on psychotics, particularly young schizophrenics. I tried it on Elly and she responded beautifully. She was still getting the disturbing stimuli schizos get—the purple balls floating in the room with tiny people; the secret radio messages, the electrified telephones, and so on.

But on the phenothiazines the stimuli were pushed way in the background, like an annoying buzz saw now operating two miles away. You know it's there but it doesn't bother you."

He gave me an appraising look while his huge lips made a lopsided oval. "She had been okay since? No episodes or violent incidents?"

What did he mean? I asked with a smidge of surprise.

He was a little uncomfortable. "Sounds like a stupid question. If she had you wouldn't be here finding out about her for a sensitive job, would you?" But something was nagging him; he had to nail it down. "She hasn't killed anybody, has she?"

I said: "She must have been some case!" I didn't want to have to start lying to him so soon.

He let me get away with it. "Schizophrenia is a humbling business for the psychiatrist. Every ten years or so some big shot comes out and says, 'We're really standing at the beginning of a new era of research and understanding of the disorder.' And the next ten years proves he's wrong."

Roughly one out of every hundred people in Western society, he went on, becomes schizophrenic sooner or later. There were about two, three million American schizos and proportionately fewer in Europe, where they use tougher standards, so a lot of U.S. schizos would be labeled as "severe emotional problems" in Europe. Still, in both places the end results are the same with the adolescent schizos: a third got better, a third remain the same, and a third get worse. They were still arguing if it was inherited, if it was caused by family interactions or what some of them called the double-bind message: your voice says you love me; your stance shows hatred toward me. With such confusion all around a lot of kids run into a fantasy world with its own crazy rules so they know where they stand.

Elly's case was stranger than most. "You know the drugs we use on the schizos don't cure them. It helps them become more functional, concentrate better, adjust more normally. Some patients get better *without* drugs. No one knows why."

Like all schizos little Elly had her own fantasy world: paranoia, hallucinations, delusions, terrible anxiety, and frequent emotional outbursts. But she had some unusual factual components to exacerbate matters.

"I'd see her about an hour a day. I'm not a Freudian so I was never analyzed but sooner or later you pick up their psychoanalytical wavelengths just as they pick up ours. With the medication I could get her to talk. First, about her father. About six months before her admission to the clinic she found out from her mother that her father was not the supposedly dead Bricha but a traitorous German Jew who betrayed her mother and her friends. Something to do with Communists, I think. Well, that was a helluva trauma for the kid. Her mother had all kinds of surprises for little Elly. She didn't like her to see Grandma Celina anymore because she was a bad person, who had done terrible things, unspecified. You tell that to a youngster you're bound to arouse active curiosity. So Elly is off first chance to grandma's house—her mother allowed her to visit a couple of times a year—to confront the old lady. 'Grand-mère, mama says I shouldn't have anything to do with you because you're bad and did terrible things.' "

Grandma curses her disloyal daughter, calls her a Communist fool, and then takes the child to her and cries and cries and says yes, yes, it's all true. I was a terrible person but I couldn't help it because awful men made me do it.

What she told the child, Hug recalled, sounded like a replay of that old white-slave-trade classic, *The Road to Buenos Aires*. She was an innocent girl from the midlands of England who was seduced into a life of prostitution by wicked men from Paris and Argentina. They forced her into a life of degradation. She was able to break out by killing her chief oppressor and afterward she was able to build a respectable life of her own.

"That's a helluva emotional load to put on a kid but somehow Elly asked her grandmother about her husband, Elly's grandfather. All she got was that he, too, was a terrible person, one of her oppressors. So by the end of that emotional teary session what the kid has is that (a) her father was a weak man, a Jew, working for the Nazis, who betrayed his friends and comrades, and (b) her maternal grandfather was a man who betrayed young women and forced them into a hateful life of prostitution.

"Elly's mother is dead and her grandmother is now her guardian and when she comes for visits I discuss guardedly some of the child's 'fantasies' about her father and grandfather. Madame Ricks said they weren't all fantasies. As she put it: 'The men in our family have been weaklings and worse.' About this time there's a big thing in the States with family therapy in which you got the schizoid patient and his entire family together to let it all come out, accusations, blame, charges, so that the therapist sitting in on the session can see the direction of forces that worked on the patient. But I'd never done it and I really didn't think I could mediate a session between grandma and grandchild because there simply was too much here I didn't know about. Also, the girl was getting better on medication and I didn't want to press my luck."

Elly finally went home in 1957 and she knew she'd have to take the chloropromazine tablets for a long time, possibly the rest of her life. If she stopped, the hallucinations and the strange commands from the purple balls floating in the room would commence again.

The last time he saw her was in 1963 when she was a student at the University of Geneva. He was in town for a meeting of the Society of Swiss Psychiatrists and he ran into her near the old League of Nations building. "She had become very pretty and I asked how things were. She was busy at the university and was using the League library a lot because she was doing a thesis on the League's efforts to control the white-slave trade in the Twenties. Her grandmother was in good health and she saw her every few weeks and she now found that she didn't need the pills anymore. And no hallucinations or purple people.

"I should have walked away from the encounter congratulating myself on a remarkable patient recovery, one of the blessed thirty-three percent who make it out of schizophrenia as good as before or even better. But I was uneasy. The girl was operating with great screens that I couldn't penetrate, certainly not in a ten-minute talk. There was something in her still that worried me."

The doubts he had about the case, and a lot of others, made it easier for him to join his brother-in-law in their present clinic operation with cell therapy for worried middle-aged men and women, trying to delay the onset of age and its attendant problems.

"I keep up with the literature on schizophrenia and they're arguing the same old points, only with more vehemence: genetic origins, family psychopathology, vitamin therapy; and why one kid in the family is hit and not the others. In short, we're still floundering around in a rough, improvised craft on a sea of ignorance. Very discouraging."

We had coffee, brought in by one of the white-coated women clerks, and he was consciously assessing me.

"I've almost certainly violated several professional-ethical codes in talking to you so freely about a patient—without her permission. Particularly," he grinned, "when I find it hard to believe she's being considered for a sensitive post with the U.S. State Department." Well, he didn't say *directly* I was a liar.

"My excuse, I suppose, is that I've long wanted to talk to an outsider about the case. It's always troubled me. You think you can tell me what's really up?"

You improvise. Elly was involved in an intense relationship with an important U.S. public figure, a high elected official. The man was married, I said, and there were all sorts of complications setting in. His work was beginning to be affected and some reporters were starting to get wind of it. It was important to find out much more about her, if for nothing more than to find out if she was working for the Russians, perhaps.

I don't think he really believed me but it was for the moment a socially acceptable way out for both of us.

Of course, it was time for the great courtroom hypothetical question, the kind the DAs and defense attorneys rehearse in murder cases with insanity defenses. "Now, doctor, given a patient with the symptoms, etiology, and prognosis you've described: is it possible such a patient although seeming to have a total recovery could still be disturbed enough inwardly so that she carries through a series of deliberate, cold-blooded murders in several countries? Is it possible that such a patient could be motivated to thinking that she owed it to the tens of thousands of innocent women who had been abducted or seduced into involuntary prostitution, into a modern form of slavery, far from their homes and families, to destroy the males involved; if not them, their sons, or even their grandsons? Is it possible, doctor, and on and on. . . ."

The trouble with such hypothetical questions is, of course, that they are made up of answers, which I wasn't prepared to provide. Whether *he* thought it possible for such patient to have done such-and-such under certain circumstances didn't matter that much anymore. I knew she had.

I promised to let him know what the final outcome was. I took a room in a hotel in Clarens and slept twelve hours.

13

March 11, 1973. New York.

Before leaving Geneva I phoned the U.S. consulate in Zurich. I was a relative of David Quittle's. Had the body been flown to the States? Yes. Were the police certain that the cause of death was a heart attack? No doubt. Because Mr. Quittle had been a former government employee a special pathology report had been prepared. A copy had been sent to Mrs. Quittle.

The only useful part of the return trip was a *New York Times* copy of Saturday, March 10, a stew let me have. I turned the pages with little comprehension until I came to a half-page ad for the *New York Times* cookbook. I kept looking at the ad and wondering why I did. I don't like to cook and I'm not an epicure. What held me on the ad? An annoyingly wispy, wobbly image floated through. I was in a kitchen with a *New York*

Times cookbook and there was something wrong with it. The image grew a little sharper. But I still couldn't see what was out of place. The book still had its dust jacket and didn't seem overly used. But there was a bulge behind the front cover. Some clippings were stored there higgledy-piggledy. So what. My mother kept recipes that way in the Rombauer cookbook. Millions of women do—the millions who don't have neat little index-card boxes for new recipes or careful file folders marked: SOUPS, DESSERTS, and so on.

And Elly? An indifferent cook by her own admission, someone who really wasn't happy in a kitchen or fooling with the oven. Would she collect recipes from newspapers and magazines? A hope chest? Silent pledges to change, become interested in cooking? Out of character.

The answering service said she was still out of town and expected back Wednesday.

The book, the only cookbook in the kitchen, was resting on a small shelf above the built-in dishwasher. The front was as I had recalled: random recipes from newspapers and magazines. They had been torn out boldly and erratically, not neatly excised by scissors. And between them was a collection of Robert Carrier Cookery Cards ("Cakes, Sweets & Puddings"). Each was about 4 × 6 with rounded corners, and numbered. The numbered front of each card had an enticing color shot of the dish and the reverse carried the ingredients necessary and the recipe. Below that was two or three inches of blank space. And on all of the cards the blank space had been used for sets of cryptic notes.

Assume the cards' numerical system corresponded to the *goel hadam* note numbering. Mine was 13. Number 13 on the cookery cards was Pears in Pastry Sabayon and they looked very tempting. The back of the card had in tiny, almost indecipherable, writing:

> Max Hanan (x) (df)
> Robert (x)
> Warren (x)
> Harry (!) Memorial ca 1/7/73
>   Dilau 1/19

Most of it seemed fairly simple. The (x) following the name clearly meant a dead Hanan. The (!) following mine looked like sign language for strike. The dates: I entered Memorial on January 7. "Dilau" surely meant Dilaudid and the poisoning attempt on January 19.

Tougher was the (df) following Max Hanan, the evil progenitor. I played with various possibilities. The strongest was that (df) referred to some specific file. Presumably not in the apartment itself or then why have two sets of information around? If I were doing it I'd keep the family dossiers in a safe deposit box.

Card number 15, Fruit Medley. That should correspond to the death of Harald Christy in Tampa, which I assumed was only intended to divert our thinking and interfere with any linkage we might have worked up by then. The back of the card showed a sparse, cryptic humor. There were no penned notes, no genealogies or (x)s or (!)s. Just a penned, heavily shaded drawing of a duck. A black decoy.

What about 16, Pineapple Peach Cobbler? The victim we hadn't heard about yet. His name was Lewis Franklin and he was descended from Morrie Franklin, who was dead, and from Julius Franklin, also dead. Next to Julius Franklin's name the file code was (rg) (chi). Lewis Franklin with the (!) after his name also had another clue attached. It went: Tor but 1st tue bran. wh. ok.

She had a calendar on a teak desk—no entries beyond conference jobs —and in March the first Tuesday was March 6, two days hence. I took the cooking cards, and closed the apartment.

Home by 5 PM. I phoned Sam, back from Washington. I said I thought we needed an emergency meeting that evening at my apartment. I knew who the next victim was going to be. Was Vogelsang back? He ought to bring him. Say 8 PM. Sam had one question:

"I got a hunch," he said, "and if it's as good as I think it is I ought to get credit. Somebody out of a Chicago family?" I said he must have been doing some real deep research at B'nai B'rith headquarters in Washington. While waiting I ordered some pastrami sandwiches and an order of onion rings from the deli. I put a bottle of Asti Spumante in the freezer compartment. It was the last of my brother's stock. He would drink anything. Just as I eat anything.

Where was Lewis Franklin? tor . . . The gazetteer in the back of my brother's dictionary had a lot of "tors," including Torgau (E. Ger.), Torino (It.), Toro (Spain), Torquay (Eng.), Torrance (Calif.), Tornio

(Fin.). But the best bet for us was surely Toronto (Ont.). Isn't that where Elly was on a conference job? Assume Toronto. But on the first Tuesday of every month Lewis for some reason goes to bran wh. ok. Back to the gazetteer. Disregard the Brandenburg (E. Ger.) and the Brandvlei (S. Afr.), and Brandon (Eng.), which left Brandon (Man.) and Brantford (Ont.).

Brantford, a big manufacturing center, southwest of Hamilton, had twice the population of Brandon, a prosperous farm and manufacturing center. It could be either but the odds would be on Brantford, only 50 miles away; Brandon was some 1,400 miles distant. The other distinction had to be the "wh. ok." Ok was okay, yes, sure, of course. What else? Get cute. Ok is also oke which is also oak. So "wh." might be "white." A hotel or motel named White Oak?

The information operator said there was no White Oak motel or hotel in or around Brantford. The Manitoba operator said there was a White Oak in Brandon and gave me the number. I phoned, asked the desk clerk if they had a reservation for Lewis Frankin for Tuesday. He checked. Yes, Mr. Frankin was due Tuesday.

I rehearsed my condensed version of the events, the items that pointed to Elly. What wasn't so easily resolved was: do I tell Sam and Vogelsang I slept with her? Or do I simply leave my getting into her apartment one of those surreptitious skills Agency people are supposed to have. I'd leave it to the mood at the time. If you overwhelm people with fascinating detail a lot of necessary questions sometimes don't get asked.

They came within a few minutes of each other and took in the great park and skyline evening view from the fourteenth floor. I had become so accustomed to it that I almost forgot the giddy wonder it induced on first sight on a clear winter night.

I had the percolator going and I brought out Scotch, brandy, and soda and ice. Hanan the Handy Host. We got settled and I gave them my little précis. There were ten seconds of explosive silence.

Vogelsang came out of it first. "Elly! I wanted to marry her. I was going . . . You sure? Elly, a crazy killer?"

I said I knew it was hard to accept. All of us had grown very fond of her but after all, I was the one she had tried to kill. I was sure.

Just as they were turning on me for a "Hey, what's this?" I remembered I'd never told them about the poisoning attempt and I provided the details and a half-hearted apology for not telling them earlier. Sam said, "What else you holding back?" I said that was it.

Sam came on. "It adds up, more or less. At the very least she's a very real possibility, you gotta see that, Peter."

Vogelsang nodded sadly. "I *see* it. I can't *believe* it."

"All right," Sam went on. "Let's play it as if she's the one for a little while. Who's next on her list?"

I explained how I come up with the name of Lewis Frankin, who was due to get it, probably, in the White Oak Motel in Brandon, Manitoba, on Tuesday when he went there for his monthly visit. I hadn't been able to check him out—probably Sam could get some phone answers from Toronto contacts on Monday—but my hunch was he was a successful Toronto businessman with a plant or branch office in Brandon. One he visited once a month or so. Why was she planning to do it there rather than on his home grounds of Toronto? My hunch was it was the same kind of operation she pulled on the first known victim, Howard Lucksig, the California accountant who was found drowned in his hotel bathroom in Los Angeles while he was at a convention.

"Men at conventions are particularly vulnerable and easy," I went on. "An attractive women who doesn't look like a hooker lets herself get picked up, not too easily. She gets him to his room. They fool around. She suggests a bath together, some new sex wrinkle maybe, and after he gets in the tub she suddenly raises his knees. His head stays under a few minutes and then she lowers his knees. She dries, tidies things up, wipes surfaces, takes the extra glass and so on, and beats it. She's probably going to pull the same thing in Brandon. It would be a little harder for her to pull it on his home ground, Toronto."

Vogelsang walked a little unsteadily to the bathroom and we heard him heave a few times. Sam and I looked at each other, uncomfortably, and we waited for Peter's return. He came back with a towel around his neck. "I'm sorry. The image of her killing him made me puke." He looked at me sourly. "I think I'd give a hundred thousand dollars right now to prove you're a goddam liar."

I said I knew a little how he felt. I was glad I'd chosen the more aseptic version of how I managed to get into her apartment.

"When you two youngsters are over your wounded egos or secret lusts," Sam said, "we can talk about some tough decisions that have to be made pretty fast."

Vogelsang looked puzzled. "What's to decide? If Hanan's right"— I'd been Harry to him for two months and now I was back to a colder Hanan—"if he's right all we have to do is call the DA, tell them what Hanan's got on Elly and they arrest her, indict her, and that's it."

Sam gave him his sad, idiot-child-of-mine look. "Let me handle this, Harry. He's still mad at you.

"Vogelsang, my friend and fellow *apparatchik*, there are a few unpleasant facts of life lying around we better take a painful look at right away."

Peter sat upright in the velvet lounge chair. The look on his face was one he probably last used when, long ago, an important client explained why he was leaving for another ad agency.

"First off, the evidence Harry gathered here and abroad makes a good case to me. It adds up—a little cockeyed here and there—but it adds up. But I'm not the cops or the DA or Interpol or what have you. *Legally*, you couldn't make a case against Elly that would stand up against an ounce of Jello. Sure, we could draw up a time-chart showing she was in certain cities at certain times. Great. But so were thousands of others. How do you prove legally she had anything to do with those deaths? Two, three, four years later you start looking for eyewitnesses?

"Second off, we're lucky we can't make a case against her that would stand up because that would mean having to go to court, which is the last place we want to be with this *goel hadam* thing. She gets tried for murder—and try to figure out which murder in which country?—and it's all got to come out: why she felt she had to kill the male descendants of the despoilers of nice Jewish girls. What a show trial that becomes! She becomes a Cause. Women's libbers get in the act. And all the professional anti-Semites and a dozen top criminal lawyers who could use more publicity get on stage. We get that and our bosses, the Committee people, would be justified in having us excommunicated, for starters."

Vogelsang rumbled a *cri de coeur:* "She gets away with it?"

Sam got up to look at the park admiringly. *"That's* a city," he said, turning back to face us. "Now we get down to primitive tribal customs.

Either of you two *boychicks* fraternity men at college?" Only Vogelsang;
he was a Beta Sig at NYU.

"Good," Sam went on. "You took an oath, brotherhood and all that;
grips, pledges?" "The usual," Vogelsang said, puzzled.

"What we got to do here is start a new very small little fraternity.
Only the three of us are eligible. And the first thing we have to do is
make sure we can *trust* one another all the way."

Vogelsang's puzzlement was leading to annoyance. "What the hell
you getting at?"

It was time another heavy got in the act.

"Remember, Peter, the first time we met at your office? I got the *goel
hadam* note and was puzzled and then annoyed at all the mystery and
the cloak-and-dagger stuff and you said, 'Trust me, Hanan, *we're all on
the same side.*' "

He nodded.

"What Sam's getting at, and we didn't rehearse this, is we've got to
make sure we're still on the same side. Because now we decide on action
and it looks like we're not going to be able to agree maybe we ought to
split up."

Vogelsang Came to Realize, as they used to say in the movies.

"What we're going to do about Elly?" I said that was a big part of
it.

"But who says *we* decide? Don't we take all this to the Committee,
pour it all out, and let *them* decide?"

Heavy number 1 got back in the ring: "There are thirty people on the
American Hebrew Leadership Council. Six are on the subcommittee we
report to. The ones who know all about the *goel hadam* up to date.
They're very busy men. It would take, easy, a week to get them together
for a few hours' talk. By that time another miserable descendant is
knocked off. Also, I was given private instructions by the Committee
chairman: the faster and the *quieter* this thing was *re*solved—and not
just solved—the better all around. To me, that means we don't go on
the *David Susskind Show* to argue pros and cons."

Vogelsang asked another foolish question and I was beginning to
write him off totally. He was also breathing a little too heavily. "You got
that in writing, Sam?"

Sam opened his arms to the ceiling. What do you do with *Idioten?*

"You're chairman of the committee, *you* put that in writing?"

Vogelsang wanted to suggest phoning the chairman but he also sensed that if he did he was out of our little fraternity, uninvited to the special party.

Sam gentled his voice for a new tack. "There's another way out, Peter. You leave now and as far as Harry and I are concerned you never attended this meeting. Maybe it's better that way. You're married, respectable, you got money, and this isn't something you should be involved in from here on in. Harry and I are single and not very respectable in a lot of ways. Your job was coordinator of all the efforts to find out who or what was behind the *goel hadam*. Okay, we think we found out. So your official job is over."

I fixed myself a drink. I didn't want to watch Vogelsang go through the struggle.

Finally. "I can't bow out now. I'm the one who brought Elly into the inner circle."

That kind of absolution was easy. "Harry and I are the only ones who know *that*. It doesn't have to go further."

He didn't want absolution—or an out. "*I* know. I started on this and I'd like to finish." He was either quite admirable or he really hadn't thought the problem through to the end.

Sam threw me a quick look: we still push him out?

One final try. "If you're in, Peter, the ground rules have to be clear. Majority rule. Sam and I can outvote you and you'd be bound by that."

"I know. I'm still in."

A random, unkind thought filtered through. Maybe, just maybe, he'd really like to see Elly punished for having turned him down once. But I really didn't think that was it.

Ground rule number 1, Sam said, was, we're operating now on our own, which means no phone calls to committee chairmen and, of course, no phone calls to Elly Bricha.

Sam had to say that, of course, but I winced empathetically with Peter. He nodded. "Nobody gets phoned. Period."

Ground rule number 2 would have to be decided quickly.

"We got to stop Elly from knocking off Frankin, who's number sixteen or so on her little list. No debate on that?" Peter nodded.

"Okay, we stop the killing and then what? What do we do with our little murdering *mishugeneh?* Any ideas, Peter?"

He had one. "Maybe we get her committed for a long time so she can't kill anymore?"

Sam grinned crookedly. "You want the ACLU down on us? On what ground we get her committed? As far as the world is concerned, what's she done that's crazy and committable? She works hard, travels, is now worth a million bucks or so, and she's very attractive.

"Go further. Say Harry is able to twist that psychiatrist's arm in Switzerland. He takes his professional life in his hands, comes forward, and testifies when she was twelve little Elly Bricha had a schizophrenic breakdown but recovered two years later. There are hundreds of thousands of adults around the world who had schizophrenic breakdowns and are now okay."

Reluctantly, Vogelsang admitted maybe that wasn't such a good idea. But in a minute he had another.

"We confront her with the evidence, the cards and the funny coincidence of all her trips and the killings. We ask her to sign a solemn pledge to end the murders. We also get her to give us a signed confession. If she breaks her word we turn the confession over to the police and the DA"

Sam's face said, this hurts me almost as much as it will you:

"So we give her another free bite. And that lets all hell break loose. The next dead man's family comes after us. Yah, you stupid bastards knew this nut was a killer and you didn't do anything about her, worse, you kept quiet, so not only are we gonna sue you and your Committee for everything you got but we're asking the DA to prosecute all of you on the ground you had knowledge of a homicide about to be committed and you kept your dumb mouths shut."

Now in a very tight corner, Vogelsang still had the guts to say the dirty words. He looked at both of us, a child's appeal.

"Then the only thing left . . ."

Sam put an arm around his shoulders. "It's easier in the movies. Sam Spade tells Bridget O'Shaughnessy he's turning her over to the cops for his partner's murder but maybe she'll be out in ten years with a little luck and he'll be waiting for her. Didn't Mary Astor say, oh, it's so unfair or something?

"You met my grandson, the one at Yale Law? I'm out there a couple weekends ago and he's home with a little ethical problem for me. It bears on our little tussle here, Peter. Called the Case of the Spelunkean Explorers and it was invented by a Harvard law prof. One time another every law student gets to crack his brains on it.

"Five young explorers are trapped in a cave and cut off from the outside. They have food and water for five days only. A rescue party taps a message through the thick wall between them and tells them they'll break through but it'll take ten days. And the kids don't have enough food. What to do? Well, they're very realistic and one of them says we'll throw dice to see which one of us will be killed in order to feed the rest until the rescue party breaks through. They're about to throw dice to see which one gets it when the one who originally suggested it says, now, I got a terrible hunch it's gonna be me so I want no part of it. But the other four roll the dice anyway and sure enough the lad who wanted out is it. He's killed and eaten and the other four are finally saved. Okay, you're the defense attorney, make your case for them at the trial."

I made it more personal. "Peter, she *did* kill your old army buddy, Monash. Even if she tried to make it look like suicide."

He was still fighting. "You're *sure?* You saw him pushed out the window?"

Sam looked at his watch. "It's getting late and I need my beauty sleep. You have a *useful* alternative, Peter?"

Shaking his head, Vogelsang hung on: "She just disappears? What's the CIA vocabulary? Termination with extreme prejudice?"

I said: "All the years with the Agency this was the first time anyone *really* tried to kill me. Peter, I like her a lot. And so do you and so does Sam but what the hell else can we do? She's a perambulating menace, a time bomb going off every few months. She's only thirty and she could go on this way for the next thirty years. God knows how many little genealogical dossiers she's got hidden away in some vault; for all we know she's still adding to the list."

Vogelsang went for his coat. He'd aged a few years. "All right, I agree. You don't need me for details. But I'm in it. The three of us unanimously agree." He shook hands solemnly and left.

Sam slapped his forehead. "I forgot to tell him what a smart kid I was down in Washington, how I figured out sooner or later the next *goel hadam* victim was going to be someone named Frankin."

I said I didn't think Vogelsang really cared any more but *I* was interested.

The Max Hanans of Chicago around the turn of the century were Julius and Lewis Frankin, brothers. They were kings of the West Side Levee. As one report had it:

This public emporium of immorality and degradation exists by virtue of a regularly organized "protective association" whose members laugh at law, successfully defy those who have tried to cope with them, and, through some mysterious influence, are enabled to continue their traffic with a license and abandon that makes the West Side Levee an open brothel.

But Julius Frankin, unlike Max Hanan, was a hypocrite. He was the president of a congregation on Twelfth and Union streets. The man who broke up the racket and got Frankin ousted from the synagogue was a determined B'nai B'rith national president, Adolf Kraus, a prominent Chicago lawyer. He was helped a lot by Rabbi Emil G. Hirsch of Temple Sinai who delivered several thundering sermons on the subject. And the *Jewish Daily Forward*, which ran several exposés. One of them went, partly:

Julius Frankin, self-confessed owner of disorderly houses, is the head of a Jewish congregation! . . . A Jewish synagogue, a holy temple, which should be the cleanest, the loftiest, the most beautiful place and institution in our lives—such an institution gives away its most honorable rank and post to a man who lives on the money earned by girls and women reduced to the dregs of humanity. . . .

Sam had been dipping into the B'nai B'rith Chicago records and clippings because "I was wondering how come we had no Chicago descendants on the list. I knew the place was second only to New York in the organized prostitution setup. There, like New York, the Jews were paying off to corrupt *goyishe* police inspectors and prosecutors. Well, they cleaned it up for a while but then Capone's mob got in and started it all over again but this time the Jews were pretty much out of it, like in New York."

Sooner or later, he knew the *goel* would get around to the descendants of the Frankins and he did some genealogical work on his own from Washington. Julius's son, Morrie, was so ashamed of the notoriety he moved his family to Toronto. He started a building-supply firm which his son, Lewis, took over and expanded. They have branches in Brandon and Winnipeg and Lewis visits both once a month. Lewis is forty-six, married, and has two kids. From people Sam talked to in Toronto he's on the up-and-up and a very solid citizen.

I congratulated Sam on his prescience. Now we had to get down to specifics: how to save Lewis Frankin from being killed in Brandon and how to stop Elly, the self-appointed Avenging Angel.

The simplest, we agreed, was also the trickiest. Sam, somehow, persuades Lewis Frankin to skip his trip to Brandon *this* month. Get him to New York for a vague, big deal in building materials? Tell him the whole story and have him stay in Toronto an extra week? Both had too many problems attached.

If Frankin goes to Brandon, obviously one or both of us would have to be on the scene to save his life, *quietly*. Long ago the idea of calling the police in had been discarded. His habit of staying at the White Oak made things fairly manageable. We could use that fact just as Elly intended to.

If the Frankin death was averted—without his even knowing he had been a marked victim—that left us with the final problem: our much-traveled *goel hadam*. She had to be killed in a way that didn't make too much fuss, cause too much investigation. For example, it had to be done in such a way that Frankin wasn't suspect. If she worked it her usual way there was a good chance someone at the large motel would see them together briefly—the coffee shop, bar, or maybe the heated indoor pool. I assumed she'd pick him up at one of those spots.

We explored possibilities. "I did some preliminary checking," I told Sam. "She and Frankin get to Brandon the same way, probably. She flies to Winnipeg and rents a car for the hundred and thirty-five miles to Brandon. She parks the car outside her motel room and I could probably cut her brake cable so that it broke completely on her drive back to Winnipeg but it's nearly all flat road and the chances that she would lose complete control and kill herself in a smashup aren't that dependable. Whatever we do has to work first time.

"Possibility number two. I still have the poison pill she slipped into my Dilaudid-pill container, the one I had tested in minute part on the rabbit. . . . We have a drink and I slip it into her glass, but once we've aborted the attempt on Frankin's life she'll know we know and if she sees us there she's on guard two hundred percent."

In addition to the pill, I told Sam, I also had in reserve my own personal L pill. L for lethal. Standard equipment for most foreign operational Agency people and it was usually kept in a special container in one of our three-way safes. We were held accountable for the pill. I held on to mine when I left Ankara for New York and there were times after the short-stopped cancer operation when I had thought of using it. Sooner or later, I said, someone at Langley is going to find out that our own Mr. Hanan on leave still owes us an L pill. But it could be used on her if necessary.

Third possibility: she has an "accidental" drowning in her bathtub at the motel, just as she planned it for Frankin. But very tricky. Yes, it seems like suicide but what is a pretty Swiss-born woman who lives in New York and travels a lot doing in a Brandon motel? Who did she come here to see? All you need is one imaginative provincial detective and a couple of breaks and some connection to Frankin is established. Also, I couldn't see her quietly submitting to an "accidental" drowning, which might mean shouts and noise and interference. No good.

"What's left?" Sam asked.

"What's left is very tricky and has a lot of loopholes so before I go into it if you have any other solutions, Sam, now is the time."

He thought the death ought not to take place in Brandon; that the car brake-cutting was too uncertain—and too easily detected afterward by the highway policy; or the rental car's insurance investigators.

"I get the feeling it has to be done here in New York, on her home ground, more or less. Lots of murders and suicides here; too many to merit top-notch investigations. Plenty break-ins in those brownstones. Every week someone gets killed by the bastards breaking in and discovering there's someone home after all. Or she gets it in a hit-and-run but that means accomplices and trailing her and a repair place that won't ask too many questions about a badly dented grill or front end. Anyway, I don't know who could do it that way. I couldn't."

It was becoming clearer there was a lot about killing Elly neither of us could do. I gave Sam a strained smile: "Some hit men we turn out."

Sam said: "I love her. She makes me feel good. What a lovely grand-daughter she'd make, I once told myself. How do you make up your mind you just kill her someplace?" Tears were forming in the eye corners. I was now the ultimate heavy.

He wiped his eyes. "I'm pulling a Vogelsang on you, huh?"

We looked at each other awhile. Total communication. Total frustration.

To break it up a little I said: "Well, we could go over to the Temple Emanu-El and put in an hour of hard prayer that God in His Infinite Wisdom Smite Down This Wicked, Murderous Elly Bricha."

A big sigh. "That's Shorsh's department. This is my responsibility. She's not going to try to get you again, once she knows you know. You go back to work and forget the whole thing, you want. You got into the act because she marked you 'victim.' That's out now. I'm past seventy and I've led a pretty interesting life and if I have to kill her, that's it. But unless it's done very smart and sneaky it ties into me and that means it ties back to the Committee and we're in the mess we've been trying to stay out of."

By now all the complicated things had been said—and unsaid—and all I had to add was: "I have a few weeks before I run back to being a brilliant, conniving deputy director of plans, some of which involves indirect murder routinely. Meanwhile, Sam, I owe you. If you hadn't gotten me so involved in this investigation I probably would have taken that L pill long ago. So I owe you—and Whatever or Whoever helped arrange my little medical miracle."

I explained my plan, giving the pros and cons fairly. "Tricky, but it could work. It does, we're off the hook and the murders stop."

He grunted: *"Boychick,* do I wanna believe you!"

"It's worth a try. If it doesn't . . ."

"Then it's up to me, whatever I can dream up. . . ."

"All yours. I bow out and go back to work in a quiet little bureaucratic job which I will love because I'm a born conniver. We'll have dinner once a year, the fraternity reunion, and tell stories about that lovely confused woman in our lives, Elly Bricha, who departed this life suddenly."

We'd both go to Brandon. I'd try my stunt and if it aborted Sam would be a backup. I'd done some phoning to Air Canada and there was no scheduled way to fly into Brandon. Most people flew to Winnipeg and rented a car. I thought we couldn't do that just in case we ran into Elly on the plane, in Winnipeg, or even on the road to Brandon. Instead, we'd go on a scheduled morning flight to Minneapolis on Tuesday, and then take an air taxi, a Beechcraft Baron, from there to Brandon, which had a small airfield. We'd get there by 1 PM. I had done some phoning and the tab for the charter plane would come to $722 plus $6 an hour for waiting time if we were going back with him. I told the service we'd want him to wait about twelve hours. This way we'd avoid running into Elly on the Trans-Canada Highway or even at the Winnipeg airport. Sam insisted the Committee pay for everything, including the air taxi. "Everything works out, the best bargain they ever got."

14

March 13, 1973. Brandon.

She's here. Lewis Frankin is here and so am I. Sam is not at the White
Oak Motel with us. He's registered at the Starlight Motel a mile away.
Frankin's in 128, she's in 151, and I'm up on the second floor overlooking the handsome cloverleaf indoor pool. I also overlook the bar, the
coffee shop, and a little "outdoor" pavilion adjoining the coffee shop.
Before I checked in I scouted the place for a room where I could see
out over the indoor plaza, the heart of this large modern caravanserai,
six miles south of Trans-Canada No. 1. It's 150 feet from my curtained
window, across the pool to the coffee shop.

   I got a look at Frankin about 4:30, shortly after he returned from
several hours at the All-Canada Building Supply Co., Ltd., not far from
a Canadian Pacific siding near Highway 10. Sam had been scouting the

building and phoned me when he left. He described Frankin—"Razor-cut red-brown hair, fashionable longish, blue blazer, gray slacks, full face, brown moccasins, canary button-down shirt, red-patterned tie." I told Sam he could work for me anytime.

About six Frankin dropped into the bar for a drink. A few minutes later, Elly, who had been seated on one of the pavilion's wrought-iron chairs, got up and went into the bar, too. Thirty minutes later they both went into the more formal dining room, the Manitoba Room. Room service took care of me with a few sandwiches, coffee, and fruit salad. I kept vigil at the slit in my curtains and at 8:30 they left the dining room. Three minutes later Sam phoned. From the side parking lot he had been able to keep both their rooms in view. Calling on the house phone he said the light had gone on in Frankin's room. I gave them five minutes and used the interior dial system to phone Frankin. When he answered I deepened my voice and said, "Mister, my wife's in your room. She's not outa there in two minutes I come in shooting."

I gave her ten minutes to be ushered out and get back to her room. I knocked on her door. "Yes?" she asked. I said, Harry. Long pause. She opened the door. Her face had an agitated sullenness. I pushed into the room, closing the door.

She sat down heavily in the green-tweed easy chair opposite the TV set. "I should have guessed," she said. We stared at each other. She kept rubbing her fingers, making and breaking little teepees. Gradually the sullenness left, a retreating tide.

Ever helpful, I said: "Well, it's too late now to say, 'and what's the goddam meaning of all this, Mr. Hanan?'"

She looked at the TV set and talked to herself, barely audibly.

"That bitch Solca in Zurich."

I was louder. "Also Dr. Ernest Hug in Clarens."

She looked at me sourly. "So now you know."

I nodded. "Sam, too."

"He's here?" I waved to the parking strip outside her back door.

"Vogelsang?" I said he knows, too, but he's in New York.

"What now?"

I said that depended. Peter Vogelsang thought the best thing would be if she took a solemn pledge to stop killing and gave us a signed confession of all her "misdeeds"—the euphemism came with a silly smile—that we would give the police if there were any more "incidents."

She dismissed that with a scornful shrug.

"Sam thinks, very, very reluctantly, that you have to be killed quietly so that the *goel hadam* business is brought to a final conclusion."

"And you?"

"Well, I'm more sentimental. Maybe because I'm the only one of us who's spent twelve great—and grateful—hours in bed with you. Still, I agreed with Sam that you had to be killed."

She crossed her hands in front of her breasts instinctively. "That's what you're here for?"

It was getting harder. The one Agency contract-killer I knew said it was better if you never spoke to the victim.

"There may be a way out."

"American ingenuity to the rescue?"

Not *that* ingenious.

"I had a half-assed notion that maybe, just maybe, we could get you to solve our problems—and maybe yours, too—by taking this pill." I took out the tiny plastic box in which I kept the poison pill resembling my Dilaudids. "The very pill someone dropped into my pill bottle that afternoon in Vogelsang's office when I nearly passed out from pain. A hundred years ago."

She tilted her head to take me in from another vantage point.

"I had an instinct about you from the start. Not this one, I told myself. He's dangerous, dangerous."

"My work?"

"No. I just knew you were dangerous. When I heard about your spontaneous remission I took it as a second warning. God was telling me something. I had to listen. I decided I'd let you go if you were right for me in bed."

"I was?"

"Very."

"I passed some test."

"But it was too late, even then. I knew you wouldn't stop until you found out everything. I was certain when my *avocat* called from Zurich.

He had been to see Madame Solca to let her know that she was going to get ten thousand francs instead of five because I didn't want any bad feelings. She took the money, signed the release, and told him that some American lawyer had been to see her with some nonsense my grandmother had a half-sister in the U.S. My lawyer got a description of the man and I knew it was you poking around."

"Frankin was going to be your last job?"

"I should say, yes . . . but . . ."

"You don't know when the itch to finish the list might come over you again?"

"Harry, it would take me days to explain and maybe even then I couldn't do it."

"So we're back to the same problem." I put the open plastic pillbox on the small desk near her.

"I don't want to die."

I nodded. "You got a million dollars to live for now. But Lucksig, Morden, Faucon didn't want to die, either. Even if you distributed your inheritance to all their families it wouldn't be much compensation. Also it would raise a lot of peculiar questions."

"I *deserve* to die. I've killed many men."

I pointed to the plastic box.

"Haven't you killed men and women, or had them killed by your people?"

I said probably, but that was different, I thought. Mine was sanctioned by the Agency, my government. Yes, they might be killers and I might be one and I'd heard all the arguments.

"Elly, we can go around on this all night. I might have bought Vogelsang's idea of letting you go but there was no way we could assure ourselves you wouldn't pull another killing and that would make all of us—Peter, Sam, me, and the Committee—equally guilty with you. We could have stopped you effectively and we didn't. And they'd be right."

"I want to stop but I can't—not by myself."

"You mean get you another psychiatrist or something?"

"No, not them."

"Who?"

"You."

It was a small girl's voice. The schizophrenic adolescent talking.

"You could take care of me. We go away. Far away. No lists, no dossiers. If I got nervous, panicky sometimes, you'd pat me and love me. Maybe after a year, two years it would be gone and I wouldn't get the urge anymore and then you could go away."

Happy sunset fade-out. "Elly, you know enough about me to know what a real disaster I am with women. In bed, okay. Very experienced, virile, et cetera, but apart from that . . . look at my marriage. You know about that. I'm no psychiatrist and I'm probably not much of any kind of emotional bulwark for the long haul. That part of me is under-equipped. How could I be of any good to you that way?"

I was surprised at myself asking the question.

"You'd be good for me. I know. And it's not the adolescent schizophrenic talking now, Harry. This is me, the whole mixture. Elly Bricha, thirty, very mixed up."

It was the moment to embrace and kiss her deeply and say, yes, yes, that's what we will do, my love. But I said:

"We get out of here and run away. We travel. We make love. I keep an eye on you. If you're out of my sight a few hours I've got to start checking airports. . . . Elly, don't you see how impossible it is? And when you're near me half of me has to be wary: she tried to kill me once, why not again? We'd make a great pair, all right. Every night I check under your pillow for a knife and you wait for me to drink the martini before you know it's safe. Great."

She cried softly. "You were the invincible one, the one I couldn't kill, the one God blessed." A tiny smile breaking through the tears. "My own messiah—the one with the natural circumcision."

It hurt to look at her anymore. This was killing *me*.

"I once did a conference in Frankfurt on criminology. The death penalty and pardons and all that." The voice became an eager child's. "You know what I found?"

What?

"In Switzerland in the eighteenth century a prisoner condemned to death could win his pardon if a virgin asked to marry him. He would be freed but the couple would be banished. If there weren't virgins around he could also be freed if a woman who had borne seven sons would cut the rope of the doomed man before he was dropped. And in Germany they had another way. If a woman ran naked nine times around the marketplace or three times around the prison where the criminal awaited his execution, why he would be freed."

She wouldn't be dull, for sure. All that fascinating trivia acquired from years of conferencing. . . .

"Elly, I'm not a virgin and I don't have seven sons and I'd gladly run naked around the motel pool three times if that would help but . . ."

She brightened. "All you have to do is run away with me and care for me for a year or so."

I held up the plastic container.

"You really want me to take it, Harry?"

"It's *a* solution. Not a great one . . ."

"I got you a cup of water last time . . ."

I went to the bathroom, jerked off the cellophane on the glass sterilized for my exclusive benefit, half-filled it, and went back. She held the pill between two fingers. "After I take the pill will you hold me, Harry?" I said I'd hold her. "I love you, Harry." I said, I love you, Elly. More than I loved anyone. She put the pill back of her tongue, sipped some water, closed her eyes, swayed, and I held her. When she grew heavy, I put her down on the bed.

I opened the back door a little and walked out to Sam in our rented car.

"She took the pill three minutes ago. She's now on the bed. There's some cleaning up to do here, first. You go back to your motel, check out right away. Turn the car in at the Winnipeg airport. I'll take the air taxi back. I don't want us traveling together."

Sam cried: "Poor Elly."

I said I'd be away for a while so he wasn't to worry. We gave each other the fraternity grip and he drove off. I went back to the room, kissed her gently on the cool lips, and sat down in the easy chair. It would be several hours before the Dilaudid's soporific effects wore off.